Parlor Games

Parlor Games

Jess Michaels
Leda Swann
Julia Templeton

AVON

An Imprint of HarperCollins*Publishers*

P- 06

19ºº pⁱˢᵗB

This book is a work of fiction. The characters, incidents, and dialogue are drawn from the authors' imaginations and are not to be construed as real. Any resemblance to actual events or persons, living or dead, is entirely coincidental.

PARLOR GAMES. "Fallen Angel" copyright © 2006 by Jess Michaels, "Parlor Games" copyright © 2006 by Leda Swann, and "Border Lord" copyright © 2006 by Julia Templeton. All rights reserved. Printed in the United States of America. No part of this book may be used or reproduced in any manner whatsoever without written permission except in the case of brief quotations embodied in critical articles and reviews. For information address Harper-Collins Publishers, 10 East 53rd Street, New York, NY 10022.

HarperCollins books may be purchased for educational, business, or sales promotional use. For information please write: Special Markets Department, HarperCollins Publishers, 10 East 53rd Street, New York, NY 10022.

FIRST EDITION

Designed by Sarah Maya Gubkin

Library of Congress Cataloging-in-Publication Data

Parlor games / Jess Michaels, Leda Swann, Julia Templeton.—1st ed.
    p. cm.
    Contents: Fallen angel / Jess Michaels—Parlor games / Leda Swann—Border lord / Julia Templeton.
    ISBN–13: 978-0-06-088229-7 (pbk.)
    ISBN–10: 0-06-088229-8 (pbk.)
    1. Erotic stories, American.   I. Michaels, Jess. Fallen angel.   II. Swann, Leda. Parlor games.   III. Templeton, Julia. Border lord.

PS648.E7P37 2006
813'.01083538—dc22   2005055876

06 07 08 09 10   RRD/WBC   10 9 8 7 6 5 4 3 2

Contents

Parlor Games

Fallen Angel

Jess Michaels

For Michael,
who makes me feel like a romance heroine
even when my hair is scary

1

London, 1815

John Valentine strummed the fingers of one hand along the bar top while in the other he clenched a tumbler of whiskey. He stared at the clock behind the bartender's head, watching as the moments bled away one by one.

Glowering at the hated timepiece, he let out a string of low curses that didn't raise an eyebrow from the gentlemen and ladies surrounding him in the crowded room. In fact, most didn't even notice his frustration as they talked, kissed, and . . . He shifted as he glanced down the bar to watch one gentleman, a powerful figure in Parliament, lift the young woman in his company up on the bar to have easier access to the swell of her breasts beneath the low curve of her scandalous gown. Valentine couldn't help but stare as the woman dipped her head back with a loud sigh. The sigh turned to a moan as her companion pushed the neckline even lower until the dusky rose of one taut nipple popped over the lacy edging.

Valentine turned away, his erection lengthening beneath

the bar. Arabella Nichols's underground haven of sex definitely lived up to the rumors surrounding it. Since his arrival,
he had seen so much that this latest exposure to sin and sex
seemed tame. How much more did the legendary Miss Nichols think he could take?

"Mr. Valentine?"

He started as a feminine voice, along with hot, sweet
breath, brushed his ears. He turned to find a lovely auburn-
haired woman standing at his elbow, a broad, flirtatious
smile on her face.

"Yes?"

"Arabella is ready for you."

The young lady's smile grew as he got to his feet and her
gaze swept over him. He ignored her blatant regard . . . and
the equally blatant offer in her expression. With a grin, she
turned and led him from the room, past a crowded parlor
where even more ladies and gentlemen congregated for erotic
foreplay, and finally through a ballroom with a stage where
scantily clad ladies danced for the pleasure of the men and
women in the crowd below. Valentine kept his eyes focused
straight ahead on the lace-clad back of his companion. His
head wasn't so addled by drink and sex that he couldn't remember this was business.

Or at least try to remember. It wasn't easy when temptation waited around every corner.

His companion led him upstairs and down a long hallway. Through the closed doors, Valentine heard the moans
and cries of couples, perhaps even groups in some rooms,
acting out the pleasures hinted at below.

"Are you warm, Mr. Valentine?" his pretty guide asked as
she glanced at him over her shoulder.

His lips thinned at the teasing glimmer in her eyes. "No."

She laughed as she paused at an ornate door at the end of

the hallway. "Then you are a stronger man than most." She clicked the door open. "Arabella? Mr. Valentine is here."

"Come in."

Valentine did as he was told, even though the response came from a formless voice. As the door closed behind him, he glanced around. The chamber didn't look like he would have guessed based on the establishment's reputation. He'd expected a tacky display of erotic delights. A room dominated by a bed, perhaps clad in red with satin all around.

Instead the chamber was tastefully outfitted, from the rich oriental carpet beneath his feet to the expensive furniture and exquisite art that filled the room. There was no bed in the sitting room, but he assumed his hostess's bedchamber was through the closed doorway across from him.

Still, he could not find the infamous Arabella Nichols.

"You kept me waiting for over an hour," he said, his eyes darting from corner to corner. They finally settled on a high-backed wing chair by the fire. It was turned away from him, but a slender female hand lay on the armrest.

Still, she did not rise, or even move at all. "I am fully aware of how long you waited, Mr. Valentine."

Irritation sluiced through him, tamping down some of his earlier arousal. "So you don't care how my time was wasted? Is this how you run your business?"

The hand curled into a fist before its owner pushed to her feet and turned to face him.

Valentine caught his breath. By God, Arabella was even more beautiful than the gossips and rogues said she was. Long golden curls cascaded over her shoulders and down her back, draping over full breasts that were barely covered by a scrap of white satin that might laughingly be called a negligee. The long slit up one side gave him a good look at her slender, lithe limbs, the kind a man couldn't help but imagine wrapped around his waist.

And then there were her eyes. A stunning, captivating midnight blue that pierced through his own. There was a spark of intelligence, of challenge, in their depths that excited him as much as her exposed skin and husky voice did.

"Keeping you waiting is *exactly* how I run my business, Mr. Valentine," she said softly, her voice a little breathless and sensual. She obviously knew her full mouth and the words she formed with it were just as much a tool of her trade as the lush curves of her body or the heat of her sex.

He folded his arms and carefully, methodically, reined in his shocking animal reaction to this woman. He already knew what those urges could do. He had once vowed to never again be overcome by them.

"I am not a man accustomed to being kept waiting," he growled.

She gave him a small and knowing smile before she slid forward in a movement both graceful and enticing. "*That* I did know about you, though little else. You see, Mr. Valentine, I had to be sure about your character."

Valentine snorted. "*My* character?"

Her smile faltered a fraction and her voice was tighter when she replied, "Yes. My business is delicate. I could not bring a man into this world who would frighten away my patrons with his glowering disapproval. And I couldn't hire a man who was unable to control himself when the ladies who work and play here offered themselves to him. You had to be tested."

She came closer with each word until she was mere inches from him. Her body heat reached out, curling around him, addling his mind as it warmed his pounding blood. Valentine's fisted hand stirred at his side. He yearned to reach out and smooth his fingers along this woman's silken skin. To claim her mouth. Her body. Make her stop talking and start moaning in pleasure.

What the hell was wrong with him? Why was he so affected by the pounding sexual tension that coursed through the room? Under any other circumstances, he would have just departed, but practicality interfered. There were few people who would hire a disgraced former Bow Street Runner. And he needed this job, whatever it was, almost as much as he desired the woman who offered it to him.

"Why does a woman like yourself wish to hire a man like me?" he asked, surprised his voice didn't tremble with pent-up desire.

Arabella's body language shifted. From the erotic temptress, she changed to an unsure, frightened lady. The transformation was brief, but Valentine saw it. And it inspired a strange desire to take care of her.

"I need your protection, Mr. Valentine," she said, and it was *her* voice that trembled, but not with desire. "Someone is trying to kill me."

Arabella shuddered as she said the words, but it wasn't only fear that caused her to shiver. It was strange . . . she hadn't had such a visceral reaction to a man in a long time. But John Valentine, with his focused, intense brown eyes, scruffy whiskers, and hair too long for current fashion, aroused her utterly and completely. Considering why she was hiring him, that could be very bad.

Or oh, so very good.

Valentine cocked his head, but he didn't seem any more moved by her statement that her life was in danger than he did by her presence. Except that when she glanced down, the outline of an impressive erection was clear against his fitted trousers. Still, he remained cool. Impassive. How she longed to crack that shell.

"Tell me more," he said. "Tell me all the details."

She stepped back, using the business acumen she had honed for so many years to rein in her emotions. Motioning him to the settee by the blazing fire, she crossed to her bureau and withdrew a little wooden box. When she turned back, she saw Valentine had gone to the settee but hadn't taken a seat. He simply stared at her, his body outlined by the fire in a most appealing way. Dear God, but he was a handsome man.

With a shake of her head, she crossed back to him, letting her body brush his as she took the seat he would not. Still, he did not join her.

"It began a month or so ago," she explained. "With a letter left nailed to the door of this establishment. It explained in vulgar detail what the sender wished to do to me. I ignored it."

Valentine looked down at her. "Why?"

She smiled, though the answer gave her no pleasure. "I am sorry to say that I receive many such letters each year from various people who want to see me gone from London. Whether it be people who have not been allowed membership to this place, ones who have had their membership revoked for bad behavior, or the occasional ladies society that wishes to end my 'reign of sin,' threats are a part of my daily existence."

"Then why take this one seriously?" he asked and advanced a small step closer.

The spicy scent of his skin filled her nostrils and her heart rate increased tenfold with the intoxicating effects. She shook her head. What was wrong with her?

"I didn't until another letter arrived. Then another. One was even slipped beneath my bedroom door while I slept." She trembled at the thought that someone had been in her home, had such easy access to her. "Still, I hoped this person would simply go away . . . but then—" She broke off as she held out the box filled with the letters she had saved.

Valentine hesitated as he stared at the spot beside her on the settee. Then he seemed to surrender, for he sank to a seated position. Once again, she was surrounded by his scent, his masculine body heat. Both gave her a strange feeling of comfort.

"Then?" he asked as he took the box filled with the words and promises of her stalker. His voice was softer this time. As if he understood her pain. Her fear.

"The threats turned to attempts on my safety and life," she admitted. "Someone put burrs under my mare's saddle to make her shy when I rode around Hyde Park. A fire was set in my bedroom . . . deliberately. Only the quick reaction of a servant kept it from raging out of control. And one night someone fired shots through the window of my main hall. They were aimed at the area where I always sit."

Valentine's face pulled into a scowl. "So whoever this is, their behavior is escalating from threats to actual violence."

Slowly, she nodded. Hearing him say those words brought reality home to her. No matter how much she'd been trying to deny she was in danger, trying to keep the truth from everyone around her, she could do so no longer.

"That is why I called upon you. I require assistance, I cannot face this danger alone. I need someone who can protect me and investigate what has been happening to determine who is responsible. I know you were once with the Bow Street Runners." She was surprised when his face twitched with displeasure at the reference to his former employers.

"And why choose me?" he asked, his gravelly voice suddenly strained. "If you know I was a Runner, you probably also know I was dismissed in disgrace."

For a brief moment, the displeasure she saw in his eyes turned to raw anger and hurt, but then the emotions were gone. Arabella took a deep breath. Clearly she would have to tread softly over these delicate subjects.

"I also heard the charges leveled against you were unfounded," she said softly.

At that, his face lost its anger, gentled. She sucked in her breath. Without the tension in his every muscle, Valentine was even more appealing. For a wild moment, she wondered how to permanently temper the rage that hung around him. How to release it with more pleasurable pursuits. Then she dismissed that surprising reaction.

"W-will you take the job?" she asked. "The payment is generous."

His eyes darted to her face, then slid lower, sweeping over her with undeniable interest. Her blood heated in reaction as her nipples tightened and wet desire flooded her already tingling pussy. She wanted to know what this man tasted like. What his cock felt like when it slid home inside her. She wanted to know how much pleasure he could bring. From the reined-in sensuality in his eyes, the way he held his broad, strong body . . . she guessed it would be as much as she could handle and more.

Slowly, she leaned forward until her barely clad breasts brushed his arm. His stare darted to the point of contact and she had no doubt he saw how hard her nipples were. Certainly she could not ignore his swelling cock. But would he allow himself to act on his desire, this man who seemed so capable of denying himself?

"If you wish it, there could even be other benefits to doing this for me," she whispered.

Valentine's expression shifted, unreadable beyond a flash of indefinable strong emotion. She found herself wanting to touch him, but held back. Until she had his answer, she was not going to pursue anything further with him.

"Very well," he said softly, though he seemed to take no pleasure in accepting her offer.

She wrinkled her brow. The man clearly desired her, but he did not respond to her in the way she had come to expect. He could have already had her on her back. She wouldn't have resisted . . . But instead he pushed off the settee, away from the brush of her body, and paced to the fire.

Clearing her throat, she said, "I do not wish anyone to know about our bargain, Valentine. No one can know you're protecting me."

His brow wrinkled. "Why?"

Arabella felt the blood drain from her face. There were many reasons why she kept secrets. Most she could not, or would not, reveal. "It would frighten the young women in my employ if they knew I was under attack."

His eyebrow arched. "They didn't realize the threat when you were shot at?"

She shook her head. "I told them the shots were fired by a drunken reveler."

"Hmmm." He looked displeased by her lies and she felt strangely compelled to explain herself.

"Any hint of danger would hurt my business. I work in the arena of fantasy and pleasure. Any danger found within these walls should only be erotic and easily vanquished with a word or a touch." She sighed. "No one must know the truth."

"I see." He folded his arms across his broad chest, drawing her attention to the muscular definition of both. "How do you propose I protect you if no one can know I'm here?"

She smiled. "By pretending to be my lover," she explained. "Part of why I chose you for this job is that you are exactly the kind of man I would take to my bed."

And that was no lie. In fact, she hadn't realized just how true it was until Valentine entered her chamber and made her wet and wanting with just a few words. "If you cleaned up a bit."

"Cleaned up?" he repeated, his eyebrow arching as he digested her request.

Rising to her feet, she closed the distance he had put between them with a few steps. He straightened up, tensed as she lifted her fingers and brushed his cheek. Rough stubble raked her skin and she hardly kept herself from moaning out loud.

"Yes. If you shaved." She lifted her hand higher, almost forced to stand on her tiptoes to glide it through his silky hair. "Cut your hair." She smiled as she forced herself to pull away. "Nothing to scar you permanently, I assure you."

"I see," he said softly, and for the first time since he came into her chamber, a small smile lifted one corner of his full, utterly kissable lips. Her heart thudded in response.

Yes, she would have to be very careful with this one. If she managed to get him into her bed, which she had no doubt would happen and happen soon, she would need to repeat her mantra every moment. No heart. Only body. Pleasure without emotion.

"Very well, Arabella Nichols," he said, and the sound of her name coming from his mouth made her knees turn to the consistency of warm jelly. "Do your worst."

2

Valentine shifted in a hard wooden chair in Arabella's bedroom as he watched her make mysterious preparations. The scent of exotic spices hung heavy around him, addling his mind and making his already erotic thoughts about Arabella even more disconcerting.

How could he have agreed to pretend to be her lover? There was no doubt he would make that fiction a reality within days . . . hell, hours, given his attraction to her and her sensual signals. And she was exactly the kind of woman he couldn't dare to lose himself in.

She turned to him, a bowl in one hand, a straight razor in the other, and a wet towel draped over one arm. Water had splashed on her thin satin nightgown in a few areas, and where it had, the fabric clung to her skin, nearly transparent.

If he lasted more than three-quarters of an hour without taking this woman, it would be a Herculean feat.

"I'll place this over your face if you don't mind," she said as she set the bowl and razor on a table beside him. She lifted the towel and covered his face. It was warm, meant to soften his rough whiskers before she shaved them. "I'll cut your hair while we wait."

"You will?" he asked, his voice muffled by the towel.

It was alarming enough to be plunged into darkness by a woman he didn't seem able to control himself around, but to add sharp scissors to the equation made it even worse.

He heard the smile in her voice. "Yes. I promise not to do permanent damage."

He made his best effort to relax, but when she touched his scalp with light fingers he came back to full attention. Tingles shot through his bloodstream, heat pulsed to his cock and every other nerve ending. With just one light, benign touch, Arabella set him at the ready.

As she began to snip away hair, Valentine fought for purchase over his desires. But it was a losing battle. The only thing his foggy mind could conjure was Arabella's earlier statement to him. She had offered him "benefits" for taking this position. He had ignored that offer at the time, but now it sank beneath his skin, despite his best efforts to pretend otherwise.

With her delicate hands smoothing through his hair, he could not ignore the images that promise inspired. He could only imagine how good it would feel to bury himself in Arabella's slick heat.

And *that* was exactly the kind of thing that had gotten him dismissed from the Bow Street Runners. Valentine groaned.

"Too hot?" Arabella asked, her gentle fingers slipping beneath the hot towel to graze his jawline. His cock throbbed in response and he gritted his teeth.

"Much," he muttered before he cleared his throat. "No," he said louder.

Her fingers moved away. "Tell me if I hurt you."

He knew just how easily that could happen. And he also knew the only way to combat his steadily growing desire was to focus on the job she had hired him for. To find out everything he could about Arabella Nichols so he could determine who would want her dead.

"Tell me about this place, Miss Nichols," he asked, shifting in the hopes he could conceal his erection.

She hesitated, her fingers stilling in his hair. Then she cleared her throat. "Arabella."

"Arabella," he corrected. "Tell me about this . . . would you call it a club?"

"Yes, though others call it a pleasure palace, a den of sin, and a hundred other names."

"And you're the mistress of the whores here?"

She stiffened. "They are not whores and I am not their madam," she snapped. "There are women who live in this house, who mingle with the patrons, fulfill their darkest desires. And, yes, they are paid. But they are not peddling their bodies to the highest bidder."

He wanted to pull the towel aside to look at her face, but resisted. He had a feeling she was using the cloth as a shield, and truth be told, he needed that buffer just as much as she.

"My intention was not to offend," he said softly.

She sighed. "I'm sorry. I've not been sleeping well of late. The idea that I run a common house for lightskirts rankles me." She snipped a few more pieces of hair before she continued. "Those who wish to congregate here and enjoy the pleasures and freedom my domain offers pay a membership fee, just as they do at White's and a dozen other clubs in the city.

Once they have paid, they may do as they wish, as long as it isn't illegal or violent. That fee is how I pay my employees."

"And what is the membership fee?" he asked.

"Five hundred pounds."

"Five hundred?" he sputtered, nearly choking on the towel as he sucked in a breath of shock. "That is more than some people have to live on each year."

He felt her shrug. "I realize that. But what they find here is freedom without judgment. Exploration of their darkest desires. And utter anonymity. Every member knows if they reveal the identity of any other, they'll lose their own membership and every activity they participated in will be publicly exposed. For those who wish even more protection, they can disguise themselves entirely. As for me, I've built a long-standing trust with my patrons. I will never divulge those who hold membership here." She paused in her work. "You must promise the same."

"My job is not to watch the others here, it is to watch you," he reassured her. When she returned to her work, he thought about the club she had formed. Even for members of the ton such utter freedom without consequence was rare. "I have heard rumors that your clientele includes many in high society. Even Wellington, Princess Charlotte, and the Regent have been linked to your establishment."

"I would never tell you if that were true, Mr. Valentine," she said with a light laugh.

"But if it were, that would mean you have powerful people in your midst. Ones who would be very powerful enemies."

"Yes." Her laughter faded and he thought he felt her hand tremble. Once again, a strange desire to comfort her filled him. To make her feel safe.

He shook off that reaction. Business. This was business. "Why do *you* believe someone is trying to kill you?"

She hesitated again. "Perhaps for my records that involve those very powerful people. Perhaps because someone is angry I revoked their membership. Perhaps someone upset over the end of an affair. Perhaps because they know—" She stopped and her fingers jerked away from his scalp.

Valentine reached up and gripped the edge of the swiftly cooling towel. Pulling it aside, he looked at Arabella. He'd known she was standing close to him; after all, he'd been able to smell the scent of her skin, feel her warmth . . . But *seeing* her so near was still a shock. She was so very lovely and his body rocketed to painful awareness in an instant.

She met his stare with an even one of her own. It might have been called challenging if she hadn't caught her full lower lip between her teeth and nibbled nervously. He watched her tongue sweep over her swollen mouth and his cock swelled ever hotter.

"I—I should shave your whiskers," she murmured, grabbing blindly for the bowl on the table beside her. It clattered, but she managed to grasp it in clumsy fingers.

As she stepped closer, her legs brushed his arm. Valentine shut his eyes, murmuring a silent prayer that he wouldn't humiliate himself before he touched her. He felt like he could explode with the slightest touch.

She lathered her hands with shaving soap and began to stroke her fingers over his cheeks.

Valentine knew about desire. No one could have called him a saint and kept a straight face. He had given and received all kinds of pleasures . . . even had desire used against him. But he hadn't fully realized the power of such a simple touch until now. When Arabella glided her soapy fingertips across his cheek, his jaw, every nerve ending exploded. Every fantasy melted in comparison.

And he wanted her more than he had ever wanted any woman.

More to the point, she wanted him. Her nipples puckered beneath the thin sheath of her gown, thrusting against the satin in an invitation he would soon be unable to refuse. Her cheeks filled with pink heat, her eyes glazed, and a little sigh escaped her lips as she lifted the razor and smoothed the first of his scrubby whiskers away.

Valentine shut his eyes, but it was folly. Until he could shut his nose to her delectable scent and his ears to her rasping breath and all his other senses to the nuances that made her so attractive, Arabella Nichols would continue to weave a wicked spell around him.

The moment she finished her work with the razor, Valentine shoved out of the chair, using the damp towel to wipe his face clean as he moved as far away from her as he could.

Slowly, he turned to face her. "I don't mix business with pleasure, Arabella," he rasped, the break in his voice belying his every word.

"You deny your body?" she asked with a tilt of her head. "That is a rare quality in a man, at least in the ones I've observed."

He shrugged one shoulder. "Perhaps. But it remains true."

Arabella watched him for a long, heavy moment, then took a slow step in his direction. "My business *is* pleasure, Mr. Valentine, so I'm afraid it is not possible for me to separate them. I have learned the trick is not to deny yourself, but to prevent emotion from creeping in . . . taking over."

He watched her slip toward him, an angel, a siren, a temptress all at once. His body swayed, his heart throbbed. He swallowed past a lump in his throat. "Desire can blind."

That slowed her advance and a sadness crept into her expression that made his heart ache in a different way.

"True. Too true. But only if you allow it. And I promise you, I will not. Ever."

Valentine wrinkled his brow at her vehemence. But then she covered her emotions with a soft smile.

"Consider this a part of the job you have been hired to do, Mr. Valentine," she continued. "If the world is to believe we are lovers, the best way for us to be convincing is to make that fiction a reality. I promise I'll make no further demands once you have finished your investigation and I feel safe."

Valentine stared. He was lost. He knew it. There was no way he would deny her. He wanted her. He wanted to taste her in every way. Fill her until he felt fulfilled. Claim her until she would never forget the sensation of him pulsing inside her. Even when she'd had another lover . . . even after a hundred more.

Arabella must have sensed that silent surrender, for her hands lifted to the scandalously thin straps of her negligee. With a smooth motion, she slipped the gown away to pool at her feet and stood before him, utterly naked.

Valentine wanted to shut his eyes, but the glory of her body did not allow it. She was all curves, soft and glowing like Botticelli's Venus. Hers was a body made for touching. Her skin looked like fine creamy satin. Her full breasts would overflow his large hands. Her hips called out to be gripped as he took her. And the soft curls of blond hair at her mound demanded to be smoothed away to reveal the wet heat of her sex.

He drew in a harsh breath. He was going to have this woman. He couldn't control that fact. But there was only one way to be sure he wouldn't lose his senses, to be sure he wouldn't be used or betrayed again.

And that was to utterly dominate their sexual encounter. To make her understand, without words, that he would not be at her mercy. That she could *not* control him with the twitch of her hips or the offer of her kiss.

He took three long strides across the room and dragged her into his arms. His mouth came down and met hers without prelude. His kiss was harsh, bruising, but she didn't draw away. Indeed, her lips parted to meet his passion with one equal in every way.

Their tongues tangled, tasting, teasing, but Arabella felt more in this kiss than a promise of passion. It was a test. For both of them. Valentine was set on controlling her; she had to be just as strong about doing the same to him.

She crooked one leg, lifting it high on his hip so the heat of her damp sex rested against the throbbing tip of his erection. Even through his trousers, she felt the steel of his cock swell larger.

A little smile tilted her lips as Valentine dragged his hot mouth to her throat, raising goose bumps on her arms as he gently suckled the delicate skin. This man might be accustomed to control in the rest of his life, perhaps even with other women . . . but she could easily make him let go. Surrender.

And she had thought John Valentine would be a challenge. Bah! She would win this war.

As he trailed his mouth to her collarbone, grazing her with nuzzling kisses that heated her blood to the boiling point, she dipped her head back and gave herself over to sensation. After he'd had his way for a bit, she would take over. Turn the tables. Until then . . .

She sucked in a breath as his mouth captured one nipple. Valentine swirled his tongue around the sensitive bud, laving it with humid heat, then nipping gently until pulsing desire shot from the point of contact to her pussy. The man knew how to use his mouth, that was clear.

She clenched his shoulders as he slipped his hands down her back, trailing rough fingertips along her sensitive spine before he cupped her backside and lifted for better access to her aching breasts. Arabella bit back a cry of pleasure as he treated her opposite breast to the same torment as the first, then pressed his lips to the valley between.

To her shock, she felt herself slipping into a haze of desire and need. This was a place she hadn't found herself in for a long time. Years ago, she had learned from brutal experience just how a man could use her body against her. Since then, she no longer fully let go. Her pleasure was always muted, always kept at a distance.

But with Valentine, she struggled for control as he massaged her backside, lifting her as he took a few strides toward her bed.

She shook her head, fighting the overwhelming need. She'd gotten overconfident and allowed herself too much pleasure. She needed to reclaim control of the encounter. Now.

Valentine laid her on her bed, dragging her down to the edge where he wrapped her legs around his hips. She moaned as the apex of her thighs brushed his hard stomach, then struggled to sit up as he leaned forward. She grasped his cheeks, pulling him in for a hot kiss. Unfortunately, claiming his mouth did nothing to reduce the fire burning in her belly. If anything, he seared her, branded her even more.

Frustrated by desire and lack of control, Arabella gently sucked his tongue while she yanked at his shirt buttons, pulling the linen away from his broad shoulders and tossing it on the floor behind him. She pulled back to stare. He was even more magnificent than she imagined. All sinew and muscle, built from hard work that had also given his skin an olive tone. She shivered before she pulled him toward her.

Valentine fell against her, pinning her down with his body weight, holding her in place with his hands as he ravished her mouth yet again. As he claimed her lips, he parted her legs with one knee. Arabella arched helplessly, her sensitive sex colliding with the rough wool of his trousers. The fabric rasped against her, creating delicious friction that brought hot, wet arousal flooding to that area.

She caught her breath, but it was too late. A loud, harsh moan escaped her mouth, vibrating against Valentine's lips. He chuckled. By God, she was the most responsive lover he'd had in a long time. Just the lightest touch had her skin flushing, her nipples pebbling, her sex flooding as it awaited his cock.

And, oh, how he wanted to fill her. He lifted his head to look down at her. Through the dewy need, her blue eyes sparkled with challenge. Slowly, she worked one of her hands free from his grip and trailed her fingertips across his shoulder, placed her palm flat against his chest before she moved it down, down over the curves of muscle on his stomach, lower to his hip. And finally, she slipped his trousers open and captured his cock.

Valentine groaned, tensing his arms so they didn't buckle and send him crashing down on top of her. She gripped him, just testing his weight, his girth in her palm. Then, with a wicked little smile, she stroked him from base to tip.

He couldn't hold back a gasp of pleasure. Arabella knew exactly how to please him, as if she knew his body as well as he did himself. Her second stroke was just as sure and spots of black began to cloud his vision.

"Lie back," she whispered, pushing him to roll off her and lie down on her pillows. He blindly followed her guidance as she stroked him yet again.

Arabella smiled, letting her thumb swirl a gentle circle around the sensitive head of his erection before she kissed his mouth. He hardly had the strength to return the kiss when her fingers were doing such magical, mesmerizing things. But then her mouth was gone, drifting down, down. She lapped her rough tongue over one flat nipple, mimicking what he had done to her earlier. His body bucked, the sensation going straight to his cock. He was surprised by how he ached with disappointment when she withdrew her lips.

But the disappointment fled, replaced by anticipation, when her lips brushed his stomach, and finally her hot breath caressed his straining, throbbing erection. Blue eyes lifted, filled with promise and heat, snagging his until he could see nothing else.

He watched as she blew warm air on the tingling head of his cock. Then glided her tongue out for a teasing lick. He tensed, gritting his teeth and balling his hands into fists as pleasure tightened all his muscles. He wanted her hot mouth on him. But he wouldn't beg for it. That was all the control he had left.

Arabella didn't make him beg. With a sly wink, she wrapped her lips around him and took him deep into her throat. Valentine's head strained into the pillows and his back arched as potent, heated pleasure nearly had him blacking out. He felt like he would spend already, like a green youth with his first woman. It took every amount of effort and experience to keep from doing just that.

She didn't make it any easier, setting a hot, sensually slow rhythm with her lips. She alternated between deep strokes and swirls of her tongue, gliding her hand in time with her mouth and bringing him closer and closer to the brink.

His breath came in shorter and shorter pants and control went from wire thin to almost nonexistent. There was no denying the explosion about to come. And he was going to enjoy every damn minute of it.

Opening his eyes, he stared upward and started in surprise. There, mounted above Arabella's bed, was an ornate silver mirror. It was as large as the bed itself and now it reflected Arabella's blond curls bobbing around her bare shoulders as she pleasured him.

But more than that, it reflected his own reactions. He watched his stomach tighten with every stroke of her tongue. His back arch. And his face showed . . . utter surrender. He was at the mercy of this woman.

"No," he groaned as he sat bolt upright. He grasped Arabella's shoulders and dragged her up his body.

"Valentine?" she panted, struggling in his arms as her eyes widened in surprise.

He refused to let her escape as he flipped her over on her back. "Not like this," he growled. "Not on your terms."

Arabella didn't get the chance to respond. Not before he grasped her hips and slid inside her in one, long stroke. She couldn't hold back a cry of pleasure. Valentine's cock stretched her, filled her. It had been many months since she'd had that pleasure. Only her own fingers, her toys, had been her companions at night. But there was nothing like a man's cock.

And Valentine's was a fine specimen.

His eyes were wild, burning with need as he stared down at her, unmoving. She arched in the hope of forcing his thrusts, but he held her steady, pushing her shoulders down into the mattress.

"Not by your terms," he repeated, gentler this time. "You watch, Arabella. Watch in that mirror above us while I take you. Because I am *taking* you."

He tilted her chin with one big, hot palm and she gasped at the vision over his shoulder. At the way his big body looked covering hers. Her leg was draped over his hard, muscular calf, some of her blond curls had caught on his arm and fell over his back in a yellow ribbon.

"Valentine," she whispered.

He didn't answer. The muscles in his backside clenched as he withdrew and thrust forward. She screamed, pleasure cycloning in her chest, in her belly, between her thighs. It was intense, out of control. Normally, she had to touch herself, finger her own clit to find completion, but with Valentine, she was already on the edge.

He withdrew again, the glide of his erection stroking her perfectly on both edges of the thrust. Bringing her closer to heaven and stealing whatever thin line of control she'd captured for herself when she took him in her mouth.

Every rational part of Arabella screamed at her to fight. Fight Valentine's possession. Fight for control. But that voice was blocked out by the singing of her nerves. By the burning rush of blood in her ears as Valentine took her again and again.

Release was coming. It crested inside her on a wave, building higher and higher in her lower belly as heat spread throughout. She could not fight it, not while she watched Valentine's hips in the mirror above. Not while her fingernails bit into his sweat-misted back.

But then her view was blocked as Valentine moved his face into her line of vision. The cords of muscle in his neck were taut, his face reflected the strain of waiting, taking, as much as she supposed her own did. He stared at her, holding her gaze without slowing the pace of his hips.

"Arabella," he groaned. "Let go."

She arched, attempting to fight utter surrender one last time, but she couldn't. The fire roared out of control and she screamed as pleasure wracked her. Valentine caught her roar of release with his lips, swirling his tongue around hers as he clutched her closer. Their lips broke contact when he groaned, filling her with his hot essence.

Panting, Valentine collapsed onto her. Arabella wrapped her arms around him, smoothing her fingers along his spine. A satiated warmth filled her, making her limbs heavy and clouding her mind. She hadn't felt so fulfilled in . . . actually, she couldn't remember when. She certainly didn't feel this good when she pleasured herself, and no man had taken her over the edge with such skill.

Valentine let out a sigh as he slipped from her embrace and withdrew from her body. Arabella winced at the sudden chill, the emptiness his departure left behind.

Her stomach clenched. That was exactly the problem. With a man like Valentine, she was opening herself up not only to surrender and pleasure . . . but to the certain emptiness bound to happen when a woman gave a man more than her body.

And that was something she could never allow. Not if she wanted to maintain her dignity. Not if she wanted to keep her secrets.

3
___

"You took her to bed?"

Valentine reached over to pound on Bennett Caruthers's back as the other man choked on a swig of whiskey. As his friend gasped for air, Valentine tried to clear his head of the images Bennett's words conjured.

Arabella on her bed, spread wide to his lips and hands and cock. Her mewls of pleasure as he took her. The way her hot body milked him when she found release.

"Dear God, man," Bennett gasped, finally able to speak again. "I never thought *that* was what she required when word arrived she was looking for a man to do a job. If I'd known, I would have gone myself."

Valentine's gaze snapped to his friend's handsome face. Even though Bennett grinned, there wasn't anything funny about Valentine's reaction. He hated the idea of his best friend being the one to take Arabella's body. To touch her.

Shaking off the uncomfortable response, he strode away to look out Bennett's window to the street below. Jealousy?

What the hell was his problem? Arabella Nichols had hired him. That they had shared a wild night of unrivaled passion didn't mean anything.

It couldn't.

"She didn't call me there to share her bed," he managed to grumble. "If she wanted a partner, she has more than a few choices in that club of hers."

"Then what did she want?" Bennett asked.

"Someone is trying to kill her. She wants protection and to find out who and why." He turned to face his friend, hoping his expression didn't reflect how much Arabella had moved him. "And that's why I need your help. I can investigate within her walls, but I'll need your assistance if I'm to stay by her side for her protection. Can I ask you to use your resources within the Runners?"

Bennett winced and Valentine fought not to do the same. They rarely spoke of their mutual affiliation with the Bow Street Runners. The group was how the two men met, how they became friends.

But that was over now. Valentine had been dismissed more than six months before. Disgraced by the charge that he had aided a ring of thieves rather than brought them to justice.

Others in the organization claimed to believe his innocence, but only Bennett had stood by his side. Fought to prove the charges were unfounded. Not even his own family had done that.

Valentine frowned, itching to refill his empty drink. But he'd been drowning his anger and disappointment for far too long. Arabella Nichols's case gave him an opportunity to prove his worth again. Even if it couldn't clear his name.

"You know I'll do anything to help you. Of course I'll work on the outside," Bennett said with a sad nod.

"Thank you." Valentine turned away to avoid seeing his friend's pity. He hated that above all else.

Bennett cleared his throat. "I've heard Arabella Nichols is the most beautiful woman in the Empire, but I have only seen her from a distance. Is she truly the fallen angel some claim?"

Valentine thought about Arabella. Of her cascading blond hair, the intoxicating, spicy scent of her satin skin, of the captivating blue of her eyes. "Yes," he said softly. "She's even more beautiful than described."

Bennett tilted his head, searching Valentine's face until he shifted uncomfortably. Valentine wasn't sure he wanted his friend to see the whole truth about his encounter.

"And you took her to bed." Bennett shook his head. "I must say, that surprises me."

"Why?"

His friend shifted. "Because a woman . . . your desire for a treacherous woman . . . is what led to your dismissal."

Valentine shut his eyes. He didn't need a reminder of that fact. Laurel Talbot had played his desire and his emotions like a fiddler at a country dance. He had given all of himself to her . . . only to discover she was the doxy of the leader of a ring of thieves. That every word she said was a lie, that every time she lay in his bed, let him take her body, it was done to aid her other lover.

And in the end, she made sure everyone believed Valentine was a willing participant in their deception. That he was part of their ring. Had given over duty for sex.

"I realize that," Valentine said softly. "But this is different. My eyes are wide open. I know what Arabella is. Who she is. She doesn't want anyone to know of her plight, so she wants me to pose as her lover. You know that when you take on a role for a case, it's best to make it as real as possible." He shrugged, dismissing the night he spent in Arabella's bed as nothing but investigative cleverness. when in reality, it was so much more. Too much more.

Bennett nodded. "I trust you know her. And yourself. Just remember that a woman in the business of pleasure must know how much power her flesh yields. Don't let any skills she possesses let you forget that fact."

Valentine clenched his fist at his side. That was the trouble, wasn't it? When he was in Arabella's arms, he *had* forgotten that fact . . . just briefly. Pleasure and emotion had ruled his wild mind. And it was only by the grace of seeing his surrender in the reflection of her mirror that he'd been able to take control of that powerful encounter.

"Yes, that may be true, Bennett," he said through clenched teeth. "But I know better than to trust any warm words or tempting touch she tries to use against me. I will keep a tight rein on Arabella Nichols."

His friend nodded, but as Bennett launched into a detailed outline of what information they would need to gather in order to protect Arabella, Valentine winced. Keeping a tight rein on her wasn't the challenge. Based on the night they had shared, the difficulty might be restraining himself.

This was only the second time John Valentine had been in Arabella's room, but already he owned it. She clenched a fist as she watched him pace around the perimeter like a sleek, dark tiger surveying his territory. The room, her things . . . even *her*, he had claimed them all the moment he arrived. And now he was going to share this chamber with her until he felt she was safe from her would-be killer.

There would be no respite from his distracting presence . . . no break from his tantalizing touch. She shivered.

Valentine didn't even notice her reaction as he turned a page in one of the letters he held. "Are these all of them?"

Her shiver turned from one of desire to fear. "No."

His brown gaze shot up with his eyebrows, ensnaring her own. "No?" he repeated in surprise.

She forced a smile, hoping to keep up the façade of a jaded lady. Very few saw her real self; Valentine could not be one of them. "As I explained last night, I only began to save them after the first attempts on my life."

"And does anyone else know about them?" he asked, setting the pile aside.

"I've confided my fears to one other person, my closest friend, Lydia Bartlett. She's seen them and even begged me to depart London."

He nodded, his expression grim. "She may well have been correct. This person, whoever he is, is serious. I don't believe his threats are idle . . . and they are escalating."

Pure terror ripped through Arabella and she dipped her head with a choked sob. Clenching her fists, she turned from Valentine and tried to pull herself together. With effort, she bit back her emotions, tamping them down deep in her chest.

But he had already seen her weakness. Silently, he crossed the room and placed his hands on her shoulders.

The touch did aid her in forgetting her fear, but it inspired a new reaction. One just as dangerous. Desire. With just a benign, comforting gesture, Valentine lit a fire in her belly. The same one he lit the night before. The one she had been trying to convince herself wasn't as hot and powerful as it seemed.

She was wrong.

Slowly, he turned her to face him and she caught her breath, this time not on a sob, but a sigh. A moan. How could the man do that with just a touch? With just the scent of his hot skin?

It was too much.

Shrugging out of his embrace, she paced to the fire. A cold substitute for his hands.

"Now that you have seen the letters, perhaps you'd like to join me downstairs?" She glanced at the clock on her mantel. Half past eight. "It is late enough that many of my patrons will have arrived for the nightly festivities."

"And you wish to show them your newest trophy?" he asked with a sly smile she didn't expect from the normally stoic John Valentine.

She laughed, some of the tension around them fading. "Yes."

"Do you think it will be difficult to convince them of our affair?" he asked as he offered her an arm. She took it, starting at the spark that snapped between them when they touched.

"Perhaps. It is well-known and often discussed that I've been alone for a long while." When Valentine's sharp gaze flashed to her, she turned her face. That was twice he'd made her blush in as many days. "To keep suspicion from being raised, yes, we will have to prove our passion for each other."

As he opened the door and led her toward the main stairs, his smile grew and turned dangerously animal. "Then I will endeavor to be convincing."

Valentine's eyes darted from corner to corner in the large main hall as Arabella led him through tables and past groups of people. Her smile was broad, welcoming, as she waved and called greetings to some of the most powerful people in society. But as she motioned to a private table against the back wall of the hall, he saw tension around her eyes. She might play the part of sparkling hostess, but there was more to her than that.

Just as he'd seen in her bedroom a few moments before, fear darkened her face. Not that he blamed her. The letters from the person threatening her life were graphic and pointed. And in his estimation, not to be trifled with.

But who was the person willing to take Arabella's life? And why?

He settled back into the leather chair, straightening his legs beneath the large table until they were hidden beneath the long tablecloth, and looked around.

Arabella always referred to the person set on taking her life as someone outside her inner circle. A thwarted lover, a blackballed patron, a zealous moralist . . . but he knew well that often it was the ones closest who were most capable of treachery and betrayal. Anyone in this room could be responsible.

Though at present, no one around them seemed very interested in taking a life. No, they seemed more focused on taking each other. Music played in the distance, soft, sensual, and set the mood for the activities around them. At the closest table to Arabella and himself, a man kissed a woman in a mask with unbridled passion as his fingers slipped below the neckline of her gown and teased her full breast. She writhed beneath his caress. Valentine couldn't see below the tablecloth, but by the way her arm jerked up and down, he believed she was stroking her companion's cock with no thought of who could see.

Farther away, but still within clear view, a woman served drinks to a table of raucous gentlemen. Her gown was utterly sheer and she wore no undergarments. When one of the men pulled her down to straddle his lap, she didn't protest. In fact, she threw her head back with a laugh and began to grind against him.

But up on the raised stage in the distance, the real entertainment of the night had begun. A large screen glowed from the lamps and candles that had been lit behind it. Behind the screen, the silhouette of a couple was clear. The man was on his knees, pleasuring his female companion. Her shadowed hips jerked and hands clenched in his hair with every motion of his head. Finally, the man slid his lips up the apex of her body, turned her around and speared his erection inside her.

Her scream of pleasure echoed in the hall around them, despite the buzzing of the crowd, the moans of other couples enjoying the public pleasures allowed them. Valentine shifted. His cock was already swelling from the presence of the woman beside him. Seeing all this sin and sex, hearing the moans, he only became more aware of Arabella. Of the spicy scent of her skin. The brush of her unbound hair against his arm.

"Valentine?" she whispered, leaning up to brush her lips against his ear.

Color exploded before his eyes as the desire in his bloodstream raged out of control. He turned his face toward hers and took her lips in savage possession. She gasped, clearly surprised by the intensity of the kiss, but when he cupped her chin and tilted her head for greater access, she acquiesced with a sigh of pleasure.

He stroked her mouth with his tongue, mimicking the way he had filled her the night before. But memories of that heated joining also made him remember other things. Their struggle for control. His near surrender to her demands.

He couldn't let himself get so close to the edge again.

Pulling back, he looked into blue eyes soft with desire.

Arabella's breath came short, lifting her breasts with each one, and her nipples were outlined clearly against the silk of her low-cut gown. He groaned when he realized she probably wore no underthings.

"Valentine?" she whispered again.

"We need to prove we're involved in a passionate affair?" he asked, his voice rough with desire and lack of breath.

She nodded slowly, but before she could say anything else, he surged forward and took her mouth again. He stole her words with a kiss, her resistance as he slipped his hands down her waist and drew her flush against him.

Arabella groaned and her voice vibrated against his tongue, sending shock waves of pleasure to heat his blood and harden his already steely erection. He wanted nothing more than to lay her out on the table and have his way with her. She wouldn't resist. The way she arched and clawed at him told him she wouldn't.

But doing so, having her publicly, would do more than relieve his need. It would mean surrendering to her terms. Losing control. He needed *her* to be the one to beg. To writhe.

A wicked smile turned his lips as he glided them away from hers. Lower to her throat. Lower to her breast, where he blew hot through her thin gown. Lower, lower, as he slipped to his knees beneath the table.

"Valentine!" she gasped, shock and desire equal in her voice.

He lifted his eyes just once, letting her see his intent before he ducked his head beneath the tablecloth. The heavy fabric muffled some of the sound and light of the hall. It cocooned him in a prison of warmth and the heady fragrance of Arabella's growing desire.

He only teased for a moment, running his hands over her

legs through her gown. She sucked in her breath above him, tensing against his fingers. He wanted her on the brink of anticipation. The edge of reason. He wanted her to reach for his lips, his hands, his touch.

His need called to him, but he pushed it aside. When he tasted her, it wasn't going to be about *his* need. It would be about hers. Only hers.

He lifted the hem of her gown, revealing the dainty slippers and hand-stitched silk stockings she wore. Both were dusky blue, matching her gown perfectly. He pushed the skirt up with one hand, shifting his position on his knees so he could stroke the back of her calf.

Her legs trembled, though she no longer said his name. She held back and he had to admire her for that. He knew the value of staying in control. A woman of her position, a woman of her reputation, had no choice but to do the same. And that was why making her lose that control was all the sweeter.

Her skirt inched higher, revealing the curve of her knee, the lower sweep of her thighs, which she still squeezed tightly together. That wouldn't do at all. Valentine forced his shoulders between them, inching them open, even as he ducked his head for clearance beneath the table.

"You wouldn't dare," Arabella hissed above him, the table shifting as she gripped it, scrambling for purchase.

He smiled as he reached the top of her stockings and spread her legs further.

"A challenge," he whispered as he revealed the soft nest of blond curls that hid her feminine core. They were already dark with needy moisture, her outer lips swollen and pouting for his touch.

She tensed, pushing back against his shoulders, but to no avail. He was far stronger and forced her to open wide. He pulled at her hips, bringing her to the edge of her seat and taking the last fraction of access she refused him.

Gently, he smoothed her curls aside, opened her sex to his eyes, his fingers, his tongue. She shivered again, her thighs quivering against his arms, her breath panting in and out.

Then, breathing in a deep whiff of the perfume of her desire, he pressed his mouth against her and tasted her.

4

Arabella bit back a moan, even though other moans echoed around her. To voice her pleasure might not bring any more attention than Valentine disappearing beneath the table had, but it would give him the satisfaction of knowing how much his touch affected her.

Not that he wasn't fully aware. Even before he pressed his lips against her, speared his tongue inside her, her desire had been wet against her thighs.

And now that he was tasting her . . .

She dipped her head back, clawing at the table as he swirled his tongue around her clit for an all-too-brief moment of bliss, then returned his attentions to her weeping slit.

It was too much. The pleasure was far too focused, building too fast for her to keep up. All she could do was try to hold back her release as long as possible. Try to regain some control, though she had no idea how that would be possible. It wasn't like she could touch him in her vulnerable position.

Nothing she did could entreat him to come back to her level, give her some chance to entice him.

She sighed as he lapped at her and her hips jolted in response. Long had she used pleasures like this against her partners. Used orgasm to bend them to her will. Gave, but only because it let her take. She used her body against her lovers . . . without them ever knowing.

But Valentine knew all her tricks.

A gasp bubbled free as he suckled her clit and starbursts lit before her eyes. She felt his smile against her pussy before he went back to firm, teasing strokes of his tongue within her folds.

Valentine was using her own tactics against her, making her pleasure the center of his world. It seemed selfless, but in reality this act was designed to have her slipping under. Surrendering.

And God help her, she was doing just that.

She arched as his strokes grew harder, but he withheld what she craved. Release taunted her with its closeness, but he seemed to purposefully avoid her clit and keep that ultimate pleasure from her.

"Please," she moaned, hating herself for it. "Please."

His chuckle was muffled by the fabric separating them. "Please give you what you need?"

"Yes, damn you," she ground out, thrusting her hips helplessly against his ever torturing tongue. "Yes!"

He didn't smile this time. Instead, he glided his hands up her sensitive inner thigh. One, then two, he slipped thick, rough fingers into her clenching channel. She groaned at the fullness of the invasion, though it wasn't nearly enough.

But he was no longer tormenting. He pulled her tight against him with his free hand and went to work on her clit with his devilishly skilled tongue. Swirling and suckling, he gave her tingling pleasure, all while pumping his fingers inside her.

Arabella's release built fast and hard, a wall low in her belly that was growing brick by brick until, finally, in an explosion so massive that she blocked out everything around her, she came. The table rocked with the force of her release as her hips bucked wildly against his still strumming tongue and working fingertips. She bit her lip, tasting her own blood as she held back screams.

The waves crested, lapped, and with a final shudder, subsided as she went limp against the leather seat.

Valentine pulled her gown down over her legs, his own heartbeat throbbing so hard in his chest that he was surprised it didn't burst free. He'd never wanted to fill a woman more, but he held back. He'd proven a point by making her beg. He'd gained control. Now he had to keep it. Keep sex on his terms. And they didn't include rutting with her in front of the Empire.

Carefully, he climbed out from under the table and retook his seat beside her. He sucked her essence from his fingertips before he unfolded the nearest napkin and dabbed his mouth, knowing she watched his every move.

"*That* should prove our affair well enough, shouldn't it?" he asked.

Her eyes flickered with emotion for a brief moment. Was that hurt he saw in her stare? No, it couldn't have been. Arabella wanted him and she needed his protection, but a woman like her would never allow herself to become more deeply involved.

"It will," she answered softly. "If that was your only intention, you succeeded."

Valentine thought about that. Proving a point to those around them should have been his only intention. But it hadn't been. Giving Arabella intense pleasure, hearing her moans, feeling her quicken at the stroke of his tongue, quiver in release around his fingers . . . those things had moved him. In those moments, he all but forgot duty. To Arabella. To himself.

A dangerous proposition. One he could not repeat. So he cut away any remaining emotions and leaned back in his chair. Trying to forget that he could still taste her on his lips, he said, "Then the first part of my duty to you is on its way to being accomplished. Let us begin on the second. Tell me more about your past."

She tensed, the satiated posture of her body gone in an instant. "Why?" she snapped, motioning to one of the women serving in the hall. The girl brought two tumblers of sherry and Arabella took a sip. "Why would you want to know about that?"

He tilted his head. "Because someone from your past might well have something to do with the attempts on your life. It's more likely a person you know than a stranger, especially considering the venom with which you've been threatened."

She hesitated, searching his face with captivating eyes. For a moment, he thought she might bring him into her confidence. But then she shook her head. "I don't think telling you about the past will do any good. If someone from my history wanted to harm me, why would they wait until now to do so?"

He frowned. She held back. It was something far too familiar. The last woman who had inspired his passion held back, as well. She had betrayed him. Stolen everything he had. His profession. His name. And he wanted Arabella even more than he had that woman. What more could *she* steal if she chose?

"How am I to protect you if you won't be honest with me?" he snapped, much harsher than he had intended.

She started at his tone, her lips parting in surprise. But before she could respond, a woman approached their table. It was the red-haired beauty who had taken him to Arabella's chamber the night before. The one with the enticing stares.

"Arabella," the mystery woman cooed as she drew Arabella into an embrace. "You are positively glowing . . . though there is no doubt why."

Her gaze fell on Valentine and one auburn eyebrow cocked in question and invitation. He nodded an acknowledgment, though he waited for Arabella's lead on how to proceed.

She smiled. He realized it was the first genuine expression he'd seen on her face, outside of unguarded moments of desire and release. He took a second look at the woman who inspired such friendly regard.

"Lydia, there you are. I haven't seen you since you brought Mr. Valentine to me last night," Arabella said with a light laugh.

Valentine looked closer. Arabella had mentioned that a Lydia had encouraged her to leave London when the threats against her began. This must be that same woman. Her friend and only confidante.

"A difficult package to deliver, I promise you." Her eyes, green and a little catlike, focused on him yet again. "I would like a proper introduction to the man you pursued . . . and apparently won . . . so single-mindedly."

Valentine rose as Arabella introduced him. So, Lydia was close enough to know Arabella desired him for a lover, close enough to know about the threats . . . but not close enough that Arabella confided he was her protector, as well as her bedmate.

"A pleasure, Miss Bartlett." He dropped a kiss on the top of her hand.

"Lydia," she insisted. "You simply must call me Lydia."

"Lydia," he repeated. He watched as the two women began to chat. It was business talk mostly, nothing overly interesting, though he marked the fact that Lydia Bartlett was very involved in Arabella's club. He also caught the stares the young woman sent his way, appraising, cool, despite the invitation in her words and demeanor.

He might have dismissed that underlying coolness as concern for Arabella's welfare with a man she hardly knew, except Lydia also turned it on her friend. When Arabella turned away, any pretense Lydia showed of being concerned or friendly fell, for a brief moment, only to return when Arabella refocused on her.

Was that a character trait of Lydia's? A woman who made a living at pretending emotion might have difficulty doing anything but acting a part, certainly. And her words to Arabella were nothing but kind.

Still, it was a fact worth looking into.

"How long have you been acquainted with Arabella?"

Both women's faces froze at his question. Arabella turned toward him slightly, her eyes wide. Again, she wished to hide her past from him. And again, her reserve alarmed him.

Lydia's smile was forced. "For many years, Mr. Valentine. She saved my life."

He cocked his head. Interesting. "Did she? You must be very close, then."

The redheaded woman bobbed out a nod. "We are." There was a sudden sadness in her expression that seemed out of place. "We always have been."

Arabella clutched his arm, dragging him to his feet. "I'm afraid my head is beginning to ache. Lydia, darling, you'll excuse us, won't you?"

Her friend nodded, giving a brief smile to them both. "Of course. It was a pleasure making your full acquaintance, Mr. Valentine."

"The pleasure was all mine," Valentine said as Arabella began to drag him away from her friend. They weaved through the main hall, dodging the arching bodies of some of Arabella's more adventurous clientele. Valentine didn't speak as she dragged him into the hallway, but at the bottom of the main stair, he stopped, easily bringing her up short.

"I don't know what put you to running, Arabella," he said, low and close to her ear. She shivered as his breath caressed her and the response set his blood back to full boil. "But it is foolhardy. I need to know more about the people who come here, about your friends and enemies, in order to help you as you've hired me to do."

She shook her head, pulling back against his arm to no avail. He had no intention of letting her escape either his arms or his questions.

"I hired you to protect me," she answered, her hiss as low and harsh as his own. "I hired you to determine who wants me dead. Not to delve into my private affairs, or those of my friends."

He let out an exasperated sigh. "You are by no means a stupid woman, Arabella. Surely you see the two may very well be connected."

She drew in a breath and he saw that she knew exactly what he was talking about. She knew full well that he needed to know more in order to assist her.

But she wasn't willing to share it.

"You're willing to *die* rather than give away a few secrets?" he asked, drawing away in shock.

She stared up at him, blue eyes clouding with sudden and, he guessed, uncharacteristic tears. Her shoulders tensed and her arm trembled against his. Frustration bubbled inside him. And fear. Fear for her life. Fear for what would happen if she didn't surrender what she refused to give.

"You won't tell me?" he whispered. "Then I have no choice but to determine the truth for myself."

He dragged her up the stairs behind him. She squealed out a protest, then scrambled to keep up with his long, anger-driven steps.

"Valentine, slow down," she snapped as he hauled her down the hallway, through her bedroom door and slammed it behind them. Immediately, he released her and looked around.

"You really should have that door locked at all times," he said before he took a long step forward. "Where to start? I think your escritoire is a good place."

"Stop!" she shrieked, but he ignored her pleas as he sat down and began to open drawers. Letters, ledgers, pens, and ink clattered as he searched through each drawer, dragging its contents out for examination before he shoved whatever he found back inside with no thought to the order it had once been in.

"You cannot go through my private things," she insisted, grabbing for his arm as he pushed away from her desk and strode toward her bedroom. Memories assaulted him as he looked at the bed, but he pushed them aside, along with her hand.

He headed for her dresser. The top drawer revealed a variety of sheer stockings, but nothing else. The second a collection of negligees that made his blood burn a little hotter. He could only imagine drawing the lacy strap of this one over her shoulder, stroking her through the satin bodice of another.

Shaking his head, he opened the third drawer.

"What . . . ?" He gasped as he stared at what he had uncovered. A drawer filled with velvet ropes, satin blindfolds, erotic books, and explicit drawings. He picked up a sketch of a woman stroking herself as a man looked on, clearly ready to finish what she started.

"Arabella?"

She straightened her spine and stared at him with no trace of embarrassment. "This is my private collection," she explained, snatching the drawing and replacing it in her drawer before she slammed it shut and turned to him with folded arms.

"Your private collection, your private past, your private demons." Valentine ran a hand through his hair as he just barely resisted the urge to pull her against him. "Those things could get you killed. Keeping me in the dark defeats the purpose of hiring me."

The stubborn chit's jaw set in a harsh line he knew was as unbreakable as her will. It was something he normally admired, but at the moment, he hated it.

"Whether that is true or not, my hiring you gives you no right to invade my private things, to delve into matters better left buried."

"And does taking you to bed give me any right?" he asked, moving in on her. She started at his sudden advance, but didn't back down. Her chin lifted, but he saw desire mixed with the anger in her eyes. "Does making you scream in pleasure, surrender like you never have with any other man, give me the right?"

She stiffened and a swell of pride rushed through him. So his words were true. Despite her jaded past, the passion they shared was as unique for Arabella as it was for him.

He tamped back the dangerous joy that accompanied that realization. He knew nothing about her. She shared nothing. Only an illusion.

"No," she said softly. "Even if that is true, and I admit nothing of the kind, it gives you no right. You are in my employ and I'll tell you what you can and cannot pursue when it comes to this case. No man controls my comings and goings. No man controls my secrets, past or future. Not even you."

His nostrils flared at her condescending dismissal, but he didn't allow emotion to show on his face. "I'm afraid not, Miss Nichols," he sneered. "That isn't how I work."

He motioned to the drawer she had closed. "I hope your 'private collection' keeps you entertained. Because I won't be around to pleasure you for a few days."

She stepped forward with widening eyes. "What? Why?"

With a shrug, he said, "You offer me no choice. If you won't share the truth, I'll seek it elsewhere. While I'm gone, be sure you stay here where you have some level of safety. Keep your door locked and don't go out alone."

He turned, but before he left, he came back. Crowding Arabella against the dresser behind her, he gathered her into his arms. Her breasts flattened against his chest, her thighs molded to his. He ached to fill her, take her, but after her denial tonight, he knew he could never possess more than her willing body. It wasn't a bargain he could make, though it tempted him.

"Arabella, while I'm gone, consider why you hired me. Somewhere out there, perhaps closer than you realize, someone hunts you. They want you dead. I can protect you, but only if you let me past this barrier you have built."

He looked at her, so soft in his arms, her eyes dewy with desire, with confusion, with a fight to remain distant. Slowly, he dropped his lips to hers, coaxing her mouth open to taste her. Her fists clenched against his chest, her heart rate doubling. She returned the kiss readily, but immediately tried to turn up the heat. As tempting as that was, he refused to allow it, keeping this kiss a tender exploration rather than a passionate possession.

With effort, he broke away. "And remember this, as well. You may entertain yourself with that drawer full of toys and pictures, but nothing will fulfill you the way I have. Surrender is fearful, but you've experienced the rewards of it . . . and I have done nothing to prove I don't deserve your trust. And I never will."

With that, he let her go. As much as he wanted to look back, he did not, and she didn't call to him. And as he shut her door behind him, he wondered why that fact made him ache.

5

"Arabella Nichols does not exist."

Valentine clenched his fists and screwed his eyes shut. How he wished he could block out those words.

"Stop saying that," he growled, turning on Bennett with a wild expression he couldn't control. "We must be mistaken."

His friend held out the papers in his hand. "We aren't. There is no record of the woman anywhere until five years ago."

Valentine's soul howled. It was no surprise that Arabella was keeping secrets. She had all but admitted she withheld the truth from him. But what a secret! She had created an entire identity from whole cloth. Who was she really? And was her shadowy past linked to the current threats on her life?

"You're angered by this news," Bennett mused as he leaned back on the edge of his desk and looked at his friend with folded arms.

"Of course I am!" Valentine barely resisted an overwhelming urge to put a fist through the closest wall. "She lied to me."

Bennett's eyebrow arched. "And that matters to you because . . . ?"

Valentine froze. Why *did* it matter? Arabella had hired him for a duty, one that had very little to do with who she was . . . or had been. He should have been able to shrug off her deception easily, but he couldn't.

Because when he took her in his arms, he felt a connection. Tenuous . . . trembling . . . terrifying . . . but there nonetheless.

He met his friend's waiting gaze. Bennett saw too much. Valentine measured his tone carefully, removing as much emotion as he could.

"It matters because someone from her past could be responsible for the threats on her. Especially if there is a life she's running from." He drew in a calming breath, not that it did much good. "When did the identity of Arabella Nichols come into record?"

"She first surfaced as Jesterton's mistress."

Valentine turned away with a shudder. Lord Jesterton . . . a sadistic bastard who went through more mistresses than the biggest libertine. He never stayed with one woman longer than a few months and he always settled them with enormous sums. The ones who survived him, that was. A few women he had been benefactor to had disappeared entirely. Rumor said they were victims to his brutality in or out of the bedroom.

And Arabella had been one of them. What tortures had she endured? He might not know anything else about her, but Valentine knew pain was not her inclination. She must have been so frightened.

And Valentine found himself wishing to comfort her. To make whatever ugly memories she carried fade away.

But that was ridiculous! His responsibility wasn't to console her. It was to keep her alive.

"If only I knew who I was protecting," he murmured.

"What was that?" Bennett asked.

"Nothing. What about Jesterton? He's a vindictive bastard. Could he be involved in the attacks against Arabella?"

His friend shuffled some papers. "Certainly he has been rumored to take swift vengeance on those who cross him, but he's been out of town for over two months tending to some business concerns. He was not nearby during at least two of the attempts on her." Bennett shrugged. "And if he wanted to harm Arabella, why would he wait five years to do it?"

Valentine nodded. He had had the displeasure of meeting Jesterton twice when his own father was still alive, before Valentine left society. The Earl didn't seem like the kind of man who could manage vengeance as a dish served cold. He hadn't seemed the patient sort.

So who was it? He was no closer to any answers. Only to more troubling questions and long-buried emotions.

"Pardon me, Mr. Caruthers, but a message has arrived for Mr. Valentine."

Both men turned to see Bennett's batman at the parlor door, holding a folded note.

"For me?" Valentine asked as he stepped forward. "Here?"

"Yes, sir, apparently the sender stressed its urgency and your servants forwarded it."

"Thank you," he said as he opened the missive. A whiff of the perfume that hung on the fine linen paper gave him no doubt about the sender. "Arabella."

His heart throbbing, he turned to the note. His eyes widened at what she had written in her swirling, elegant hand. Anger and terror welled inside him in equal measures.

"Damn it! Bring my coat," he bellowed as he stuffed the letter into his pocket. "Hurry!"

"What is it?" Bennett asked, stepping forward.

"Keep looking into Arabella's past," he ordered as he snatched his coat from Bennett's stunned batman. "I'll call on you tomorrow if I'm able."

"Where are you going?" Bennett insisted, trailing him as he hurried into the hall.

He turned as he wrenched the door open. "Arabella has decided to disregard my order and venture out alone. So *I* am going to the opera."

Without waiting for Bennett's answer, he started down the stairs, but he could hear his friend's voice echoing around him as he boarded his waiting carriage.

"Be careful, Valentine."

As he slammed the carriage door, he scrubbed a hand over his face. Be careful. It was all he could do when Arabella . . . or whoever she was . . . was making her way into his hardened heart.

When the curtain to her private box flew back, framing Valentine at his darkest, most furious best, Arabella's heart flipped with both relief and anticipation.

Relief because although she had tried to be brave, every noise, every word, every gesture from those in her midst made her tremble. She now saw danger around every corner and Valentine's presence gave her a peace she hadn't felt since he stormed from her room with a demand she stay home.

But the reasons for her anticipation were less clear and certainly less reassuring. She knew he would be angry. In truth, she deserved the fury that darkened his brown eyes to rich chocolate. She had put herself in danger to prove a point and he would react accordingly.

But she anticipated more than his mere rage. As he stood, the curtain fluttering behind him, the light from the hall outlining his wide shoulders, his fists clenched, she realized she had *missed* him. She anticipated being with him. Touching him. Letting him touch her.

Her heart flipped as he pulled the curtain closed and stormed, silent, across the small private area. She scrambled to her feet to meet him, but he gave her no opportunity to put up a defense. Instead, he grabbed her shoulders, turned her, and pressed her against the wall behind them.

"What were you thinking?" he growled, his touch as demanding as his words. His fingers pushed into her skin, but they did not inspire fear or a need to obey. Instead, they sparked dangerous lust. Need she had forgotten was so strong in the days they were apart.

She struggled against him to no avail, so she stilled, staring up at him as she prayed he would not see what a strong hold he possessed over her.

"You left," she whispered, her tone as harsh and angry as his. "You demanded I follow your rule with no explanation. I waited for you to tell me when you would return. You never contacted me. For all I knew, you had no plans to complete the bargain we made. What would you have me do? Live under the rule of an absent lover who has made it abundantly clear he does not respect my right to make my own decisions? Live in fear of my own shadow? No, Valentine, I would not have you control me."

He barked out a laugh that no doubt carried to the boxes around them. Society would have its fun recounting this tale tomorrow.

"No, Arabella." He sneered her name and she turned away from the contempt in his tone. But when he spoke again, the sarcasm and anger were muted. "I would have you use enough sense to know I was trying to protect you. I would have you care enough about your own safety to hear my words. Your actions in coming out alone tonight were foolhardy at best."

She pushed against him, again trying to break away from the distracting press of his body. All she succeeded in doing was brushing her hips against the hard thrust of his erection. Her eyes went wide as she darted her gaze to him. He tilted his head in challenge, as if daring her to point out that he wanted her.

She didn't. Instead, she whispered, "I had no choice. People were beginning to ask why I locked myself away. If I wanted to keep the threats against me a secret, I had to come out. To be seen. And—"

She bit back what she was about to say. It was too close to the truth, too close to him.

"And what, Arabella?" he asked, his grip on her arms softening, becoming a caress rather than a prison. "You have so many secrets. What is this most recent?"

She shivered as his breath caressed her cheek, her throat. How many dreams had she had of Valentine's hands on her skin since he deserted her? Of his smile, the one he so rarely flashed. Of his cock buried deep, but also of the comfort of his hand against her back as she entered a room.

"I wanted to see you," she admitted, hating herself for telling him something that could be used against her. But she couldn't hold back. "I wanted you to come to me."

He drew back, staring at her as if weighing why she would say such a thing. Then his mouth dipped closer, his breath searing her lips as he murmured, "I'm here, Arabella. For better or worse, I am here now."

Then his mouth met hers at the same instant the orchestra below blared forth in music and the opera began. Arabella arched, no longer fighting. It had been two days since he touched her and she had thought of little else during that time. For the moment, she didn't care about surrender or the voices in her head that reminded her how foolish that was.

She wanted Valentine. She wanted him to fill the stunning, sudden emptiness his departure had left in her soul, her body, her heart.

He obliged without her asking. His mouth, which had been so rough when he claimed hers, gentled against her lips. She opened to him and, for what seemed like an eternity, they kissed. He sucked and swirled her tongue, tasted her completely. He owned the kiss, but did not use it against her as he had done in the past. It was a gift, given even as he took equal pleasure in return. For the first time since she met him, she felt like they were on equal ground, and it was glorious.

The music below swelled again, the lilting voice of the soprano merging in perfect duet with the deeper tenor. Valentine drew back, looking into her eyes. Questions lay there in his gaze. Ones about her past. Even ones about the future. But one stood out above all others. He was *asking* to touch her, without words. Without force.

She gave her answer by slipping her hands between them and shoving his heavy coat from his shoulders. He growled out satisfaction before his mouth returned to hers. Now the kiss was possession.

Valentine pushed against the wall, pinning Arabella. The luscious length of her molded to his hard body and he was in heaven. Only one thing was better. Having her admit she wanted him at her side. He ignored his better judgment and memories long enough to savor that confession.

Her arms slipped up around his neck, urging his kiss on,

surrendering, this time with no fight. It was enough to drive
a man mad. His fingers stroked her arms, swept along her
exposed collarbone, and finally found the little pearl buttons
on the front of her stunning violet gown. The one that made
her eyes midnight-blue.

The delicate fabric fell away easily in his hands, revealing
her voluptuous breasts. Valentine dipped his head, capturing
one rosy nipple and sucking hard enough that Arabella cried
out at the exact moment the cymbals crashed below them
and muffled the sound.

He glanced up. She bit her lip, trying to hold back a second
cry of pleasure when he took the opposite nipple into the
heat of his mouth. That wouldn't do. He wanted to hear her
pleasure. It was more beautiful than the opera below.

He stroked his tongue across the bud, swirling, sucking
until she was trembling. Finally, his teeth rasped gently over
the sensitized tip and she let out a moan as her trembling legs
gave way.

He cupped her backside to support her, massaging her
through the drooping satin of her gown. She arched helplessly, shamelessly offering her breasts, grinding her hips
against his swelling erection. His control wavered as intense
pleasure ripped through him.

He forgot any concern for control or the crowd around
them as he pulled her dress away, letting it pool at her feet.
She was naked beneath. Of course she was. She always was.
And he loved that she granted him such access. That she was
always ready, always slick and heated, always open for his
touch.

"Valentine," she breathed close to his ear, his name a
plea.

He did not deny her. Drawing back, he wasted no time in
divesting himself of his own clothing. He stood before her

naked, his erection thrusting proud and ready, curling toward his stomach. It tingled with every look she gave him, with every step toward her, as if his cock knew that soon it would be inside her, fulfilling both their needs.

Arabella sucked in her breath. Valentine's body could not have been molded more perfectly to her specifications, and she ached to join with him in an ancient dance of pleasure. That it was also an ancient dance of control was something she shoved aside, revolting against her rational mind in favor of her body's desire. Her heart's desire.

He reached for her and she stepped freely into his arms. Slowly, he lowered her to the floor, cushioning her on their discarded clothes. If the rough carpet was uncomfortable, she didn't feel it. She was too focused on Valentine as he knelt beneath her spread legs.

He cupped her rear end, hot fingers searing her skin. She gasped as he titled her up, spreading her sex for his hungry eyes and opening her to his every whim. As the music crashed and built around them, he fanned the flames of need by playing his fingers along the entrance to her slit. His index finger smoothed her curls, brushed teasingly over her clit, and finally delved deep within her. She tossed her head, gasping for breath as pleasure threatened to overwhelm her even with this simple touch. No other man had ever brought her to the edge, kept her there, with such ease.

But no other man had been like Valentine.

His finger pulled away, leaving her clenching body empty. "You're so hot," he murmured, his voice filled with awe and tense with desire as he swirled his wet finger around the bud of her pleasure. "So wet and ready."

She nodded, the ache inside her spiraling tighter, closer to losing control. "Yes, ready for you. Please, please . . . give me what I need."

His gaze came up and she was shocked by how intensely a fire now burned within. He gripped her hips and slid her forward until the head of his cock nudged her entrance.

"Whatever you desire," he promised as he thrust forward.

Around them, the opera house echoed with the building music of the final aria. The singer's voice grew more desperate with emotion, and so did Arabella. Valentine swirled his hips as he thrust, holding her close as he took her.

Release built like a racing stallion within her. She felt it approaching as Valentine pounded deep inside her and it raged out of control when one rough thumb pressed down against her sensitive clit.

She bit back her cries of pleasure as wave after wave rocked her. Her body tingled, her hips jerked, and all the while Valentine thrust on, his pace never ending, never easing.

She had just come down from the high of release when he leaned forward, lifting her until they were face-to-face, her legs wrapped around his thrusting hips. Still, he continued to move within her, even as he speared his tongue between her lips.

Valentine clenched at her hips, setting the pace as he thrust. She met him, her mouth scorching his, her breasts brushing his chest. God, she was so hot around him, milking him closer to release.

But he wasn't ready yet. He wanted to feel her clench and quiver again. Again. He never wanted that to stop. He was claiming her, whether she knew that or not. And he would not be satisfied until she was weak in his arms, given over to him utterly.

He broke contact with her lips and dipped his head, catching the nipple that bobbed so temptingly before his lips. Her head tilted back and she sighed. Then the sigh broke as he sucked. Her body tightened, her channel squeezing and pulsing through a second, powerful orgasm that brought him right up to the brink of control.

He thought of anything and everything to calm his racing pulse. Not yet. His possession wasn't complete. Her surrender wasn't overpowering.

Sweat slicked their bodies as he once again lowered her to the piles of clothing on the box floor. She was limp in his arms, panting as her body clenched through the final tremors of her most recent release. This time he didn't kneel as he took her, but covered her with his body, holding her close and raining kisses along the damp, flushed skin around her hairline, down her neck.

He slowed his thrusts, ignoring the shots of overwhelming, electric desire that stroked his cock each time she lifted weakly to meet his demands. He worked his hips, rotating to let her feel how fully he filled her. To stroke that secret, sensitive spot buried deep within her channel. Her body quickened with each stroke, her hands clamped against his back, nails digging at his flesh as he brought her closer, closer, closer . . .

He watched her face as he took her. She strained, tears of relief streaming from her eyes. She was close to another orgasm, one more powerful than any previous. He saw it in her eyes, felt it in the way her body reached for more, reached for completion.

He rolled his hips as he slipped his fingers between their bodies and stroked her clit between his forefinger and thumb.

Arabella screamed in time to the final note of the prima donna's aria and it was the most beautiful sound Valentine ever heard. She bucked, her hips nearly throwing him free, and still her release and her cries went on and on. Even after the singer finished her final note and the crowd rose to its feet in applause, Arabella cried out as he finally allowed his own pleasure and filled her body—as he wished he could fill her heart.

Arabella's hands trembled as she refastened her buttons and did what she could to straighten her wrinkled gown. Not that what she and Valentine had done would be a secret, even if she could erase the effects from her clothing. She had practically screamed the opera house down. But that wasn't what troubled her. She had been on public display before . . . even with Valentine.

What troubled her was how intense this encounter had been. Not just physically, though she *was* weak from orgasm after orgasm, but emotionally. Valentine had been reaching for something as he took her, something more than power or control. And truth be told, she'd reached for it, too.

Even though she had long ago promised she would not give her heart or power to another man. She peeked over her shoulder where Valentine leaned against the wall, fully dressed and looking none the worse for wear. With a shiver, she broke their stare. Breaking her promise with a man like Valentine was even more complicated and treacherous.

He pushed off the wall and she *felt* him come up behind her. When he touched her shoulders, she shuddered with renewed desire. She'd had her own plans for tonight. Ones that didn't involve utter possession on the floor of her opera box.

No, her plans involved taking control back. She'd prepared her room for Valentine. Had a plan. But he'd swept that away, and that proved, more than anything else, that she could never surrender to his will again.

Turning, she threaded her hand through his arm and blinked up with a flirtatious flutter of her eyelashes. He arched a brow at her sudden shift in attitude, but she didn't back down. She couldn't.

"You'll accompany me home, won't you?" she asked. "You aren't going to stay away again?"

He sighed and there was something pained in the sound. Something that called to an answering ache in her heart. "Of course I'll escort you. You shouldn't be out alone. You're still in danger."

She nodded, briefly sober. Somehow when she was with Valentine, it was all too easy to forget why he had come into her life in the first place.

"Did you find any new information about who might be threatening me?" she asked, dropping her voice as he pushed the curtain aside and escorted her out of her opera box.

As they entered the crowded hall and headed for the main entrance, people stared. Valentine didn't seem to notice as he guided her through the throng, always sure of each step. She wished she were as steady on her feet and in her mind.

"Not quite enough," he answered, just as low. He drew in a long breath and looked unhappy to be broaching the subject. "Who are you?"

She started. "I don't know what you mean."

His scowl deepened as they walked through the thinning crowd and through the doorway to the street. Her carriage was parked in front and the footman hopped down to open the door as they stepped toward it. But before they reached the vehicle, Valentine came to a halt, turning her to face him.

"You know," he said, his voice little more than a harsh whisper. "You know exactly what I mean. Your name isn't Arabella Nichols. What else have you been hiding?"

_____

Valentine watched the blood drain from Arabella's face, as she realized exactly what he was saying. She yanked her arm from his and he winced as she stumbled away.

"I—I—" she stammered, her blue eyes darting around wildly as her hands trembled.

"Please don't deny it," he said softly, somehow still longing to pull her into his arms even though he was watching proof of her deceptive practices play out before his eyes. "I have seen enough proof that I won't believe you. And I don't like to be treated like a fool."

Her breath came sharp, but her trembling had subsided and she managed to control her expression. In fact, she looked at him in challenge now.

"I won't deny it. Clearly you are no fool, Valentine. But that doesn't mean I intend to share my private past with you." She shook her head. "My body was the bargain, not my soul."

Pain roared through him at that dismissal of all they'd shared. As if the sex between them, which was so powerful and consuming, was only part of some bargain. But then . . . he looked at her, cool as the evening breeze, arms folded. Perhaps what they'd shared *was* only a side deal of a business arrangement.

No. He'd felt something more in the way she touched him. The way she arched beneath him. The way she lost control when he took her.

"The bargain we made was for protection and investigation, my dear," he said with a sneer. At least when he turned to anger, his chest didn't feel like it would burst. "I've done both, with little assistance from you. I deserve to know what

I'm up against. If you expect me to continue to serve you, I demand it."

"Demand?" She repeated the word as if it were poison. "You are my employee, you have no right to demand."

Valentine stood stone-still as her words of anger cut through him, burned through his frustration to his very core. He could not, would not, do this again.

"Then you'll have to find another 'employee,' Arabella. I won't work under your terms." Turning his back, he stalked away.

"Valentine!" she called after him, her voice filled with shock . . . undeniable pain. He did not turn back. He couldn't.

"Valentine!" she repeated, filled with fear. He hesitated, but wouldn't allow himself to turn. He couldn't protect her when his heart and mind were tangled in her presence. It wasn't fair to either of them.

He took another step, but was interrupted by her voice yet again. Only this time, it wasn't his name from her lips, but a bloodcurdling, terror-filled scream. His heart pounding, Valentine turned back.

Just in time to see a man he did not recognize grab Arabella's wrist and thrust a knife toward her heart.

6

Valentine didn't recall jumping forward. He didn't remember throwing his full body weight on top of Arabella's attacker and slamming him to the cobblestones below. But he found himself on top of the man, raining blows upon him with all his might. His knuckles stung from the force of each punch.

He wound back, ready to thrust another fist into the man's flesh, when from the corner of his eye, he caught a glimpse of Arabella. She was crumpled to her knees, leaning against the carriage with a pale and frantic footman beside her.

Valentine turned away from her attacker, too distracted by seeing her so pale and terrified to care anymore about the man he held down. She met his gaze, her blue eyes dull with terror and pain. Then her eyes widened.

"Valentine!" she screamed. "Look out!"

He spun back as her assailant shoved him away, slicing at him with his knife. Valentine felt no pain as he made a grab for the man, but the stranger was too quick and took off into the gathering crowd of stragglers leaving the opera house and passersby.

Valentine struggled to his feet and took a step after the man, but he was long gone. He turned back to Arabella.

"Are you hurt?" she asked, trying to stand. "Are you cut?"

He dropped to his knees beside her, elbowing her footman out of the way. "I'm fine. You were injured. Let me see."

She drew back, as if she were surprised to hear the news, but then her gaze dropped down. She looked at the handkerchief she clutched to her shoulder as if she hadn't seen it before. Valentine frowned. She was in shock from the attack . . . and possibly the wound she would not show him.

"Come on, sweetheart," he coaxed, touching her wrist and drawing her hand away. "That's my girl."

He winced at the sight of Arabella's blood slashed across the snowy handkerchief in an ugly line. The shredded fabric on the shoulder of her gown was also edged in blood. The cut was a long, deep slash across her shoulder.

Arabella looked at the bloody handkerchief, moved her gaze to her wound, and promptly collapsed against his chest.

Arabella's eyes fluttered open. Distant voices buzzed in her ear, but they seemed so far away. So removed. It was like she was lying on a cloud and she couldn't quite move to see where she was.

She shifted and a shot of pain rocked through her shoulder. It brought a dose of reality with it and memories assailed her. A strange man came out of the crowd at the opera. He lunged toward her, knife drawn. A searing pain as he pulled his weapon free, tinged with her blood, and readied himself to strike again.

Valentine. He'd drawn the man away. A fight.

She sat up, ignoring the pain.

"Valentine?" she called into the dim light of what she now realized was her bedroom.

There was shuffling in her sitting room and Valentine appeared in the doorway. His shirt was off, his muscles gleaming in the firelight.

"I'm here, Arabella," he soothed as he crossed the room to stand beside her bed. "Lie back."

She did as he asked, but grasped his hand. She needed to touch him. It was only then she noticed an ugly line across his chest. Blood and stitches.

"You were hurt!" she cried as she tried to sit a second time. He placed a gentle hand on her uninjured shoulder and kept her in place.

"I'm fine. The doctor was about to bandage me. Your wound was much deeper and you must be still."

She lay back, but kept hold of his hand. She needed to know he wasn't hurt. Staying in contact with him soothed her. Made her own pain fade.

A man appeared in the doorway behind them. "Mr. Valentine, I must finish my work."

Valentine kept his eyes on her, never withdrawing his comforting gaze. "You can finish here, can't you, Doctor?"

The doctor nodded, though he cast a disapproving gaze at Arabella as he came in. As his injury was wrapped, Valentine stood beside her. He never released her fingers and began to swirl gentle circles across the top of her hand with his thumb. Perhaps the touch was meant to soothe, but it had the opposite effect. Despite everything that had happened tonight, desire kindled inside her. And she saw it affected Valentine, too. His eyes glowed in the dim fire, reflecting everything she felt and needed.

But more than desire flickered between them now. The questions he had asked her before she was attacked still lingered. Valentine had been willing to abandon his duty . . . abandon her because she wouldn't tell him the truth about her past. That hadn't changed just because of a madman's attack.

Arabella shut her eyes on a sigh, allowing Valentine's touch to soothe her troubled thoughts. She didn't want to lose him.

Her eyes opened. He wasn't hers to lose. Their affair was based on business and pleasure. Not emotions. But hers had become involved, despite her best efforts to stay in control.

And now she had to decide if she could risk everything she had built by telling him the truth he so desired. Risk her heart by giving him her past. And trust him to protect her future as he had vowed to protect her body.

Valentine walked to the door of Arabella's bedchamber with the doctor. "Thank you," he said quietly. "Is there anything I need to know to take care of her?"

"Though her wound was more serious than yours, it wasn't deep. She should be recovered very soon, especially if you follow my instructions on changing the dressing and cleaning it regularly," the doctor replied as he peered at Arabella over Valentine's shoulder. Clearly the man knew who she was, even if he wasn't a member of her club. "The same goes for you, my boy."

"I'm fine," Valentine said with a wave of his hand.

The doctor pursed his lips. "If you really want to take care of her . . . be gentle with her. The attack wounded her shoulder, but it clearly frightened her. She may be more fragile than usual in the next few days." He arched a knowing brow. "She'll need care, not to be hounded by your desires."

Valentine clenched a fist. As if he would pursue deeply carnal desires while she lay injured on her bed. Not that he didn't want to. Need still sparked between them, despite her injury . . . despite their argument.

"Thank you," he ground out. "I'll keep that advice in mind."

The doctor grumbled his good-byes and left. Valentine closed her bedroom door, locking it to keep out the curious well-wishers who flocked outside. Lydia Bartlett was herding them away and he was sure she'd wheedle the information about Arabella's injuries from the doctor. It would give her something to do. She'd been very pale when she saw Arabella's bloody dress and limp form.

Drawing a deep breath, Valentine moved to the bed. He stepped forward and Arabella turned her face toward him at the motion. He sucked in a breath. By God, she was so beautiful. He had removed her bloody gown and dressed her in the closest thing to a demure nightgown she owned, but it still hardly covered her. With her blond hair spread across her pillows and her blue eyes wide with the remnants of fear and pain, she looked so innocent. So sensual. Fragile, the doctor had said, though Valentine knew she fought to keep from appearing weak.

So much like an angel. Fallen, but an inner light remained.

"Will you lie with me for a while?" she asked, her voice soft.

He nodded. How could he deny her? Just when he should have been pressing her for more details on her shadowy past, instead he wanted to hold her. Soothe her. Comfort her like a man who was more than her protector . . . more than her temporary lover.

Ignoring that thought, he took a spot beside her and reached out to stroke her hair aside. She shivered with that light touch and heat pulsed through him, though dimmer with the events of the evening. Even after all she had been through, she was still so responsive.

His gaze slipped to her bandaged shoulder and he winced, thinking of how he'd walked away and let someone hurt her.

"Did you recognize the man who attacked you?" he asked softly.

For a moment, she didn't answer. Her eyes fluttered shut and she merely lay there, letting him brush his fingertips back and forth across her cheek. He almost thought she'd fallen asleep when her voice came quiet.

"No. I didn't know him."

He frowned, though he kept the movement of his hand slow and steady. If she hadn't known her attacker, that probably meant he had been hired to hurt her. Which meant whoever was threatening Arabella wasn't just some deranged lunatic trying to get revenge for an insult, real or imagined.

That meant her stalker was willing to *invest* in her death, with some greater return in mind. His thoughts buzzed with the possibilities, but he wouldn't be able to speculate on any suspects until he knew everything that Arabella refused to share.

He opened his mouth to ask more questions when a tear slipped from her closed eye, trailing down her cheek in a slow, painful line. Strong protective urges rose up from deep within Valentine, crushing down his questions and fears and leaving only the strong, undeniable desire to hold her. Fix her pain, emotional and physical. Give this strong woman even more strength.

Gently, he gathered her into his arms and held her, rocking as she wept. She poured her fear out in her silent tears, her worries, her pains. And the fact that she trusted him with those things was a gift he recognized and accepted with awe. Now if only he could have her explanations so easily.

She let out a shuddering sigh after a long while and relaxed against his chest. As he held her, he finally looked around the room. Until now, he'd been too busy to truly notice his surroundings. Now that he did, it gave him pause.

"Arabella," he said softly.

"Yes?" Her voice was muffled against his chest, her hot breath warming his skin.

"What are these?"

She pulled back. When she saw he was motioning to the leather thongs that had been attached to her bedposts, the color drained from her face.

She struggled for words for a moment, then tilted her jaw up and said, "I intended to bring you back here tonight. I wanted to seduce you."

"You clearly didn't need to seduce me if you wanted me. I'm sure you remember the opera box," he said with a little smile.

He was surprised when she didn't return it. "The opera box is a perfect example of why I wanted to seduce you. Every time we make love, I've been swept away. Compelled to surrender, whether by design or weakness." She sighed. "Tonight I hoped to take your control as you had mine. To tie you down, force you to bear my touch without being able to turn the tables as you have before."

Valentine sat up in surprise, staring at her. The images her words conjured were powerfully erotic and aroused him to a painful degree. But the concepts behind those images were equally terrifying. Surrendering. Giving her everything. Turning over his trust, his body . . . even his heart.

She turned her face and the tracks of her tears glittered briefly in the firelight. Valentine winced. Arabella was a strong woman. She had to be to create a new identity. To survive being mistress to a sadistic lord. To establish a haven of sex and sin so popular that it had made her a fortune. He respected her abilities.

But he also realized she felt that strength slipping away. Because of a person who wished her dead. Because of him and his drive to keep control. She *needed* to reclaim her power in some way.

And that was one gift he could give her tonight.

Slowly, he lifted a hand and put it through the leather strap, tightening it as Arabella watched in wide-eyed surprise.

"What are you doing?" she asked, her voice barely carrying, even at such close proximity.

"Do you still want power over me?" he asked, just as quietly. "Can you fulfill your original plan, even with your injury?"

Arabella's throat worked as she swallowed hard. Then she nodded.

"Then tighten my other hand," he said as he slipped his free hand through the other thong. "I am yours."

Arabella's heart throbbed at that simple, three-word phrase. *Hers*. Even if it was only in this bed, even if it was only for tonight, the thought thrilled her. She hadn't realized how powerful her urge to claim Valentine had become.

She pushed to her knees as she tightened the thong on his left wrist, then looked down at him. Even at her utter mercy, he looked dangerous. But she couldn't go back now. She didn't want to.

Bending over him, she let her hair cascade across his body, brush over his stomach. His muscles tightened, flexed, and the erection that had bloomed beneath his trousers grew larger with the touch. She thought of the way he had used that same cock to torment her earlier in the evening and smiled. The tables would soon be turned.

She crawled to the bottom of the bed and made quick work of his boots. Then she straddled his legs, giving him a sensual smile as she let her fingers tease around the crotch of his trousers. He let out a quiet groan as he lifted his hips to chase her tormenting fingers.

With a laugh, she drew her hand away. "Not yet."

He arched an eyebrow, but let his hips rest flat on the bed again. Taking her time, she freed each button of his trouser waist and peeled the heavy fabric away. His cock sprung free, swollen and hard, ready.

She wrapped her fingers around the heavy length, remembering how much he liked it when she stroked him the night they met. That seemed like a lifetime ago, even though it wasn't long at all.

She met his gaze and slowly worked her hand from base to head, massaging lightly. When his eyes screwed shut and he let out a hoarse groan, Arabella's heart soared. Giving him pleasure was as much a gift to herself as to him.

That thought brought her up short. Her original plan for tonight was to steal Valentine's power, regain her control. But now, as she stroked him, power and control were the furthest things from her mind. So was the idea of *taking* anything from this man.

The moment she touched him, her world revolved around *giving*. Giving pleasure. Giving completion. Even giving a tiny part of her heart and soul, a part that had remained hidden for many years.

Her sigh shuddered as she leaned forward to press one kiss against the mushroom head of his erection. Valentine jolted at the contact of her lips. When she looked up, he strained against the leather ties, the vein in his neck popping as he fought to maintain calm.

She smiled. "You can let go, Valentine."

He stared at her, his gaze hooded. There was still a wall between them. One built by her secret past. Built by his painful experiences. She wanted more than anything to tear that wall down. Even if it meant giving more of herself than was wise.

But for this moment, she was content to start with her body. Her intent had been slow seduction, but she couldn't wait for that now. She wanted Valentine inside her. But she needed something else just as much.

"Tell me you want me," she said as she slid up the length of his body. She let her breasts rub against his hips, his stomach, his chest, until her face was even with his.

He hesitated, then whispered, "You know I want you."

"Do you need me?" The question was a hard one to ask, but she had to know.

Valentine drew in a harsh breath. "I need you, Arabella. More than I ever thought I could."

The tears she had cried a short while ago had been born of fear and heartbreak, but the ones that burned her eyes now were joyful. She bunched her nightgown, positioned herself above Valentine, and took him inside her, inch by slow inch.

The fullness she felt when he filled her always surprised Arabella. It was almost like a part of her was missing until their bodies joined. Then . . . completion. Fulfillment.

Shutting her eyes, she began to ride. After so many times when Valentine had controlled the pace and even the position in which they joined, she reveled in her newfound power as much as she reveled in the pleasure of rocking her body against his.

Valentine groaned as she swirled her hips and moaned with him. He felt so good, so right. Almost immediately, she found herself on the edge of a powerful orgasm, but she couldn't quite reach it. She rocked against him in frustration, closer and closer, but unable to reach the pinnacle she desired.

Opening her eyes, she looked down at Valentine. He met her gaze and she jolted even closer to release. Suddenly she knew what she wanted, how to get it.

"I'm going to untie you," she said softly.

"Why?" His eyes went wide as she freed his wrists.

She grabbed each hand, placing them on her waist before she started to move again. "Because I need you to touch me. I don't want control or to take. I want to feel you inside me. I want to feel your arms around me."

His expression softened as his arms wrapped around her. His fingers pressed into the flesh of her backside and he guided her, helping her thrust as she moved with more purpose, more pleasure. Desire coiled in her belly and began to tighten, becoming more focused, more clear, until an explosion of pleasure overwhelmed her.

She cried out as she came, but her shout was not the only one. It merged with Valentine's cry of release as he pumped hot into her body.

Valentine sighed as Arabella fell forward onto his chest in an exhausted heap. His arms came around her as he soothed sweaty locks from her cheeks and listened to her breathing slow. What had begun as a gift had turned into a powerful, emotional encounter. As unexpected as it was pleasurable.

Arabella's body relaxed as he moved her to his side and gathered her close. She was asleep, or nearly asleep.

"Valentine," she whispered, her voice heavy. "I love you."

7

Valentine watched the morning light play with Arabella's features. The sunlight reflected off her golden hair and made her skin even more luminescent than usual. He could have lain there and watched her sleep all morning, except his troubled thoughts kept him from fully enjoying the pastime.

Arabella loved him. Her admission the night before had kept him tossing and turning all night. Worse than that was his reaction to her sleepy claim. Joy had flooded him. Emotion. The very things he'd vowed to avoid after his last disastrous affair. Things he had no right to feel when he knew full well that Arabella was lying, that she wasn't who she said she was.

Her eyes fluttered beneath her hooded lids, then came open to reveal blue so pure it hurt to look at it. Hurt to observe that beauty. Especially when he knew it hid such deceptions. Ones he had to uncover . . . for his own sake as much as hers.

"Good morning." She sighed. A wince marred her expression when she stretched her injured shoulder.

"Good morning," he replied. "I'll change your dressing in a while. But before I do . . . we need to discuss what happened last night."

Her face paled and her smile faded. "The attack?"

He frowned. "No. Before that."

She straightened up, propping herself into a sitting position against the pillows. Her tousled blond hair tangled around her shoulders and she stared solemnly at him, waiting as she contemplated his statement. He had a wild urge just to put her on her back and make them both forget these issues, but he couldn't.

"You want to know about my . . . identity," she said softly.

He nodded. "Last night I put my trust in you. This morning I ask for some of the same in return."

"Trusting me with your body and your control in this bed is very different from asking me to trust you with my past . . . my soul." She fingered the edge of the coverlet as she spoke, but there were no angry sparks as there had been the previous night.

He sighed. If he demanded trust, he had to give it. He realized that now. And it wasn't even as terrifying as he thought the realization would be.

"It *is* the same for me, Arabella. Giving you control last night was a test of more than just my body." Her gaze snagged his, questioning. "You're not the only one with a painful past."

She tilted her head and he sighed. "You know I was dismissed from the Bow Street Runners. Do you know why?"

"I heard rumors." She shifted as if uncomfortable. "About you aiding a ring of thieves."

His jaw set as it always did when this subject was broached. "There was a woman. I met her during my last assignment with the Runners. She was exotic and wild and I went to her bed most willingly." Arabella's mouth twitched, but she urged him on with a nod. "I surrendered myself to the pleasure she gave, believing we had made a connection. I didn't realize until it was far too late that she was the doxy of the man I was investigating. She used my desire, my heart, against me, in order to help him in his crimes. Nothing we shared was real. In the end . . ." He trailed off. "In the end I was implicated in their crimes and ultimately dismissed from the position I loved, all because I allowed myself to surrender to her charms."

Arabella sucked in a harsh breath. "I'm sorry, I didn't know."

"Few do." He sighed. "And few who have heard the story choose to believe it." Reaching out, he took her hand. "But don't you see, Arabella? That woman was a stranger in my bed. And I've realized you are as well. Please help me understand who you are. If not for your own safety, then for my sake."

Arabella looked at him, his eyes so dark with questions and desire. He had trusted her with a glimpse of his past. All he asked in return was a bit of her own.

She sighed, then started in a trembling voice, "My name is Miranda Foxworth, I am the daughter of—"

"The Earl of Kessington." Valentine drew back, instant recognition on his handsome face. "You're dead."

She flinched, wishing she could recoil. Wishing she could keep hiding. But she couldn't. Not from this man.

"That's what my father told the world. That I disgraced my family and died from the shame. But I did neither." Her chin tilted with defiance. "*He* brought shame upon our name, upon me."

"Tell me." He brushed the hair back from her face. She smiled at the touch, so comforting. It had been a long time since anyone had touched her that way.

"I am the eldest of five sisters," she said, clenching her hands in her lap. "My father wanted sons. My mother died trying to give him that wish. Two other wives followed, but all they birthed were girls. Eventually he decided that at least we were worth something in the marriage mart."

Valentine winced. Arabella had stopped flinching at her father's cold, calculating nature long ago. "He arranged a courtship with the Duke of Waverly."

"Marcus?" Valentine repeated. "But he only took the title this year."

"No, his father."

"He was an old man," Valentine said with a frown.

She shivered. "Waverly and my father promised I would be his wife . . . but the Duke wished to test my 'wifely' skills first. He convinced me with promises, seduced me, took me to his bed."

Valentine started but said nothing.

"He was not an unkind or selfish lover. In fact, he schooled me in many of the ways of pleasure. I did not love him, but I didn't think his household would be any worse than my father's. I was beginning to look forward to the marriage when an announcement arrived."

"He had married Elizabeth Grayton."

She nodded, surprised he knew the story. But then, Valentine had once been a member of society, before his father's death. "She was the pretty, virginal daughter of a man much richer and more powerful than my father, whose fortune was tied to entail and who wanted nothing more than to rid himself of his daughters for the lowest cost."

"Why didn't he call Waverly out?" Valentine asked, his jaw set with anger. "He had every right. The man breached an agreement."

"The man also paid a significant portion of my father's debts," she said softly. "Satisfied he had received the highest return available, my father threw me from the home, claiming I had soiled my reputation, become a wanton. I had no money, no reputation, nowhere to go. Any relatives who might have taken me in could not risk their reputations. I became a mistress."

"And changed your name."

She nodded. She'd grown so used to the name she now bore, she sometimes forgot she had ever been Miranda Foxworth. That was another life, another girl.

"Yes. To Arabella Nichols. Arabella because I liked it. And Nichols because Waverly's first name was Nicholas." She winced at the memory. "I never wanted to forget what a man could do if he held power over me. If I trusted him."

Valentine's face constricted with brief pain, then he took her hand. "Jesterton, what about him?"

She let a humorless laugh pass her lips. "You have researched well, Valentine. You were a talented Runner. He was the first man who took me as a mistress. I know there are rumors about him. About his appetites, about his cruelty." She shrugged. She had long ago trained herself not to think of those horrible weeks. Not to relive the fear and the pain. "They are all true. But I survived. And he settled me very well when he moved on to the next woman. I took that settlement and invested it. And eventually, I put my money into this club. Here, the pleasures of the flesh can be explored without recrimination. Both men and women are equal partners in desire. Here I regained whatever control I lost to my father, to Waverly, to Jesterton. I let Miranda die completely and became Arabella in every way."

Valentine nodded, but the emotion she'd seen in his stare while she told her story had faded. Now there was a blank distance in his eyes. It frightened her. Had she made a mistake by confessing her past?

He raised her hand to his lips and pressed a kiss against the top. "Thank you for trusting me, Arabella. With this information, I hope I can finally determine who is trying to kill you."

Her eyes went wide as he pulled away. He shrugged into his clothing without explanation. When he turned back to her, it was with a false smile. "You must rest a while. I've arranged for a guard at your door. No one will harm you while I'm gone."

"But—" she began, shocked by this sudden, unexpected departure.

He raised a hand to silence her. "I will return, I promise. I have a few things to do, things to help solve this case. You want that, don't you?"

She stared at him. There was a double meaning to his question. He wasn't merely asking if she wished to be safe again, he was saying that the sooner the case was over, the sooner they could each return to the lives they led before they met. He was saying that despite the closeness they had shared, he could not share any more.

Her heart stung and she dropped her gaze so he wouldn't see. "Of course," she murmured. "I understand completely."

He hesitated, but shook his head. "Good. I'll see you when I return later this afternoon."

He dropped an awkward kiss on her forehead. Gone was the man who had brought her to the heights of ecstasy. The man who had demanded her surrender. She swallowed back disappointment and forced a smile as he walked to her door.

"Good-bye," she whispered as he turned to look at her.

His face fell slightly. "Yes, good-bye."

He shut the door behind him and she heard his echoing footfalls in her adjoining sitting room before he was gone. She lay back on the pillows with a sigh. What had happened?

One moment he was confessing private pains and urging her to give up her own sad history . . . the next he couldn't wait to be out of her sight. But what else could she expect? No man would want a woman with such a past. No man could truly love what she'd become.

"What are you doing?" she muttered to herself as she flopped her uninjured arm over her eyes. This was exactly the kind of thinking she had expunged when she became Arabella Nichols. There was no room to give a man . . . any man . . . that kind of power.

Even one she—

"Arabella?"

She moved her arm and saw Lydia creep into her bedroom. Her friend looked pale and drawn, but Arabella had never been happier to see anyone.

"Lydia!" she said, motioning her friend to her side.

"Thank goodness you're alive." Lydia sighed. "I had to bribe the guard to let me in. But you look upset. Is everything well?"

Arabella stared at her friend. This seemed to be the time for confessions of the soul. She needed advice, she needed guidance, and Lydia was her oldest friend. It was time to tell her the whole truth.

"I'm physically well. Valentine halted the attack on me."

Lydia's face changed ever so slightly. Hardened. "How

8

"So let me be sure I understand you . . ." Bennett folded his arms. "The woman poured her soul out to you, confessed she loved you—"

"In her sleep!" Valentine interrupted.

Bennett wrinkled his brow. "She confessed she loved you. And you *left?*"

Valentine scowled. Bennett's summation of what had happened certainly didn't put him in a very good light. And it didn't take into consideration *why* he had gone. When Arabella confessed her past, it had lightened his heart. She'd given him her trust, told him secrets no one else knew. But—

"You're in love with her," Bennett said, eyes wide. "That's why, isn't it?"

And that was the rub. Valentine had realized, as Arabella was pouring her heart out to him, that he had fallen in love with her. Despite his belief that a quick connection wasn't

lucky he was there. I thought you two had parted when he left for two days without any word."

Arabella cocked her head. How had Lydia known Valentine sent no word in the time they were apart? She shrugged, wincing at the pain it caused in her shoulder.

"I must confess something to you," she said. "Valentine *is* my lover, but that isn't the only reason why I called him here. After I was threatened, I knew I needed to take action. I did not wish to depart London as you said I should, so I hired him to protect me and investigate the attempts on my life. Valentine is a former Bow Street Runner."

Lydia drew back, her face suddenly pale. "What?" she asked, low and harsh.

Arabella nodded. "I didn't want anyone to know how afraid I was, so I kept his true purpose here a secret. But I've ruined the whole plan, Lydia." She drew in a breath. "I—I've fallen in love with him."

Hearing the words from her own lips startled Arabella. In love? She had shied away from such emotion her whole life, yet in the instant she met Valentine she'd been gripped by powerful emotions. Their attraction went deeper than the earth-shaking sex . . . there were other feelings always swirling beneath the surface. Things she had been afraid of. But that didn't change the fact that she felt them.

She was in love with Valentine. A man who had just deserted her.

Lydia shifted, drawing Arabella's attention to her. Her friend stared at her as if she had declared she would give up the club and take a vow of celibacy. She'd never seen Lydia in such shock, with such emotion flickering in her dark eyes. She waited for her to say something . . . anything. Extend her sympathies, offer her hope, but she only continued to stare.

"Lydia?" she whispered.

"Now that you are in love, do you intend to quit the club? Leave London with him?" Her friend's eyes flashed, belying the strange monotone of her voice.

Arabella's stomach clenched, both from her friend's question and her strange demeanor. "No. Valentine has made it clear from his actions that he does not return my feelings. I suppose I'll be forced to hire another guard. Perhaps even go to the authorities about the threats on my life." She forced a wavering smile. "But never fear. I shall not bend to the will of some madman. The club will go on. And I'll remain at the helm. No one can take that away."

She expected an encouraging smile, a hug from her friend. Instead, Lydia's face twitched, as if she had been keeping emotion at bay for a long time and had finally lost the battle for control.

"You idiot." Lydia's voice was harsh as her fists balled at her sides. "I tried to make you leave. I tried everything to just make you go away, but you wouldn't do it."

"What are you talking about?" Arabella asked, a sudden urge to move away gripping her. This was her friend, yet fear curled cold fingers around her heart as Lydia babbled on.

"Do you think I *wanted* to try to kill you? You gave me no choice! And then to hear you hired someone to protect you? You ruined my plans and you didn't even tell me!"

Arabella's mouth dropped open and she edged away. "K-kill me? Please tell me this is a joke, Lydia. Please tell me you don't mean what you just said."

She was close to the edge of the bed now, almost to the point where she would have a wide mattress separating her from her friend.

But Lydia would have none of it. With the quickness of a racehorse, she leapt toward Arabella, grabbing her injured arm and dragging her back across the bed. Arabella cried out

in pain, but Lydia's hand clamped across her mouth as she pulled her down to the floor in a heap. She hit the hardwood with enough force that the air was jarred from her lungs. Pain roared from her shoulder, but she struggled to regain control.

"This is no jest," Lydia hissed. "I worked hard with you to build this club to the heights it has reached, but I never received the acclaim that you did. I never got my fair share. But once you're gone, I will."

Arabella's head spun as she struggled against Lydia's surprisingly strong grip. How could this be happening? How could her best friend have betrayed her so completely? But the answers to those questions were standing in front of her. Staring at her in the form of Lydia's wild eyes.

Money. Power. Arabella had received both over the years. And Lydia would be the one to run the club, receive the benefits of her hard work, if she were to leave London, become indisposed, or die. Apparently the lure of those things had overcome the woman Arabella had rescued from the life of a common lightskirt three years before.

And now Lydia was going to take what she desired. Unless Arabella fought.

She bit at Lydia's choking hand over her mouth and her friend released her with a cry of pain. Arabella took the opportunity to shove her away, and Lydia stumbled toward the fireplace, her arms flailing as she tried to regain her balance.

Arabella struggled to her feet, but light-headedness slowed her. She glanced down at her injured shoulder to realize Lydia's violence had reopened her wound. She was bleeding. With her world spinning, she headed toward the door, but before she got three steps, Lydia's voice stopped her.

"Hold still or I'll put a bullet in your head right now."

She turned to find Lydia on her feet with a pistol leveled at Arabella's head.

possible. Despite his mandate to keep women like Arabella at arm's length and never let sex dictate his emotions.

But then she told him she would never let a man have her heart again. That she had learned through her bitter experiences that she had to use her body against the men she cared for so that they couldn't use it against her instead. Could things be different with him? Could she ever let go of her fears, her pains, and be with him on an equal footing, where control did not play a part?

Last night it seemed she had, but now he wasn't so sure.

"You won't answer me?" Bennett asked, pushing off the desk. "Then perhaps you're a coward."

That stung. Valentine spun on his friend in shock. "You are treading in dangerous waters, my friend. Be wary of what you say."

Bennett looked less than impressed. "Why, so I can help you hide from yourself? You may not like to hear it, but you've been running since Laurel betrayed you. You wouldn't even fight for your position. And look where your self-pity got you!"

Valentine winced. Bennett was right. He'd been too shocked by her betrayal, too angry at himself for allowing Laurel to weave her way into his heart, to do anything. He always said he valued control . . . but he hadn't been in control for a long time. He'd been paralyzed.

"Well, I watched in silence for a long time, Valentine, but I won't watch anymore. I can't be a party to your throwing away any more of your future. If you love the woman, go back to her. Take a damn risk." His friend slammed a hand down on his desk. "Make a damn move. Be the man you once were!"

Valentine straightened his shoulders. He'd once thrived

on risk. Danger. And Arabella was both those things, with a supple body and enchanting eyes to boot.

With a smile for Bennett, he headed for the door. But before he could go, his friend stopped him.

"I almost forgot. In my digging I found one monetary transaction I couldn't verify in Arabella's accounts. A large sum was given to a Lydia Bartlett."

Valentine froze. "Lydia?"

"Yes." Bennett double-checked the sheet in front of him. "Does the name mean something to you?"

He nodded. "Arabella's best friend. She's involved in her business." His intuition pricked, reminding him of the strange feeling he'd gotten when he spoke to Lydia a few nights ago. Of the coolness of her stare when she regarded Arabella. "And she could be with her right now. I must get to her."

Without waiting for his friend's reply, he raced for his carriage. He could only hope his intuition was wrong.

Though that was rarely the case.

Arabella screwed her eyes shut. The life she led was dangerous. There had been a few times when she knew she cheated death. But this time, with Lydia's gun pointed at her head and her friend . . . former friend . . . unwilling to talk rationally, it seemed her luck had run out.

There was still so much she wanted to do. So much to say. And most of what she'd left undone had to do with Valentine. She'd been so busy protecting her heart and her precious control, she hadn't let him know what he'd come to mean to her. If she died, would he realize that she had loved him? Would he care?

"I'm sorry," Lydia whispered as she began to depress the trigger. "I tried, but you gave me no other choice."

Just as Arabella expected the blinding pain of death to take her, the door to her bedroom flew open and Valentine burst inside. He hit Lydia with the full weight of his big body.

Arabella scrambled to her feet as Lydia and Valentine rolled across the floor, fighting for the gun that was now pinned between them. She took a step forward, but before she could say or do anything, the pistol went off.

The world slowed as Arabella screamed. Lydia was on top of Valentine, but neither moved. It was as if time froze when the bullet fired.

Shaking off her shock, Arabella flew to the two of them. She pulled Lydia away, praying Valentine hadn't been hurt. To her utter joy, he looked up at her, then tossed the pistol out of the way.

She spun to face her former friend. Lydia was dead, shot through the heart with her own weapon.

Arabella threw herself into Valentine's arms, pressing kisses along his face as she smoothed her hands over his body to be sure he was unharmed.

"I thought she'd killed you," she sobbed.

"Shh," he soothed. "You're bleeding."

"I don't care," Arabella insisted, hugging him close and not even feeling the pain of her reopened injury. "All I could think about was that I would never get to tell you how much I need you. How much I love you."

Valentine stiffened and Arabella's heart sank, but she clung to him nonetheless. If he didn't return her feelings, so be it. At least she had taken the chance of loving him.

Slowly, he pushed her away so he could look at her. His eyes, so dark with emotion, speared her. Held her in place, unyielding in their scrutiny.

"Do you love me, Arabella? Truly?" he whispered.

She nodded without hesitation. "I realize I promised you I would demand nothing when this was over, but—"

"Shhh," he said, but his wide smile gave her a hope she had never felt before. "Listen to me."

With effort, she shut her mouth and waited. Praying, hoping for a dream she had let die long ago. A dream of love. Of a future with one man at her side.

"I love you, Arabella Nichols. Despite my best attempts to pretend otherwise, I love you. But I cannot be with you unless you take another identity."

Her heart sank. Was he asking her to go back to being Miranda Foxworth? To return to the drab, frightening world her father had created for her?

"What identity?" Her voice broke.

"Mine. I'll only settle for loving Arabella *Valentine* for the rest of my life. I will only settle for having you as my wife."

She smiled as tears filled her eyes. "And the club?"

He shrugged. "Keep it if it gives you pleasure." The smile turned wicked. "It certainly gave me much pleasure. It led me to you, so I have a soft spot for it."

"Soft?" she asked as she reached out to cup him with teasing fingers. "Not likely."

He sucked in his breath as he helped her to her feet and held her close. "We can explore that after I bandage your wound again."

"And what about after we explore that?" she whispered.

"I will go about clearing my name. But first, marriage." He kissed her nose. "And much, much love."

"Forever," she breathed as she tilted her face up for his kiss.

Jess Michaels always flips through every romance she buys in search of "the good stuff," so it makes perfect sense that she writes erotic romance where she gets to turn up the heat on that good stuff and let it boil. She loves alpha males, long-haired cats (and short-haired ones), the last breath right before a passionate kiss, and the color purple (not the movie—though that's excellent, too—the actual color). She also firmly believes that Cadbury Cream Eggs should be available all year round and not count against any diet.

Jess loves to hear from readers. You can find her online at http://www.jessmichaels.com or e-mail her at jess@jessmichaels.com.

Parlor Games

Leda Swann

1
_

Sarah Chesham pushed open the door to the coffeehouse and stumbled over the threshold. The interior smelled heavenly—of dark-roasted coffee beans and mouthwatering grilled meat—but it was dark and smoky, and her tired eyes took a few moments to adjust to the dimness of the light.

She made her way through the gloom to the closest table and sat down at it, settling her skirts over the tops of her sturdy work boots. Elbows resting on the table and her head in her hands, she concentrated on catching her breath and calming the overrapid beating of her heart.

A buxom young woman in an apron bustled up to her. "What can I get you, dearie?"

Sarah raised her head. "A ha'penny cup of coffee. And a chop," she added with reckless haste, just as the serving woman had turned to walk away.

She counted out three pennies with careful deliberation and placed them to one side on the table. Her purse was left anxiously light, but there was no help for that. A girl, even an unemployed girl with scarcely a shilling in her pocket and no prospect of getting more, had to eat.

Her plate, when it came, was piled high with more meat than she usually ate in a month. The smell as the chops wafted past her nose was so delicious that she almost fainted with the joy of it.

Still, she shook her head and pointed to the three pennies on the table. "I can't eat all that. I only wanted the tuppence ha'penny dinner."

The young serving woman winked broadly at her. "You look like you need feeding up. I won't tell if you won't." And she set the entire plate of food down on the table in front of her.

Sarah had been brought up to eat daintily, but she was too hungry to remember her lessons. She wasted no more time arguing in the face of such unlooked-for good fortune, but tucked into her pile of chops with gusto, barely remembering even to use her knife and fork in her haste to fill her belly.

The serving woman pushed the door of the study closed with the toe of her boot. "There's a girl out in the front parlor who looks a likely prospect."

The older woman sitting behind the desk took off her spectacles and laid them aside on the blotter. "Is she pretty?"

The younger woman screwed up her nose at the question. "Of course she is. Pretty as a daisy, though a mite scrawny. I gave her a decent feed," she added defiantly.

The older woman frowned and tapped the end of her pen on the desk. "Her age?"

"Young enough, but not too young. Nineteen, twenty, maybe. No older."

"Her situation?"

"Talks like a toff, and nice manners, too. She's been brought up good, even if she's fallen on hard times now."

The older woman's frown cleared a little and she stopped the tapping. "She was hungry, you say?"

"Half starved."

There was silence as the older woman thought for a moment, her hands steepled in front of her. Finally she gave a decisive nod. "We could use a pretty new face."

Tom Wilde slouched in the darkest corner of the corridor, his hands in his waistcoat pockets and his top hat pulled down low to shade his face. Checking once more that the farthest reaches of the corridor were still empty, he turned his head and peered once more through the tiny peephole strategically positioned in the ornate wainscoting to the room next door.

The knowledge of the risk he was running only added spice to his peeping. The old harridan who ran the coffeehouse knew his face too well for comfort. She would welcome the devil himself as a paying guest, but if she caught him spying on her coffeehouse guests? A sound cudgeling would be the very least of his punishment.

Coffeehouse guests. He curled his lip in a silent sneer. Old Madame Erskine did not make her money from selling watered-down hickory coffee or shoe-leather chops as the other coffeehouses did. No, her trade was in a far more lucrative business.

He swiveled his head a fraction to take in another aspect of the view. No hickory coffee for Madame Erskine's guests. No, indeed. He took one hand out of his waistcoat pocket to adjust his trousers, which had suddenly shrunk several sizes. She traded in some of the most tempting morsels a man could hope to find on this side of paradise.

Scant wonder that his quarry, the right dishonorable Member of Parliament from Stoke-on-Trent, visited her establishment so often. The merchandise was tempting enough to give the Archbishop of Canterbury an irresistible itch to pull up his cassock and have at them with all his might.

The premier grub of Fleet Street, however, was made of sterner stuff than to turn knock-kneed at the sight of a few half-naked women. They were nothing but a distraction to his real business here—evisceration. Not the messy business with a stiletto knife, but using the infinitely cleaner and deadlier weapon of a pen. He ignored the throbbing in his trousers and mentally sharpened his quill.

He wasn't called the Adder of Fleet Street for nothing. A little bit more research to pad out his salacious pamphlet, a bit more dirt-digging that turned up another juicy tidbit like this one, and Sir Richard Eddington, the right dishonorable Member from Stoke-on-Trent, would be the laughingstock of all London.

He smiled to himself in the darkness. His writing was not only poisonous, but also highly profitable. Salacious pamphlets were the most lucrative market in his line of business, and he was well-known for writing the best of them. All those who had something to hide, politicians and business tycoons alike, shuddered at his name.

Sir Richard Eddington might not know it yet, but his well-deserved disgrace would keep Tom, the Adder of Fleet Street, in comfort for six months or more.

Sarah carefully laid her knife and fork down on her plate atop the pile of chop bones and dabbed at her mouth with the napkin, slightly ashamed of her greedy haste now that her desperate hunger was appeased. Slowly she drained the lukewarm dregs of her coffee and set the cup down on the table. The last excuse she had to linger in this oasis of warmth and food was now gone, but she could not yet bear to leave.

The kindness shown to her by the serving woman had touched her heart as well as filled her belly. Kindness had been a rare commodity in her life of late. She blinked back the tears that threatened to spill over. Self-pity was an indulgence she could not afford.

Reluctantly she pulled her checkered woolen shawl around her shoulders and stood up, leaning on the back of her chair for support. She would be strong, and somehow she would survive. She was still too young and too full of hope that her life would one day be more than drudgery and starvation to welcome death.

The serving woman in her clean white apron bustled up to clear away Sarah's dishes.

Sarah clenched her fingers tightly over the back of the chair. "Excuse me, miss, if you don't mind me asking, but would you be needing another girl to help in the kitchens?"

The serving woman stopped still, dirty dishes in her hands. "You're out of work?"

Sarah lowered her eyes to the table. "I am," she confessed, ashamed of her need. "I was trained up as a milliner, but there's no work for us this winter and we've all been laid off with no pay and can't find no work anywheres, so I'm looking for a different sort of position."

"What can you do?"

"I'm healthy and strong and I'll turn my hand to any kind of work you wanted done."

The serving woman bustled over toward the kitchen, Sarah on her heels. "Well, we *could* do with another girl around the place, but I doubt the work would be to your liking." She shook her head slowly back and forth. "It wouldn't be what you were used to."

Sarah's heart leaped at the tantalizing prospect of being allowed to stay. "I'm not proud, though I was brought up a curate's daughter," she said, trying to quell the desperation in her voice. "I'll scrub hearths and wash dishes and wait on the rudest gentlemen ever so politely."

"A milliner is used to earning good money," the serving woman said doubtfully. "What wages would you be wanting?"

To her horror Sarah found herself weeping. "I wouldn't ask for any money," she sobbed. She sank to the floor and clasped her arms around the serving woman's knees. "Please take me on. You won't be sorry. I'd work from dawn to dusk for a corner of the kitchen floor to sleep on and a morsel to eat. Anything to keep me off the streets. I'd die there, I know I would."

The serving woman patted Sarah's head with a comforting hand. "Now then, dearie, don't take on so. There's many a girl who's had to go on the streets before you and has come out again none the worse for it."

Sarah sobbed into her shawl, her shoulders heaving with every breath she took. "I couldn't go on the streets, miss. Not with my father being a curate and all. He'd turn in his grave to see me brought so low."

"We'll have to see what we can do about getting you a position here then, won't we, dearie. Now, come on and dry your eyes and I'll take you to see Mrs. Erskine. She's the lady as owns the coffeehouse and she'll be the one who says whether you can stay or no."

Sarah dragged a cotton handkerchief from her skirts and wiped her eyes as she slowly got to her feet. "I didn't mean to take on so," she whispered, ashamed of her sudden outburst.

"Truly, I didn't. It's just that Emma from the milliner's shop who got laid off just before me got so desperate she went on the streets last week." She gave a sniffle. "Nobody's seen her since."

"Don't worry about it." She pushed open a back door that led into a dark corridor and shooed Sarah along. "Now come along sharpish, dearie. You can wait for Mrs. Erskine out back in the sitting room. It's nice and private there, and you won't be disturbed."

The corridor echoed hollowly under her tread. Sarah stumbled quickly after her, hurrying to keep up. "Do you really think Mrs. Erskine might take me on?"

The serving woman gave a little laugh. "Soon as she sees your pretty face, dearie. Soon as she sees your pretty face."

The door at the far end of the corridor opened, letting through a shaft of dim light. Two women appeared silhouetted in the doorway for a moment, before the door shut behind them. Their footsteps clattered on the bare wooden floor as they came toward him.

Tom shrank back into his corner and stayed as still as a statue. Thanks to the gloom of the corridor, he remained invisible as a ghost.

To his relief they did not come the length of the hallway, but opened a door halfway down, the door that led to the empty salon. He knew it was empty. It had been the first room he'd checked out when looking for the right dishonorable MP for Stoke-on-Trent.

"Wait in here, dearie," he heard one of them say to the other. "I'll let Mrs. Erskine know you're waiting and she'll be with you presently."

One of the women went into the salon, and the other

tripped her way back along the hallway and through the
same door the pair of them had come in by.

As soon as she had gone, Tom came a little ways out of his
corner and stretched his cramped limbs. Clearly another
pretty little bird was about to be snared in Mrs. Erskine's
nets. He was curious to see her up close to see if she was as
attractive as the girls in the other salon. From what he had
seen so far today, Mrs. Erskine employed the best-looking
girls in London. No other girls could match them.

His hands outstretched, he felt for the tiny peephole he
had found earlier. His fingertips found it almost right away,
and he crouched down to look through into the salon beyond.

He shook his head at the irony of his position. How his
fellows would laugh if they saw him, the Adder of Fleet
Street, behaving just like any two-a-penny peeping Tom.

Sarah sat on the edge of one of the sofas, waiting in trepidation for Mrs. Erskine to appear. Would she be a kindly woman
who would give her a chance to live a decent life, or would
she be rough and cruel and send her away again, her hopes
dashed to the ground? She clenched her fists tightly together
to stop herself from trembling. How she hoped that her luck
was at last about to change, and that Mrs. Erskine would
welcome her into her household.

She waited for some time wrapped up in her own thoughts,
but Mrs. Erskine did not appear. Eventually she raised her
eyes and looked around her, curious at last to see what kind
of a household Mrs. Erskine ran. Maybe the room held some
clues as to her character that would help during the coming
interview.

The room was more sumptuous than she had realized on

first entering. A large ornate rug covered the floor, while around the walls half a dozen sofas peered into the middle of the room, as if it were a stage.

She rose from the sofa to take a look around. At the far end of the room stood a pair of sideboards. One of them was covered with books and journals, casually resting in untidy piles. The other sideboard held a liberal collection of cut-glass decanters filled with spirits. She was tempted to take a hasty nip to calm her nerves, but she did not want Mrs. Erskine to think her a drunkard or a thief.

Instead, she idly examined the painting on the wall behind. One glance at the subject matter and she let out a gasp of shock before bending her head to look at it more closely— at once shocked and fascinated by the graphic detail. A man and a woman were locked in an intimate embrace. Her clothing, if you could call mere draperies clothing, had fallen largely away, displaying her wanton nakedness. His hands were on her bare stomach, and her naked breasts, artfully framed by the falling draperies, were clearly visible.

She bent her head closer. Even more shockingly, the man's phallus could just be seen, poised on the brink of entering the woman from behind.

She straightened up, her face burning, and moved hastily backward, not knowing what to think. Mrs. Erskine must be a brave woman of singular tastes to display such a picture in her public sitting room.

Her gaze wandered to safer ground, to the sideboard beside her. Next to a highly polished silver tray holding an intricately detailed crystal decanter was a brass and wooden contraption with lenses at one end, and a place to rest the forehead and an arrangement for holding photographs at the other. A stereoscope viewer, she thought with budding excitement. She had heard tell of these in the milliner's workroom, but she had never thought she would get the chance to look in one.

She glanced around the room and listened for any sign of Mrs. Erskine's return. Hearing nothing, she carefully positioned herself so the yellowish gaslight was behind her and placed the viewer to her eyes.

No sooner had she focused on the image than she hastily removed the viewer, thinking her eyes had deceived her. Expecting a picture of Greek ruins or maybe of Tuscan landscapes, instead she had seen a three-dimensional image of two women. Naked women. Women who were entwined in a private embrace.

She put the viewer back up to her eyes, this time gawping openmouthed at the wanton pose of the women. It was more shocking even than the painting on the wall. This picture was real. It was no artist's fantasy, but a picture of real women, doing real things to each other.

The women's hands were on each other's breasts and pussies, caressing each other in the most intimate fashion. What disturbed her most was that they were clearly enjoying themselves, looking intently into each other's faces with lust-drugged eyes.

She could hardly drag her eyes away from the photograph. What would it be like to have a woman do that to her? The wicked thought caused her own pussy to prickle with heat and a dampness to form under her skirts.

Her face hot with embarrassment mingled with excitement, she was about to replace the viewer on the sideboard when she noticed a prettily inlaid walnut box just the right size for holding the stereoscope photographs. Lifting the lid, she found a number of photographs tidily arrayed inside.

The temptation was more than she could resist. Keeping a

nervous ear out for Mrs. Erskine, she pulled the first photograph from the box and placed it in the holder.

The new image was even more shocking than the last one had been. In front of her eyes, as clear as day, was the image of a man standing, his trousers around his knees, while a scantily dressed woman knelt at his feet. Her hands were on his naked buttocks and his member was buried in her mouth.

Her own pussy was tingling at the naughty sight. She stroked it through her skirts with one hand, but it only made the tingling more insistent.

With shaking hands, she took out the next photograph, and again peered intently into the eyepiece. It was the same couple, but this time the image showed them in a yet more intimate embrace.

The man, dressed only in his shirttails, was sitting on a sofa looking straight at Sarah. His hands gripped the woman's waist as she sat astride his cock, his member half buried in her pussy. The woman's hands caressed her breasts as her eyes stared defiantly at Sarah, as if daring her to find fault with her actions.

Shifting her gaze slightly, she studied the room the couple were in. The rolled-arm sofa and the highly patterned wall looked eerily familiar. Moving the stereoscope viewer away from her eyes, she realized with a start exactly why. She was in that very room she could see in the image.

She looked around uneasily. Right here, right in this very sitting room, men and women fucked each other in front of a camera. Maybe she should not wait for Mrs. Erskine and inquire after employment. This was clearly not a suitable household for a curate's daughter.

Still, her curiosity was stronger than her sense of unease,

and the tingling in her pussy was greater than both together. She pulled yet one more photograph from the box and placed it in the viewer.

This image was the most shocking yet. A woman braced herself on the floor, resting on knees and elbows while a man penetrated her from behind. But his cock was not pleasuring her cunt, it was deep in her ass with her gaping pussy clearly visible below. The man rode her as he would a pony, legs astride her waist, his hands entwined around her hair as he bent over her.

What made her gasp with shock, though, was the third person in the act. He had one foot on the floor, with the other on the woman's back, and his huge member had just entered the other man. It was a picture of a man fucking a man fucking a woman.

This was *definitely* not a suitable household for a curate's daughter. A bit shakily, Sarah carefully placed the viewer back beside the silver tray and returned the stereoscopic photographs back into their oaken box. She really ought not wait for Mrs. Erskine to come and interview her.

Perched back on the edge of the sofa again, she was caught in the grips of indecision. Was it any of her business if Mrs. Erskine had a boxful of unusual and disturbing images in her sitting room? If her curiosity had not been aroused and she had not peeped at them, she would never have known of their existence.

Besides, Mrs. Erskine held out the tantalizing promise of employment. If she were to leave now, without seeing her, what would she do then? Go on the streets as Emma had done, selling her body for a crust of bread, and never be seen again?

She felt in her pocket, knowing already how little money she would find. She was down to her last few pennies. In only a matter of days she would have no choice—she would have to sell her body or starve.

Better that she work for Mrs. Erskine, however unusual the woman's tastes were and whatever she had to do to earn her keep, than go on the streets.

Yes, life was still worth living and Mrs. Erskine's household was better than the streets. There was no choice to be made. She had to wait. She sat quietly on the sofa for some time, but Mrs. Erskine still did not appear. Made nervous with idling, eventually she stood up again and moved about the room, seeking something to distract her mind from the coming interview.

Her feet were irresistibly drawn back to the same corner of the room she had been in before. She would not touch the naughty stereoscope again, but there was a pile of journals on the sideboard. Surely Mrs. Erskine would not object to her leafing through one of them while she waited.

She picked up the topmost one, entitled *The Oyster*, and retired back to the sofa, away from the naughty temptation of the stereoscope.

Her mother had been a governess before she married her father, and had taught Sarah to read. She had learned her lessons well, and could pick out the text with ease.

The story told about a pretty servant girl who had fallen on difficult times in the city and wanted to go back on a steam train to her faithful sweetheart in the country. Fortunately she was alone in the carriage when the guard arrived to take her ticket. Unable to pay, she admired the guard's uniform, told him what a handsome man he was, then sucked his member till he spent in her mouth.

The guard let her stay on the train, and in the end she was reunited with her faithful sweetheart.

The illustrations that accompanied the story were as

saucy as the words, and the prickling in her pussy had returned tenfold. Listening closely to make sure that she was quite alone, she pulled her skirts up to her knees, let her knees fall wide apart, and slipped her hand in between her thighs.

Her pussy was wet and slippery and her fingers felt so good that she had to slide them up and down over herself.

As she looked at the etching of the young girl on her knees in the railway carriage with the guard's member in her mouth, she rubbed herself gently, imagining that she was the girl in the railway carriage and sucking on a handsome railway guard's cock.

Her eyes drifted shut as she indulged in her naughty daydream.

"You like the book?"

Her eyes flew open and with a gasp of horror she took her hand out from under her skirts and closed her legs tightly together. "What are you doing here?" she demanded. She was so horrified at being caught touching herself that she was nearly in tears.

The man standing in front of her seemed not in the least perturbed. "You don't have to answer me. I can see that you did." He picked the book from her hands and studied the illustration she had been looking at. "You like the idea of sucking a man's cock?" He came closer to her, his groin on a level with her mouth. "Tom Wilde at your service. I am all yours. Please indulge your fantasies."

"Go away." Blinking furiously to hold back her tears, she pushed him away so he stumbled and nearly fell. "Go away and leave me alone."

He sat down on the sofa beside her, and took hold of her hand so she could not get free of him. "Never fear, I shall pay you well." Capturing her hand, he laid it on his groin. His erect member was obvious even through his trousers. "See what you have done to me already? I'm more than ready for your mouth and tongue."

She snatched her hand away as if he had put them on hot coals. Her fingers were wet from where she had been stroking her pussy and she wiped them surreptitiously on her skirts. "That is disgusting," she said, rising hastily from the sofa to escape him. "I will not listen to such filthy talk. You are not a gentleman to proposition me in such a dirty manner."

He gave a humph of disbelief as he grabbed her by the arm and pulled her back down and onto his lap. "Come now, sweetheart, you did not think those pictures were so disgusting just a few moments ago, did you?" He ran his hands over her breasts, making her nipples tingle under his touch. "This is hardly the place for you to have a crisis of conscience."

His free manner shocked and frightened her. All the men at the milliner's shop had treated her with the respect due to a curate's daughter. They would never have laid violent hands on her, or kissed her bare neck, or stroked her legs through her petticoats as he was doing. "Let me go," she cried, struggling to get free again. "Take your hands off me."

In answer to her entreaties he only pulled her closer into his lap until she was sitting astride him, his member pressing into the cleft between her buttocks. "I have offered to pay you well. What else do you want? Do not think you can bamboozle me with tales of your innocence," he added in a warning tone. "Mrs. Erskine's establishment is hardly a place where one would find a genuine shrinking violet, and I have no time for your teasing."

She stopped struggling and looked at him, the knowledge of what sort of establishment Mrs. Erskine ran only now beginning to dawn on her. "I don't understand you," she said desperately, hoping against hope that her sudden suspicions were unfounded. "What kind of a place is this?"

2

Tom shook his head. It was hard to believe such naïveté in this day and age. Did she think he was a fool? "What do you think it is? It's a brothel. An elegant brothel a cut above most of the others in London, but still a brothel. A place," he added brutally, "where men come and have their cocks sucked by willing young women like you."

Her eyes widened at his brutal words and she gave a gasp of horror. "No, it can't be. You're lying."

He gestured around him at the paintings on the walls, at the book of explicit drawings that she had been poring over so eagerly. "Look around you. What respectable establishment has paintings of naked people cavorting on the walls, or picture books of men and women copulating in every position you could imagine, and a few you'd never thought of before? Where else could you see stereoscopic images of actual men and women fucking each other senseless? What else could it possibly be?"

She had huddled into herself, her shawl pulled tightly

across her shoulders, withdrawing from his touch as if it were poison. "I thought . . . I thought maybe the salon was owned by a lady with . . . with singular tastes."

"Singular tastes." A bark of laughter escaped him. "That's one way of putting it, I suppose. Only it's not Mrs. Erskine's tastes that are singular, but those of her clients. She caters to all sorts here."

Her face looked utterly woebegone. "I was hoping she would offer me employment."

A tear ran down her cheek. Damn it, but he wanted the girl. Irritated though he was with her refusal, he could not help but pity her as well, she looked so miserable. He picked her up off his lap and set her aside on the sofa to remove temptation from his immediate vicinity. "You're a beautiful girl. I'm sure she will."

Her stance was so rigid she looked like she would break in two. "You do not understand. I am untouched, a virgin. Even if she does offer me employment, it will not be as a scullery maid, but as a whore." Her voice caught on the words. "I will be nothing more than a whore."

He shrugged. Why did women make such a fuss over trifles? He'd been damned glad to get rid of his virginity at the age of fifteen—even though it had been to the no longer terribly youthful landlady of the house where he boarded. "Turn her down then, if your purity is so damn precious to you." Mrs. Erskine was not the most savory woman of his acquaintance, but as far as he knew she had never stooped to kidnapping unwilling girls to work in her coffeehouse. Times were hard enough that she didn't need to.

"You do not understand." Her face was wild, like that of a tiny kitten held at bay in a corner by a vicious dog. "She will offer me employment as a whore and I do not know if I will have the strength to refuse."

He only half heard her, his mind focused on the click-clack of shoes coming down the corridor. Mrs. Erskine, he had no doubt, coming to check out her latest wares. Damn the woman. Both of them. He could take a thrashing along with the best of them, but he preferred to avoid being beaten senseless when he could.

He looked wildly around the room, which offered little in the way of hiding places. The only possibility of escaping the house without a sound drubbing was the sofa. He dropped to his knees and felt underneath it. It would be a tight fit, but luckily he was lean enough to be able to squeeze underneath.

The footsteps were coming closer. He put his finger to his lips. "Shhh, you haven't seen me," he said, as he lay face-down on the floor and scooted under the sofa.

Just in time. No sooner had he wriggled underneath than he heard the door latch open. Footsteps muted by the carpet approached his hiding place, and with an oomph that nearly drove the breath out of his chest, a heavy weight settled on the sofa.

"You are the girl that wants employment?" It was Mrs. Erskine. He would recognize that gravelly voice anywhere.

"Yes, ma'am."

"You are a virgin?"

He could not hear the answer to that question, but it must have satisfied Mrs. Erskine.

"You understand what kind of a house I run here?"

Silence, then a whispered, "Yes, ma'am."

"And you are still willing to seek employment, knowing that?"

"I have nothing else, ma'am."

"Well then, that's settled." To his relief, the weight rose off the sofa and he could breathe again. "Come with me and I will show you to your new quarters."

———

With leaden feet, Sarah followed Mrs. Erskine to a sitting room on the upper floor. The die was cast and there was no going back. She was a whore now. In order to feed her body, she had sold her soul.

Never again would she be able to see her family—her mother or her sisters. Her existence would bring nothing but shame on them. From now on, she would be as dead to them. Far better for them to think she had died and gone to heaven than for them to discover the awful truth—that she was living in hell.

A petite woman with a heart-shaped face and violet eyes, dressed in a low-cut gown of deep red, rose from the sofa to greet them with a dazzling smile and a fetching shake of her pale brown ringlets.

So this, Sarah thought to herself, is what a whore looks like. She would not have thought a common whore could be so elegant.

Mrs. Erskine gestured Sarah forward. "Polly, this is Sarah, our newest recruit. Show her around, if you please. She can have Angelina's old room, and whatever dresses we have that can be made to fit her."

Polly curtsied, bending forward to show off even more of her cleavage. "Yes, ma'am."

Mrs. Erskine unbent far enough to smile at Polly. "Sarah's a milliner—if she can make hats, she can alter the dresses herself. I will expect her to be ready for tomorrow's games. See to it that she is." And without a further word to either of them, she swept out as majestically as she had entered.

"There's no need to look like the devil will come down the chimney any moment now and steal your soul away to hell," Polly whispered to Sarah with a giggle as soon as Mrs.

Erskine had closed the door behind her. "It's not a brothel. Not really."

Sarah stared blankly at her. Surely the gentleman in the sitting room was not mistaken. Besides, everything around her screamed "brothel." The sitting room had thick wool carpet, patterned wallpaper, red velvet window dressings tied back with tasseled braids, and even a grand piano in one corner. It was grander even than the parson's house where she had been invited once to have tea, while her father, the curate, was still alive. Not that the parson would have had such shocking paintings on his walls, or such obscene statues with oversized phalluses in the corners.

"Mrs. Erskine doesn't make us sleep with the gents if we don't want to," Polly went on. "We just have to play games with 'em and tease 'em, and make 'em want it bad. They like that. That's how she makes her money." She took Sarah by the hand. "Come and I'll show you to your room."

She led Sarah along a narrow hall, gesturing at the openings hung with velvet curtains of differing colors. "This is where we girls live." A pair of dark blue curtains was drawn back on one of the openings. Pulling the door behind them open, she gestured Sarah inside. "Here's Angelina's old room. It's yours now. Sarah's room."

Sarah stood in the open doorway and gasped. "This is *my* room? Just for me?" It was far larger than the bedroom she had shared with all her five sisters in her father's cottage, and as sumptuous as the sitting room they had just passed through. The floor was covered with dark blue and red Turkish carpets, the bedstead was shiny brass, and the counterpane real silk in a beautiful shade of pale blue. Even the washstand was made of mahogany and had a marble top.

Not a brothel, indeed. What a foolish taradiddle that was, as transparent as the gauze drapes over the bed. She threw

Polly a disbelieving look. "Why do I get such a beautiful bedroom all to myself if I don't have to bring the gents in here?"

"We have to tease the gents for Mrs. Erskine, and she gives us food and lodging for it, but not a penny in our hands. Anything else is up to us." Polly giggled again and danced a few steps on the Turkish rug. "We bring the gents in here if we feel like it and give Mrs. Erskine a cut of the takings. That's how *we* makes *our* money."

A faint ray of hope began to shine in Sarah's breast for the first time since she had sold her soul to Mrs. Erskine for a place to lay her head. Polly's happiness and cheery welcome had dissipated the worst of her gloomy despair. Maybe being a fallen woman would not be altogether as bad as she had feared. Maybe, just maybe, it might even have a few good points. Polly certainly seemed perfectly content with her lot. "Food and lodging just for teasing gentlemen?" Could she but secure her food and lodging, she would have no need for money.

Polly leaned her elbows on the dressing table. "It's enough for some of the girls, but I have ambitions," she confided. "This sort of life won't last forever, and when you're too old to entice the gents, you need some money of your own to fall back on or it's the streets all over again."

"Ambitions?" Her own did not stretch much further than survival. What ambitions could a whore have beyond that? Her father had always taught her that a single misstep in a woman's life was irretrievable, and that once a woman became a whore, her die was cast.

"Some of the girls are looking for a keeper, but I don't want to be beholden to one man. I want enough money to set myself up in a business all my own. A tavern out in the country where I could grow my own vegetables and keep a few hens." A dreamy look stole over Polly's face. "That would be heaven. I'd fuck any number of gentlemen for that.

"But enough dreaming." She sat down on the sofa in Sarah's room with a bounce. "Now to business. Tell me, can you play cards?"

Cards? Sarah gulped. Mrs. Erskine had not mentioned anything about cards. "Only Go Fish. My papa did not approve of gambling."

"So much the better. You will lose quickly and that will make you a popular partner with the gentlemen. You can sew, though?"

At last something she could be proud of. "I am trained a milliner." Though she did not like to boast to Polly, she could sew better than most.

Polly bounced off the sofa again. "Come and take a look at the dresses, then, and see which ones you take a fancy to."

She led Sarah to a storage room at the end of the hallway where a dozen dresses of all colors of the rainbow were hanging. On the shelves behind lay a confusion of dainty cotton chemises and drawers trimmed with lace.

Sarah's mouth gaped open. Was she meant to wear such fine things? Nothing had touched her skin before but coarse linen in the summer and heavy flannel for the winter. Such fine garments were for rich ladies who owned their own carriage, not for poor girls like her.

Polly prodded her impatiently. "You'd better get a hurry on and choose a handful. Mrs. Erskine wants you ready by tomorrow."

Tom crept through the gloomy hallway to his dark corner once more. He had struggled with his conscience all night, but in the end it had made him return.

The young woman he had met here yesterday weighed on his mind. She was young and gently bred, the daughter of a curate, and he had left her here in the power of a noted bawd. It would be on his head if her sweet innocence was corrupted and turned to debauchery.

He should have swept her out of the salon and taken her far away from Mrs. Erskine's bawdy house. With the contacts he had all over London, he could have helped her to find respectable employment. Sweet and gentle as she looked, she was sure to be a delightful nursemaid, bathing babies and helping little children to spell out their lessons. Even if nothing else could be found, she was pretty enough to stand behind a shop counter and sell ladies' gloves and other feminine trinkets.

Such a sweet daisy as she was would surely hold out against the lure of sin for as long as she was able. Her defense would be stout—she would not yet have succumbed to vice.

Her innocence deserved a white knight to protect it. He would be her white knight—he would find her and rescue her before she fell headlong into the pit of corruption that was Mrs. Erskine's bawdy house.

Sarah clutched Polly's arm with a death grip as she walked into the brightly lit salon with the other coffeehouse girls. Despite the layers of frothy undergarments she was wearing, she felt horribly exposed. Her satin skirts, cut short to show her ankles, swished around her calves, her bodice dropped so low that her breasts were half falling out of it, and her arms and shoulders were bare. Only the fear of being thrown onto the streets stopped her from turning tail and fleeing back to the safety of her room.

A group of gentlemen in frock coats stood at the far end by the fire, watching their approach avidly. Some of them, hats in hand, started forward to meet the girls as they entered.

A shiver went down her spine as the men approached and she stopped dead, clutching Polly's arm as if it were her life-line. "Do not leave me," she whispered.

"Don't be a goose," Polly whispered back, giving her a little pinch on the arm and dragging her forward. "Just remember what I told you. Act like a lady, be nice to the gents, and everything will work out fine."

A pair of gentlemen made a beeline for the two girls. One of them took Polly's arm with a possessive air while the other, a portly gentleman whose waistcoat barely buttoned up over his large belly, made a stiff bow at Sarah. "May I?" he asked, offering her his pudgy arm.

Polly dropped Sarah's arm to cling to her partner's with both hands, and gave the fat gentleman a roguish wink. "This is Sarah. She's new here tonight."

"How new?" he queried anxiously.

"New to the whole game," Polly confirmed.

Sarah's gent took her arm and placed it in the crook of his. "Then I am glad to be the first to make your acquaintance, Sarah." His tongue rolled over her name as if it were a sweet treat. "My name is Sir Richard Eddington. You may call me Dickon."

He smelled of sweat and small beer. "I am p-pleased to meet you," she stammered.

At that moment, Mrs. Erskine stepped into the center of the room. "Welcome to my coffeehouse, ladies and gentlemen, and to the evening's entertainment."

She gestured to the round tables set up in front of the fire. "Gentlemen, please choose a partner and take your seats at the table of your choice. This evening we will amuse ourselves with a game of cards."

There was an instant rush as the men claimed their partners. Amid the hubbub, the portly gentleman led Sarah to one of the tables by the fire. She looked helplessly after Polly as she was led away by her escort to a table on the far side.

Sarah's partner gave her a predatory smile as he showed her to her chair. "I shall enjoy playing cards with you, my dear." His lips were fat and they glistened with grease where he had not wiped them properly after dinner.

The heat from the fire could not stop the goose bumps from forming on her arms. She gave him a tremulous smile back. "Thank you, but I am not very good at cards."

His smile widened noticeably, sending a trickle of icy suspicion creeping down the back of her spine. "So much the better."

Once they were all seated around the tables, a cry went up from the gentlemen. "What game? What game?"

Mrs. Erskine hushed them all with a wave of her hands. "Ecarte," she pronounced.

There was a general groan of disappointment from the gentlemen and some mutterings about how they may as well have stayed at home. Sarah felt herself relax just a little. There was nothing too scary about playing straight ecarte. Polly had explained the rules to her last night—it was simple enough if she kept her wits about her.

"We shall be playing not for money, but for forfeits," Mrs. Erskine amended, with a faint smile on her austere face. "Clothes or kisses or other favors, make them what you please."

The groans turned to cheers, her partner joining in the general revelry. "Let us play for clothes, my dear." He leered greedily at her. "At least at first. Who knows what may happen later."

Sarah felt her heart leap into her throat. Polly had warned her that playing for clothes was one of the gents' favorite games. She had hoped to escape it on her first evening, but it seemed luck was not with her today.

Mrs. Erskine approached their table, cards in her hand.

Sarah could hardly manage to give her a civil greeting. Her wits had completely deserted her—her only thought was how to keep all her clothes on her back.

Mrs. Erskine shuffled the pack and dealt a hand to each of them, leaving the rest of the pack on the table between them. Sarah stared at the cards on the table with grim fascination, silently praying that God would have mercy on her and send her a good hand.

When she had finished dealing out all the cards, Mrs. Erskine moved to the middle of the room and clapped her hands together. "I will leave you young things to play cards together now. Do not get into mischief as soon as you are unchaperoned. I shall be in the next room if anyone needs me." And with a brief curtsy to her clients, she left.

Surreptitiously Sarah wiped her damp palms on her skirts and picked up the cards in front of her. She could do this. Indeed, there was little choice about it—she had to do this.

The fire was warm on her back, but she was as cold as ice inside. She stared at her cards blankly, wishing with all her might that her father had been less set against all forms of gambling. A sketchy explanation of the rules of the most popular games from Polly the previous night was no substitute for knowing what she was doing.

Opposite her, Sir Richard was looking at his cards with a frown of concentration on his face. She watched with fascinated disgust as he absentmindedly took a large silk handkerchief from his pocket and mopped his sweating forehead. If her partner had been a little less gross and a little less leering, she would feel more comfortable. But Sir

Richard? Would she have to undress for this overblown glutton of a man?

She forced herself to focus on her cards. A pair of sevens. A faint smile crept over her face. A pair of sevens wasn't so bad. She could win this hand.

She discarded her odd card. "One, please."

Sir Richard dealt her a card and took one for himself.

Her new card was a disappointment. Her hand still only had a pair of sevens. It was good, but would it be good enough?

With shaking fingers, she pushed a chip into the center of the table.

Sir Richard grinned at her and pushed in two chips.

Her heart pounding with fear, she looked intently at her cards and bit her lower lip. Should she raise the stakes and risk losing the lot? Or play it safe and lose just a little at a time?

"Will you match me?"

The eagerness in his voice decided her. Throwing her cards facedown on the table with a grimace, she forfeited the hand. "I fold."

His pudgy hands gathered the chips from the table. "You owe me a forfeit. Three forfeits, to be precise." With a piggish gleam in his eye he studied his prize. "Turn around for me. I will unfasten three buttons from your bodice."

Reluctantly she turned her back to him. He leaned over the table and unfastened three buttons of her bodice, his fat fingers lingering unpleasantly on her neck, his whiskery sideburns scratching her skin. She turned back to him as soon as she could, brushing his fingers away.

With a look of satisfied anticipation, he gathered up the cards and shuffled them together. "Shall I deal this hand?"

———————

From the other side of the wall, Tom watched the game with growing fury.

His mystery girl of yesterday claimed she was an innocent? Hah—he wanted to spit at her dainty feet.

No innocent miss would be sitting down at a card table playing ecarte for her clothes and letting Sir Richard Eddington undress her, one button at a time. Or smiling in the rascal's face as he did so.

He ground his teeth together. Sir Richard Eddington was a rake of the first order. He had a fashionable wife and a nursery full of babies waiting at home for him, not to mention at least one pretty young housemaid who was expecting his child as well.

By God, if she was determined to act the whore, she could do better than Sir Richard.

If she wanted to act the whore, she could do so with him.

The card game continued with Sarah losing every hand. She was not the only woman to be doing so. While some of the gentlemen had lost their top hats and their jackets, and a particularly unlucky one had already discarded both his shoes, most of them were still fully dressed. The women, however, were unfastening bodices and shedding stockings and slippers at a great rate. Polly had already completely discarded her bodice and corset and was now giggling in her shift and petticoats.

At length Sarah had only one button left to her bodice— and not so much as a pair of twos in her hand.

One glance at her face and Sir Richard pushed two chips into the center.

She looked despairingly at her cards and tossed them face-down onto the table.

He grinned widely as he leaned over the table to unfasten the last button. "I have won another forfeit, I fear. Your bodice is mine, now."

All of Polly's warnings had not been sufficient to prepare her for this moment. Slowly she pushed her bodice first off one shoulder and then off the other.

Sir Richard's tongue snaked out to lick his lips.

She clasped her bodice to her chest, unwilling to let it fall.

"Excuse me, sir?"

Sarah looked up, startled, straight into the eyes of Tom Wilde. She clutched her bodice tighter to her chest with fingers that shook slightly.

Sir Richard frowned at the interruption but did not take his gaze off her chest. "What do you want?" His voice was harsh.

"You are Sir Richard Eddington?"

"What do you want?" he repeated.

"There's a messenger outside asking for Sir Richard Eddington. As I was coming inside anyway, I volunteered to fetch you."

That brought his attention away from Sarah's chest. He looked straight at Tom. "A messenger? For me? Did he say what he wanted?"

Tom coughed. "He said something about you being needed in the House for a vote. I told him I would pass the message on."

Sir Richard swore under his breath and rose from his chair with alacrity. "Excuse me," he said to Sarah. "I am needed elsewhere." Without further fuss, he clapped his hat on his head and waddled self-importantly out of the room.

Tom sat down in the chair that Sir Richard had just vacated. "Now, where were we?" he asked, a glint of wickedness in his eye. "Ah, yes, I remember, you were just about to take your bodice off." He waved his hand in the air. "Please continue."

Sarah was rooted to the spot. Her face burned worse than the hottest horseradish mustard. "What are you doing here?"

"As your partner, Sir Richard Eddington, the right honorable Member of Parliament for Stoke-on-Trent, seems to be needed elsewhere, I am playing the part of a gentleman and taking his place."

"You should not be here," she hissed at him.

One eyebrow rose in a query. "Why ever not?"

"You have not been invited."

His laughter rang out through the room. "My dear girl, anyone with money in his pocket can get himself invited to Mrs. Erskine's entertainments. I have money in my pocket, therefore I consider myself duly invited. Now, about that bodice."

She clenched it even more tightly to her chest. "I cannot take it off in front of you."

"Why not?" His voice was hard. "Is it not enough that I have paid Mrs. Erskine? Do you want me to pay you, too?"

Tears filled her eyes at the sneer in his tone. "You . . . you are not a stranger to me. I have met you. I know your name. I cannot show you my breasts."

He took up the pack of cards and shuffled them with a practiced hand. "You only fuck strangers for money? Is that it?"

Tears were rolling down her cheeks now. "You are shaming me. Do not do this to me."

He dealt the cards onto the table and took up his hand. "Come, take your cards. If you win this hand I will let you put your bodice back on again."

His kindness was more than she had expected. She looked up at him through her tears. "You will?"

"I promise."

Slowly she let her bodice drop, taking heart from Tom's apparent indifference to her seminakedness. He did not stare at her greedily as Sir Richard had done, but kept his gaze on his cards.

Her eyes widened in delight as she picked up her own hand. A pair of tens. This was the best hand she had had yet.

Hastily she discarded her remaining card and picked up another. To her disbelief, another ten stared back at her.

With growing excitement she pushed a chip into the middle of the table.

Tom watched her with hooded eyes. "What's your name?"

"Sarah. Sarah Chesham."

"You disappoint me, Sarah."

Miffed at his tone, she raised her head from her cards. "Why?"

"You are so cautious, so afraid." He pushed a stack of his own chips into the center alongside her lonely one. "You do not have the courage of your convictions but play timidly, for small stakes, when you could be bold and win everything at a single stroke."

She stared at the pile in the middle of the table. If she were to lose, she would be nigh on naked. "I do not care to win except to get my bodice back," she said with a pout. "I have no wish to rob you of your clothes."

"You do not wish to strip me naked?"

She pursed her lips. "No." His question brought all sorts of naughty images unbidden to her mind. The thought of seeing Sir Richard's naked rolls of flesh made her shudder, but

Tom Wilde was a much better figure of a man. He was lean and wiry where Sir Richard was grossly fat, and his whiskers were dark and neatly trimmed, far removed from the bushy auburn monstrosities that Sir Richard wore.

Ignoring the throbbing in her pussy, she clamped her legs together to stop them trembling at the thought of Tom standing before her with no clothes on. She was a respectable woman still, despite her dodgy profession, and she needed to remember that.

His mouth quirked into a smile at her denial. "You are a liar as well as a coward."

She was *not* a liar. She did *not* want to see his bare chest, his strong legs, or to see his member spring up at her touch. She did not want to see him as naked as the men in those naughty stereoscope pictures, or to have him do unspeakable things to her as they were doing to each other in the pictures. Or if she did harbor a secret desire, it was only out of curiosity, not lust. "You are no gentleman to say that to me."

"Even though it is true?"

She glared at him and pushed an even larger handful of chips into the middle of the table. "It is *not* true. Match that if you dare."

He counted out a stack of chips to match hers and pushed them in. "Done. Now show me your hand."

Triumphantly she laid her cards face up on the table. "Three tens. Now start undressing. We shall see how well *you* like being stripped naked in company."

He laid his own cards facedown on the table. "I think not."

A trio of jacks. She looked at them in disbelief. Fate was playing a cruel joke on her.

He reached out to the pile of chips and began to count them, slowly and deliberately. "Come here," he instructed her. "Around to my side of the table. I want to claim my forfeit."

Her gaze was glued to that pile of chips. No wonder her father had disapproved of gambling so strongly. It only led to ruin and damnation. If only she had not let Tom goad her by calling her a coward and a liar. Now she would have to undress for him until she was as naked as the day she was born. Her whole body felt hot and flushed at the thought. "You will claim them all?"

"Every last one."

3

"You are *not* a gentleman," she complained, though her pussy was already beginning to drip in anticipation. If she had to lose her clothes, she would far rather lose them to Tom than to Sir Richard the gross. Sir Richard disgusted her, but Tom? She could not quite put her feelings for Tom into words. "You are a scoundrel."

"I'm a scoundrel," he agreed complacently. "I'm a cad and a rotter and a no-good wastrel, but I have also just won a game of cards and I am about to undress you one garment at a time and I will enjoy every minute of it."

"I'm glad that one of us will enjoy it," she muttered under her breath as she rose from her chair and came to stand beside him. She could not bear to let him suspect that she was half looking forward to having his hands on her, undressing her bit by bit. His opinion of her was low enough already. Such evidence of her wantonness would shock him further.

"Tut, tut. Mrs. Erskine will have you thrown out on your ear if she hears you. Surely she pays you to be pleasant and polite and to smile at me, not to grumble like an old fish-wife."

She poked her tongue out at him. "I'm here, aren't I? Waiting obediently for you to undress me." Goose bumps formed on her bare arms as she spoke. The prospect of having him as her master and having to obey every naughty command he gave her was strangely enticing.

His green eyes were calculating as he looked her up and down. "I like obedience in a woman. Take off your slippers."

She held out her hand. "Two chips." Nobody, especially not Tom, was going to cheat her.

Not until he passed her the chips did she slide her embroidered slippers awkwardly off her feet.

"That was easy now, wasn't it," he remarked, amused at her discomfiture. "Now, come closer and let me unfasten your skirt."

He put his arms around her waist, drawing her in to stand between his thighs, and reached behind her to unhook her skirt. Her skin prickled at his nearness and she suddenly found it hard to breathe.

"You are very practiced at undressing women," she muttered at him to hide her embarrassment, as he unfastened her hooks with ease and pushed her outer skirt over her hips to pool at her feet on the floor.

Though she was not cold, she shivered as she stood there in front of him, dressed only in her petticoats, her arms crossed over her nearly naked breasts to protect her modesty. Being a naughty woman was more difficult than she had expected. The lessons of a lifetime could not be overcome in one short evening.

All pretense he had made of indifference was gone and he was gazing at her as if he wanted to eat her up. She did not know where to look. He made her feel both eminently desirable and horrifyingly debauched at the same time.

"Silk stockings with red clocks embroidered on them?" His voice was still hard and sarcastic, but his face was flushed as he reached up and loosened his necktie. "How quaint. Put your foot up on my knee and let me see them closer."

It was good to know that she had some small amount of power over him. She put her stockinged foot up on his knee, her skirts lifting with the movement.

His hands lingered over her ankle. "Very nice. Now take them off."

Timorously she reached inside her petticoats to unbuckle the garter holding up her stocking, but Tom stopped her with one hand on her arm. "On second thought, I will take them off for you."

Was he offering to put his hands up her skirts? That would never do. She pushed him away. "I don't need any help. I can take them off for myself."

"But I *want* to do it for you. And I have won the forfeit, have I not?" Reaching under her petticoats, he ran his hands up her leg to the top of her stocking. "You owe me."

"Get your hands out from under my skirts," she hissed, slapping at his hand on her leg and wriggling around to get away from him. "It is not proper."

Oblivious to her protests, he unfastened her buckle, removed her garter, and slowly rolled her stocking down her leg and over her foot. "You are not *meant* to be proper. Give me your other leg."

Sarah looked around for someone to protest to, but no one was paying them any attention. All the others were either crowing over their cards, or one half of the couple was undressing the other with much laughter and giggling.

"Come on. I'm waiting."

Modesty had no value here—indeed, it would ruin her. She had to get over her fears if she wanted to stay. Mrs. Erskine would not take kindly to her first customer complaining over her unwillingness to play the game with him. Reluctantly she took her bare leg off Tom's lap and put her other leg on his knee.

He reached under her petticoats to the top of her other stocking, caressing the bare skin of her thigh with his fingertips. "You're enjoying this, aren't you?"

Her leg was shaking under his feather-light touch. "No." He was touching her where no man but her husband ought to touch her. She ought not to be enjoying the feel of his fingers on her leg.

"You are lying again. You really must try to stop. Lying is a nasty habit."

She shivered as he continued to caress her gently. "I am not lying."

"Your neck is all red and flushed. Your leg is trembling under my hands. And if I were to reach my hand just a little higher, I would find your pussy as wet as any man could wish it. As wet as it was when you were looking at those naughty pictures in the salon yesterday."

How did he know that her pussy was dripping into her drawers? She clamped her thighs together, trapping his wrist between them so he could not roam higher. "Don't touch me there."

"Relax." He unbuckled the garter on her second stocking, unrolled it, and cast it aside. "I am only claiming my forfeit as I am entitled." His pile of chips was dwindling rapidly, and he eyed it with disfavor, suddenly losing his patience. "I never knew a tart had so many damned underclothes. Come, take off those petticoats of yours."

Her petticoats were fastened with distressingly few hooks and tapes. One by one she let them fall at her feet until she was standing in front of him wearing nothing but corset, chemise, and drawers.

A murmur of appreciation escaped him. "Turn around for me. I want to see you from every side."

Obediently she turned in a circle for him, her body burning under the heat of his gaze.

"Now your corset."

Her eyes fixed on his beseechingly. "Do you have no pity?"

"Not a whit," he replied cheerfully. "Take it off."

One by one he handed over his chips as she unhooked every last busk on her corset.

With shaking hands she cast her corset aside. Her breasts swung freely under her fine linen chemise, the dark outline of her nipples clear beneath the thin fabric. Her nipples were peaked into tight buds at the unaccustomed sensation of freedom, and the unsettling knowledge that his gaze was fixed on them. Her seminakedness was decadence itself—instead of being ashamed, her wickedness excited and inflamed her senses.

One chip was left on the table. He picked it up, tossed it into the air, and caught it again with an air of utter unconcern. "Take off your shift."

And allow the entire room to see her naked breasts? That was taking decadence too far. She crossed her hands over her chest, wanting to obey him but unwilling to violate her modesty to such an extent. "I cannot do that."

He was inexorable. "You lost the hand. You owe me a debt, and I want to see your breasts."

"Will you not take another forfeit?"

Her words piqued his interest. "What are you offering?"

She looked wildly around the room for inspiration, her gaze finding only half-naked couples in unchaste embraces. "A kiss?" she offered in desperation. There could be no great harm in a kiss. It was better than showing off her naked breasts to a room full of gentlemen, and to Tom in particular. One kiss did not make her a whore.

"Sit on my knee and give me a kiss and we will have a deal."

She had not kissed any man before—she had never had a follower to ask her to kiss him, or to steal kisses from her on the sly in a dark corner. The prospect of kissing Tom frightened her a little, but not as much as exposing her naked breasts in mixed company did.

Her heart beating fast in her chest, she perched herself on the edge of his knee and gave him a chaste peck on the cheek. "Now give me the chip," she demanded, hopping off his knee again. "I have paid the last of my forfeits."

"That was no kiss." He wrapped his arms around her and pulled her into him so she was sitting on his lap, her head resting against his shoulder and her breasts jammed against his chest.

She gasped half in horror and half in pleasure as her drawers gaped open, plastering her naked pussy tantalizingly against his rock-hard member. Only the thin cloth layer of his trousers separated her bare skin from his. Her brain felt thick and heavy, as if it were covered in a thick London fog—all her sensations were bound up in her pussy, hot and tingling at the nearness of his member.

She moved tentatively against him and was rewarded with a quiver of pleasure that shot right through her body. Did all women experience this delight when a man kissed and fondled them? Was this wondrous feeling why women gave themselves over so willingly to be whores? No wonder Polly danced around with a smile on her face if she was made to feel like this every evening.

He bent his head to hers, kissing her roughly on the lips, forcing her to open her mouth under his onslaught. With one hand he held her tightly against him, while the other crept under her chemise to fondle her naked breasts.

His mouth was hot against hers, as he forced her to respond to him. She had no breath left to protest, and no will either. His hands were like fire on her breasts and his kiss was more intoxicating than port wine.

She squirmed against him, thrusting her breasts into his hands, her nipples begging him to fondle, to touch, to taste. He obeyed her wordless commands, cupping her breasts in his hands, flicking his fingernails over her sensitive nipples and rolling them gently between his fingers.

Her pussy ached with desire and she could not resist moving backward and forward on his lap to rub it more insistently against his member. Her juices would leave wet patches on his trousers, but she was beyond caring. What did it matter if he discovered what a wanton she was if he would only go on touching her and kissing her like this forever. He made her feel so alive, so desirable, so much like a woman.

When at last he raised his head from the kiss, his breathing was labored. "I can't wait any longer," he said with a groan, his hand already at his waistband fumbling with his buttons. "Take me upstairs and let me fuck you."

His rough-spoken demand called her to her senses. Pushing his hands away, she pulled herself free of his embrace and stood up off his lap, flushed and panting. They had gone more than far enough already and she was not his for the asking, not even if her pussy was on fire for him. "No," she said, her voice shaky. "I will not take you upstairs." Enough of her good sense was still left her to refuse him the ultimate act.

"You'd rather fuck me here? With all these people around?" He sounded intrigued, but not put off by the notion. "Whatever the lady wants." He flicked open another button and rearranged himself so that his member stuck out, stiff and purple, from his unfastened trousers. "Come here and sit on my cock then, and let me fuck you right here with everyone watching us."

She stared at his huge member poking out of the top of his trousers. Did he like the thought of fucking her in the midst of a crowd of people? Would he take her to the room next door and thrust his member into her pussy while a man took pictures of them for the stereoscope? "I will not be your whore."

He stopped in the act of pushing down his trousers over his hips and looked up in confusion. "Why not? I can pay. I've already told you I have plenty of money."

Mrs. Erskine had given her a choice and she would take full advantage of her freedom. She would not throw her virginity away for mere money. She was not that desperate yet. "Because I choose not to."

"Don't be silly," he said, stroking his privates with one hand and holding out the other to her in invitation. "You cannot refuse me. You are a whore."

"I make my living playing parlor games with gentlemen, not by sitting on their cocks," she said crudely, gaining strength from his disarray. The ache in her pussy would go away if she ignored it. "Now, do you want to play another hand of cards?"

His member had grown more purple and swollen with every word they spoke. He slammed his hand down on the card table in a fury. "Damn the cards. I want to fuck you."

"I do not fuck strangers for money," she said primly, throwing his earlier words back in his face.

He gestured at the room, which had already lost a good half

of its occupants. "I doubt your friends are as fastidious as you are. They will all be upstairs fucking away merrily by now."

She shrugged. Taking off her clothes for a forfeit did not make her a whore, nor did kissing a man to pay another forfeit. Keeping company with whores did not make her one. "That is their affair. Not mine."

"You are nothing but a cock tease. I should have chosen one of the other women. Any one of them would have acted fairly by me and not left me in these straits."

Her anger rose, though she tamped it down as best she could. If he treated her as a whore, that was his mistake and his loss, not hers. "You chose poorly indeed."

"You will not go upstairs with me?" He sounded as if he still could not quite believe her.

"No, I will not."

"I will take my leave then," he said sulkily, re-buttoning his trousers and clapping his hat on his head. "If nothing else is on offer."

She inclined her head politely. "Good-bye, Mr. Wilde. I hope we will meet again soon."

He grunted at her and strode out of the salon without looking back.

Sarah watched him go with some relief. Her first client had departed, her first evening was nearly over, and she had survived. She could have wished that Tom had not picked a quarrel with her at the end, but maybe it was all for the best. His rough demands for her to sit on his cock had been easy to refuse, but if he had coaxed her and talked words of kindness and love into her ear, she shuddered to think what she might not have done for him. His member had been so stiff and proud, and her pussy was still wet with wanting him . . .

She turned back to the gathering. It was just as well that he had not talked of love to her, and that she had been able to refuse him. Giving in to him would have confirmed his bad opinion of her—that she was nothing more than a whore. Not that she ought to worry over what he thought of her. He was a gentleman and she was a parlor games girl. She would never be anything more to him.

The fire had long since died away and the salon was nearly empty, but she could not go upstairs until Mrs. Erskine had given her permission. She sat at a deserted table idly shuffling cards and was soon joined by another partnerless girl. They played ecarte together halfheartedly until Mrs. Erskine finally returned to the salon and dismissed the remaining gentlemen for the night.

Her toilette was soon made and she retired to bed, but she could not sleep. Through the walls on both sides of her she could hear the muffled sounds of sex—the rhythmic creaking of bedsprings, indistinct voices, slaps and giggles, and hoarse groans of pleasure.

Whores they might be, but they did not seem to mind their chosen profession. Judging by the noises, they were positively enjoying their life of sin.

She lay by herself in the darkness, wondering what it would be like to have Tom Wilde beside her in the bed, to have his naked body lying atop hers and his member thrusting deep into her pussy.

She fell asleep dreaming of making love with Tom in the salon while the rest of the coffeehouse girls and their partners sat around on the sofas and watched them, and a man with a camera photographed their every position to add to Mrs. Erskine's private collection of stereoscope images.

Tom strode back to his lodgings in a fine old temper. He had rescued his pretty daisy from the sweaty hands of Sir Richard Etheridge, and what was his thanks? To be shown the door with an erection so hard he could use it to break rocks.

Goddamn the little tart for being such a tease.

He'd wanted to take her right there in the sitting room, thrusting his throbbing cock deep into her willing cunt. Heaven knows, she was as ready as he was for a good hard fuck. Her pussy had left a wide patch of damp on his trousers. He'd thought only to save the scraps of her modesty by taking her upstairs where they could fuck in private—he'd never dreamed she would refuse him.

He should've stayed and played another hand of cards with her until Mrs. Erskine called the proceedings to a halt at midnight and threw all the gentlemen out. At least then he could have watched the sway of her unconfined breasts under her shift, and maybe even reached under the table and stroked her warm, wet pussy.

Dammit, he should have stayed and just *talked* with the wench. Even talking with her would have been more pleasant than going home to his empty lodgings with a cock as hard as steel and no prospect of relief.

He pulled his fob watch out of his pocket and glared at the face. It was too late to return tonight. Mrs. Erskine would never let him in at this hour.

Tomorrow, however, would be very different. Tomorrow evening he would pay a visit to Mrs. Erskine and claim the pretty Sarah as his own. Tomorrow night, wild horses would not be able to drag him out of Sarah's boudoir until he was fully satisfied.

The following morning, almost as soon as it was light, Tom Wilde strode into Mrs. Erskine's office. His temper was not improved from having slept badly, visions of Sarah keeping him uncomfortably hard all night. "Your new girl, Sarah Chesham. I want her."

Mrs. Erskine laid her pen down on her blotter. "And good day to you, too, Mr. Wilde."

Her chilly tone was a reminder for him to mind his manners, but he was past caring about such petty games as manners. "I'm serious. I don't want her playing your games with anyone but me."

Her gray eyes were hard as steel. "I am a businesswoman, Mr. Wilde. I do not keep the girl out of charity."

"I will pay."

"For what?" She studied him intently, her fingers steepled together. "I do not run a brothel, Mr. Wilde, but a house of entertainment. I will not sell her to you."

"You cannot tell me that your girls are all virgins," he scoffed.

"I would not be so foolish as to make that claim," she said with a small smile. "But I have not prostituted a single one of them. If they choose to take a man up to their bed, they do so of their own free will, and it is naught to do with me."

"Are you telling me that I cannot buy her into my bed?"

She shrugged. "Do not ask me. She is not mine to sell. You will have to deal directly with the girl herself on that matter."

If he had to ask Sarah, then ask her he would. There was no use wasting any more minutes with Mrs. Erskine. He turned on his heel to walk out and find Sarah as the old bawd suggested, but she stopped him with a word. "Wait."

He crossed his arms across his chest and waited.

"You can buy her time, if not her body. For a small monthly payment," and she named a sum that made his eyes pop out of his head. "I will ensure that the other gentlemen who frequent my house understand she is not available to play with them."

"Highway robbery," he muttered. "I should just carry her off and be done with it."

"The other gentlemen will no doubt be grievously disappointed if my new girl is snatched away from them before they have had any opportunity to play with her," she continued in an even tone. "She was promisingly popular last night. Sir Richard Etheridge made a beeline for her as soon as he saw her, and he is well-known as a connoisseur of fine women."

Sir Richard Etheridge ought to have his cock pulled out by its roots and fed to the pigs. He gritted his teeth and tossed a handful of guineas onto the blotter in front of her. "I will pay."

"Of course, you realize that your payment only buys you her time," she added with a malicious look on her face as she tucked the guineas away into a pocket in her skirts. "If she should choose to take another man to her bed, you must understand that it is quite out of my control."

Sarah came down to the salon the following evening in a very different frame of mind. Earning her keep by teasing gentlemen was less fearsome than she had supposed it to be. The work was not as respectable as millinery, to be sure, but it was better than walking the streets, and it had its own compensations. While she was not saving any money, she was living splendidly, with plenty of food, fine clothes to wear, and even a bedroom to call her own. Really, she had no cause for complaint.

Maybe Tom would be there again tonight. She hoped he would be, and that he claimed her before anyone else could. Especially Sir Richard. She did not like Sir Richard, with his fat fingers and his sweaty forehead, and the way he smelled of nasty things under the heavy cologne he wore. Even though Polly had confided to her that morning that he was as rich as Midas and a very good catch, she did not want to engage his interest. Wealthy or not, he still sent shivers of disgust racing down her spine.

As soon as she entered the salon, Mrs. Erskine pulled her aside. "Your services have been engaged for the month," she said quietly in Sarah's ear.

Her heart gave an uncomfortable lurch. "So soon?" According to Polly, a girl had to work hard at gaining a gentleman's interest and please him very well in bed before he would pay for her exclusive services. She hoped her new protector would not expect so much from her—particularly not the bed part. "Who has paid for me?"

"Tom Wilde. See to it that you treat him well." She gave a rare smile. "You have done well. He has paid handsomely for the privilege of having you to himself."

Some of the tension escaped from her body. Far better Tom Wilde, for all his rascally ways, than Sir Richard the fat. She could almost enjoy playing parlor games with Tom, if he did not try to take them too far.

Barely had she turned away from Mrs. Erksine than Tom was at her elbow. "Take my arm."

Orders, even orders to do exactly what she wanted to do anyway, always rubbed her the wrong way. It was on the tip of her tongue to refuse him, until she caught sight of Sir Richard waddling her way, his piggy eyes fixed on her. Hastily she tucked her hand into the crook of Tom's arm. "Are you always this autocratic?"

Placing his free hand over hers, he walked her toward an empty corner of the room. "Yes."

Secretly his attitude thrilled her. "You make no apology for it?"

"I wanted you to myself. It seemed the fastest way of achieving my goal."

"Ruthless as well as autocratic," she muttered, completely forgetting Mrs. Erskine's injunction to be pleasant to him.

He barked a short laugh. "And are you, Miss Sarah Chesham, always this rude to gentlemen who have paid through the nose to spend time with you?"

She shrugged, not liking to be reminded that her time, even if nothing else, was for sale. "As you are the first such gentleman, I can hardly say."

"As you are so unaccommodating, I am hardly surprised you are not overwhelmed with admirers. Would you be as rude to anyone else in the room?"

Mrs. Erskine's injunctions forced themselves in on her remembrance all of a sudden. "I have not been rude to you at all," she protested guiltily, knowing that she lied.

"Would you be as rude to Sir Richard Etheridge, for example? He has a good deal more money than I do, and he is a baronet to boot."

"Sir Richard the fat?" Her face crinkled in distaste. "I would not care to talk to him at all." That at least was no lie.

He entwined his fingers with hers. "Is it just me who rouses your ire, then? Did our acquaintance start out on the wrong footing?"

She could not think of their first meeting, when he caught her with her hands under her skirts touching herself, without blushing to the tips of her ears. "You are an acknowledged scoundrel. You bring out the worst in me."

His fingers squeezed hers affectionately as he maneuvered her through the room. "You are so pretty I cannot believe that your worst is so very bad."

The insincerity in his voice grated on her feelings. "Do not waste your breath with empty flattery," she said wearily, suddenly in no mood to play games with him. "It is not necessary. I will spend the evening with you regardless. You have paid for my time and Mrs. Erskine will not allow me to cheat you of that."

Without her noticing, he had steered her to a quiet corner of the room where they could talk undisturbed. "I trust you enough to believe you would not try to cheat me."

"What do you know about me? That I work in a coffeehouse that doubles as a bawdy house, and that I am the closest a woman can get to a whore without being one? Why should you trust me?"

"You are pretty enough to make me forget all that and trust you anyway."

Would he not give up his condescending flattery? Could he not see that its hollowness was insulting? She took her hand out of the crook of his arm. "Then you are a fool."

To her surprise he did not get angry with her. Instead he leaned against the wall, crossed his arms in front of him, and looked at her in genuine admiration. "You are an astute woman."

Her irritation could not be dismissed so lightly. "What do you mean?"

"As pretty as you are, I do not trust you one whit, but I trust Mrs. Erskine to not let me be cheated."

Even though she had goaded him into making such a bold statement, his honest words still irked her. "Why do you trust her and not me? Is she so singularly honest? Or am I so particularly untrustworthy?"

His smile spoke volumes. "It's very simple—she has more to lose than you do. I could destroy her coffeehouse with one malicious pamphlet, and she knows it. I have no such hold over you."

Uncomfortable though his words might be, she much preferred him when he was telling her the unvarnished truth instead of pacifying her with lies that a child could see through. "You are a writer?"

"I am. And a moderately successful one, too." His pride was evident in his tone of voice. "I write the news sheets and contribute to a number of periodicals."

His open pride in his profession surprised her. "My father always said that writing was barely a respectable way to earn one's living."

Tom's brow darkened. "Your father must have been a paragon of all earthly virtues to turn up his nose at writers."

Judging by the black look on his face, she had offended him without even trying this time. "He was a curate, a man of God." She shrugged uncomfortably. "Things were either black or white to him."

"And are you equally uncompromising? Do you consider me beneath your notice now that you know I am a working man, and earning my living in a barely respectable way?"

"Why should I?" She spread out her arms in a gesture that invited him to share the irony of her situation. "I am a working girl myself, and my profession is a far less respectable one."

"You are no helpless ornament. You at least *have* a profession."

"One I am not proud of. How could I be proud of this?"

"Earning a living is better than giving up and starving on the streets."

"Is it?" She shot him a shrewd look. "My father, for one, would not think so."

"And you? What do you think?"

"I am here, aren't I?" The corner of her mouth creased in a mirthless smile. "Not starving in the streets or laboring in the workhouse for a pittance with no hope of ever getting out again."

"I admire your spirit. You are brave. A survivor."

Bravery would have been holding her head high as she died by inches in the workhouse. True courage would have allowed her to forget the needs of her body while she took care of her soul. Bravery was not selling her body for bread because she was afraid of hunger and cold and want. "I took the easy way out. There is nothing brave about that."

He came nearer to her, and traced down the line of her cheek with his forefinger. "Is it so very bad, being here?"

"I am glad you have bought my time for the month," she confessed, in the spirit of truthfulness that had overcome them both. "You are easy to talk to and you do not stare at me like Sir Richard did last night. He made me feel somehow dirty."

He grinned at her. "You forgot to mention that I am a far finer figure of a man than he is and that you like me immensely."

"Sir Richard is a fine figure of a man," she protested with an answering smile. "Well, anyway, he is very fine."

Tom made a face. "And he cuts a perfectly ridiculous figure in his gargantuan striped satin waistcoats. He is as big as a house. You could put a tasseled saddle on him and ride him about town, and pretend you were in India riding an elephant."

She suppressed a grin. Really, she should not think of Mrs. Erskine's guests in such a way, but Sir Richard *did* look uncomfortably like an elephant. "You are a scoundrel."

His eyes brightened. "You like me in spite of the fact that I am a scoundrel?"

She could not help but laugh. "It is very wicked of me, but I suspect that I like you all the more because of it."

A movement behind her caught his eye, and a groan escaped him. "Speak of the devil."

She turned in the direction of his gaze to find Sir Richard the fat bearing down on them, huffing and puffing like a steam engine.

He bore down on Tom, fixing him with a steely eye. "You called me away last night to no purpose. There was no vote in the House last night."

"Was there not?" Tom lifted his eyebrows in surprise. "I must have been mistaken. I do apologize."

Sir Richard Etheridge was not appeased. His chubby fingers were clenched into tight fists at his sides and his breath came in even shorter bursts than usual. "There was no mistake about it. You called me away on purpose."

"Why would I do that?"

Sir Richard Etheridge jerked his head in Sarah's direction. "You wanted the wench," he ground out between clenched teeth, "so you thought to get me out of the way with a damnable lie."

"Don't be so melodramatic, my dear old fellow. All's fair in love and war."

"I am not your dear old fellow." Sarah was almost frightened by the vicious ice in Sir Richard's voice. "I claim no acquaintance with you. You are not a gentleman."

Tom examined his fingernails with a show of interest. "True, but then neither am I a fat lecher."

Sarah stifled a horrified gasp as Sir Richard's face went as purple as a peony at the insult.

He turned to Sarah with as much dignity as he could muster and offered her his arm. "Come, girl. You can see your companion has no breeding. Will you not do me the honor of your company instead?"

Sarah shook her head, not knowing what to say that would

not make the situation worse. Really, Sir Richard looked as if he would be struck down with apoplexy, he was so angry. Tom was such a scoundrel to tease the poor man so.

"You're too late," Tom said before she could gather her wits sufficiently to reply. "She is not mistress of her own destiny at the moment. I have made arrangements with Mrs. Erskine."

Sir Richard took back his arm and glared at Tom, thwarted malice writ large in his piggy eyes. "You have not heard the last of this," he warned, as he turned on his heel and waddled away. "I am not a man to be lightly crossed."

Sarah shuffled uneasily at his threats, but Tom merely roared with laughter. "He is not a man to do anything lightly," he sputtered, loudly enough that Sir Richard could hear.

Judging by the sudden stiffening of the ramrod posture of his back and the increase in pace of his waddling, Sir Richard heard this last insult only too well.

Sarah was saved from replying to Tom's latest sally by Mrs. Erskine, who called the company to attention. "Make yourselves ready, ladies and gentlemen," she called. "For a game of blindman's buff."

4

Sarah watched as one of the gentlemen set a hard-backed chair in the middle of the room, with a small table covered in a lace cloth beside it. With dignified ceremony, Mrs. Erskine placed a large-figured hourglass firmly on the top.

A round-faced fellow with a pronounced look of mischief in his eye promptly plumped into the chair with an emphatic "Me first!"

Mrs. Erskine tied a thick black blindfold firmly around his head, covering his eyes. "Can you see anything?"

He waved his hand in front of his face. "Not a thing. It's as dark as midday in a London fog."

With this confirmation, she reached over and turned the hourglass over, starting the flow of sand.

One of the coffeehouse girls stepped forward. With a deliberate gesture, she removed the pins from her coiffure and leaned over the seated gentleman, shaking her long dark hair down over her shoulders and allowing some stray strands to caress his face.

Leaning toward her, he breathed in her scent, looking for all the world like a pouter pigeon stretching its neck out for a tasty morsel.

"I do declare," the pouter pigeon said with a series of appreciative sniffs. "We appear to have Mrs. Isabella Beeton in the parlor this evening. No one else, I am sure, could smell so deliciously of home and hearth and all other good things."

A snigger ran around the room. Sarah joined in the laughter. Aside from the Queen herself, a less likely player of blindman's buff could not be imagined. Mrs. Isabella Beeton's *Book of Household Management* had been like a second Bible to her mother. The very thought of such a pillar of respectability taking part in naughty parlor games was positively sacrilegious.

Egged on by the gentlemen, the girl started to undo her bodice, releasing the buttons one by one. Sarah stifled a gasp of shock as she realized the girl was wearing only the thinnest lawn chemise under her bodice. Her exceedingly generous breasts were practically bare.

The girl leaned into the temporarily sightless man seated before her and pressed her bosom to his face, nigh on smothering him with her attentions.

The pouter pigeon chuckled wheezily, his face buried happily in her chest. "Surely this cannot be the breast of our honored Prime Minister, William Gladstone. Even *he* could not be this liberal."

The assembled men roared with laughter at the idea that the devoutly religious Prime Minister should be thrusting his naked bosom into anyone's face.

Showing no sign of wanting to move his face away, the pouter pigeon chuckled again. "Besides, I do not think I will ever see the day when England's Prime Minister has such a delightfully bountiful chest as this."

Sarah did not think it was *such* an absurd idea as all that, but the gentlemen evidently did. Their laughter redoubled at the very notion that a woman would ever be Prime Minister.

The laughter quickly turned to a cheer of delight as the girl removed her bodice altogether and tugged her chemise low enough for her breasts to fall free. She teased the seated man's mouth with her nipple, brushing the tip of her breast against his lips and then withdrawing before he could taste her properly.

Sarah watched in trepidation as the sands in the hourglass diminished rapidly. The girl's display as she twirled before the cheering men, her large firm breasts completely exposed and nipples crinkling with the attention, made her palms sweat. Would she be called on to do the same? To prance around half-naked before the whole assembly as they called out indecent suggestions?

"Relax," Tom whispered in her ear, sensing her nerves. "You are mine, remember? If you are called on to perform, it will only be for me. I will not demand more than you freely offer."

"You will not?" Although she was hardly experienced at being a coffeehouse girl, she did not think it likely that any gentleman would pay a vast sum of money to have her at his disposal for an entire month and then not pressure her to lie with him. Polly had warned her that she would not be able to keep her virginity indefinitely or she would soon lose her popularity. A new girl with a new face would join their group and Sarah would lose her novelty value. Teasing the gentlemen, Polly warned her, would only take the customers so far. Eventually they all wanted to be fucked.

"Not tonight." He drew her closer to his side until she was pressed up against his thighs. "After all, I am in no hurry. I have a whole month to tempt you into offering me everything."

"I will not offer you everything however long you wait," Sarah said, turning her head away from him. His confidence irked her. He ought not be so sure of himself and of his powers of seduction. Whatever he may think of her, she was *not* a wanton.

"We shall see."

Sarah tossed her head at him and focused on the game again. The victim was still searching blindly for the girl's breasts as she teased him mercilessly, never letting him have more than a fleeting taste. As the last grains of sand trickled through the hourglass, she placed a nipple at his mouth in a final tease. There was no time for him to give the proffered nipple more than a quick lick before the sands of the hourglass ran out and the gentlemen all bellowed "Time!"

The girl darted away from him and skipped around the room in victory, her breasts bouncing in the gaslight.

The pouter pigeon groaned as Mrs. Erskine approached to remove the blindfold. "Maggie, you are a cruel wench to torment me so."

Maggie stopped dead. "You knew who I was all along," she accused him.

"Of course I did."

"Then why didn't you say so?" she asked with a pout. "Didn't you want to win my company for the evening?"

He stood up again, his sight restored, and surreptitiously adjusted his trousers as he moved toward her. "Your breasts were too delicious. I had rather lose the game than guess your name and give up the taste of you a scant second too early."

Maggie giggled, her hurt vanity appeased. "You are a flatterer," she said, allowing him to take her arm.

"And you are a tormentor. You know how to whet a man's appetite and leave him hungering for more. Will you let me taste you again?"

In reply, she simply giggled again and led him to one of the outer sofas.

Mrs. Erskine chose the next victim, Sir Richard, and bound him to the chair, blindfolding him securely. A sweeping glance through the room and her eyes lit on Polly, who came forward to stand before the corpulent politician.

As soon as Mrs. Erskine overturned the hourglass, Polly grabbed Sir Richard's hand and sucked his index finger, taking it all the way into her mouth and slowly withdrawing it again.

Sir Richard grunted, whether in pleasure or impatience Sarah couldn't tell. Though she had grown up in a country vicarage, she had never learned the art of translating the speech of pigs.

Polly released his finger, moved in front of him to stand astride his knees and lifted her skirts over his head. When her skirts were at their highest point Sarah plainly saw, for the briefest of moments, that Polly wore nothing underneath.

Sir Richard's hands moved under Polly's skirt and, with a sudden movement that nearly caused Polly to topple, he pulled her toward him.

The gentlemen cheered and called out encouragement to him when Polly arched her back and let out a moan of pleasure. Sir Richard's hands and head were plainly busy underneath Polly's skirts.

Sarah put her hands over her eyes, spreading her fingers the tiniest bit so she could still see through them. It seemed there was to be no end to the debauchery she would have to witness in Mrs. Erskine's house.

What Sir Richard was doing under Polly's skirts she didn't like to conjecture, but Polly certainly seemed to be enjoying it. As the sands in the hourglass ran inexorably out, Polly writhed and moaned under his attentions, her head thrown back and her eyes closed as if in the throes of ecstasy.

The room held its collective breath as the last grains of sand in the hourglass slithered toward the funnel. With uncanny timing, Sir Richard let out a muffled "Polly!" just as the last grains fell.

Polly squeaked with delight at being guessed and lifted her skirts to release Sir Richard's head. With a sly look, she turned toward the audience of gentlemen and lowered her skirts a tad too slowly, affording the entire room a view of her neatly trimmed bush.

Sir Richard released the blindfold himself and stood, Polly's juices clearly visible on his chin. "I believe I have won your company for this evening," he said as he pulled her away to a darker corner of the room. Polly followed him with a squeak and a giggle, not at all loath to oblige.

Mrs. Erskine walked through the crowd of gentlemen to choose the next player. Though Tom and Sarah were standing toward the back of the crowd, she bypassed the eager gentlemen at the front and took Tom by the hand. "Let us see how you perform, Mr. Wilde," she challenged him.

He allowed himself to be led to the chair where he was duly blindfolded.

As soon as his sight was obscured, Mrs. Erskine took Sarah by the elbow and propelled her inside the circle of watching men. "Mr. Wilde will not pay for your company forever," she whispered into Sarah's ear as they made their way over to the chair. "It is time you began to learn what pleases the men who come here. You are not a Polly, to flit carelessly from flower to flower. You will want another protector to secure you as soon as Mr. Wilde loses interest in you."

With shaking hands, Sarah overturned the hourglass.

There was no point in worrying just yet about Tom losing interest in her—he had paid for her for the month.

Though she did not want to attract the men who stood around her watching, she wanted them to be amused and entertained with the game. Mrs. Erskine would be displeased if she bored them.

Most of all, she wanted Tom to know, not just to guess, that it was she who stood before him.

As she stood there, irresolute, the men around her began to turn their heads away and titter. The cause was easy to divine—they were distracted by Sir Richard Etheridge and Polly, who were getting very intimate in their dark corner. The esteemed politician was half lying on the couch, his trousers around his ankles, while Polly sat on top of him, moving rhythmically. Her voluminous skirts could not hide the fact that she was fucking him in the corner.

They were making no effort at concealment. To Sarah's horror, and the amusement of the gentlemen, Sir Richard grunted with Polly's every downward thrust, sounding remarkably like a pig at the trough. Even Tom, blindfolded as he was, was facing the direction of the noisy couple.

Sarah could not compete with such an open and public display of intimacy. Nor did she want to. Instead, she wanted to tease, to entertain, and to allow the men's imaginations to complete the picture.

She grabbed Tom's hands and held them to her face. Would he know her by his sense of touch alone? She guided his fingers over her eyes, round her ears, down the nape of her neck, shivering at the intimacy of his touch. Though he was only touching her face, his caress was more private and more sensual than all the thrusting and grunting that was emanating from Sir Richard's corner.

Tom's hands rested on the nape of her neck as she repeated the caress on him, running her hands over his face and neck, learning every ridge and hollow of him with the sensitive tips of her fingers.

In turn Tom gently ran a finger up Sarah's throat, over her chin, and gently parted her lips where she kissed his questing fingers.

Her fingers mimicked his as they explored each other in gentle caresses.

The surrounding crowd had gone quiet and were watching them intently, ignoring the overt display in the corner.

Intent as she was on caressing Tom, she did not notice the hourglass until the last grains of sand were falling. She squeezed his earlobes hard in a silent message.

His lips curved in a smile. "Miss Sarah Chesham," he said quietly, just as the last grain of sand fell.

The men in the audience applauded loudly as she removed the blindfold and, to her own surprise, planted a chaste kiss on Tom's lips.

He took her by the hand. "I have won your company for the evening?"

Sarah nodded, her mouth dry. Out of the corner of her eye she saw that, thankfully, Sir Richard and Polly had finished their display and were lying quiescent on the sofa. The thought of providing such a wanton display made her breathless with fear, and also, she had to admit, with excited anticipation. She could never behave like that in public. Not with Tom. He would think she was a shameless tart.

Maybe one day when she had lost her virginity and was a whore in every way, maybe then she would feel ready to take part in such public fucking. Maybe one day she would lie on a sofa in the middle of a crowded room, spread her legs wide apart and invite a man to climb on to her and fuck her.

Her pussy began to grow shamelessly hot at the thought of watching them watch her fucking. But she was not ready for that now. Not yet. "I will not—"

Irritated, he cut her off. "I know. You won't fuck me on the sofa in the corner. Believe it or not, I wasn't going to ask you."

A wave of what almost felt like disappointment swept over her. "What were you going to ask for?"

"Your company and your conversation. Is that too much to expect?"

"No."

"Good. Then stop scowling and try to look as if you are enjoying yourself."

If Mrs. Erskine had not been watching her suspiciously, she would have stamped her foot. "I am not scowling."

"Far be it from me to contradict a lady. You must simply have a particular way of smiling that I mistook for a scowl." He dragged her to the closest sofa and pulled her down next to him. "Come sit down on my lap and whisper sweet nothings in my ear. I guarantee that will wipe the scowl off your face."

Though she would rather have bitten him, she had little choice but to obey.

To her surprise, the evening passed quickly in Tom's company. Although he kept her anchored on his lap, he did not press her to get more intimate with him than that. Content to sit and talk with each other, they passed the evening in remarkably good cheer, paying little attention to the rest of the room. Though Sarah could not help but notice that the games of blindman's buff got increasingly rowdy and debauched as the evening wore on, Tom's attention remained on her alone and their corner remained quiet.

The salon had all but emptied when Tom suddenly whispered an invitation in her ear. "Walk with me."

Sarah looked up at him in astonishment. It was well after

midnight, and the streets would be as black as ink. "What did you say?"

"Walk with me," he repeated.

"Surely you do not want to go for a walk at this hour of the night?" The streets of London, even lit up as they were with gas lamps, were no place for a midnight stroll. There were too many ruffians abroad at that hour, and too many dark alleys where danger lurked. Besides, she was far too warm and comfortable sitting on his lap to want to move.

As if he could read her mind, he hugged her tighter to his chest. "Not now, you goose. Walk with me tomorrow to the park."

She did not know quite what to read into his demand. While working at the milliner's, she had been asked many a time by the butcher's boy in the next street to take a walk with him in the park. The leer with which he'd asked had left her in no doubt as to his intentions. She had not liked his loud voice and his casual cruelty to the young apprentices in the street, whom he lorded over as if he were a king, and had always refused him.

Did Tom mean to court her? He had been so abrupt and unloverlike in his demand that she could not credit it. "Why do you want to walk with me? Do you have something you wish to talk about?"

His hands were wandering across her bodice, but for once she did not slap them away. There was something so comforting about being held like this.

His hands brushed her breasts with tantalizing gentleness. "I don't particularly. I'd far rather that you took me to your bed."

"Will you stop asking me that," she said with some irritation, knowing how desperately close she was to giving in to him. Just the feel of his arms around her as she sat on his lap and the touch of his hand on her breast were enough to make her nipples harden to an uncomfortable tightness and her pussy to weep anew.

After all the games they had played and watched this evening, she was desperate to take him upstairs to her bedroom, to let him undress her and to welcome his thrusting cock into her burning pussy, but she would not do so. Taking him into her bed would be as good as a confession that she was no better than a whore. However much she desired him, however much she melted at his touch, she would not humble herself so far. "You know I will not agree."

A great sigh escaped him. "I know. Which is why I have hit on the notion of walking with you instead. I am at the sorry stage where I would rather have your company fully dressed than not at all."

He really was trying to court her. Her insides curled pleasantly at the thought that he liked her company as well as desiring her body. "I do not know if we are allowed out to go walking," she said doubtfully.

"Pshaw. Tomorrow is Sunday and even the lowliest housemaid gets a half-day on a Sunday. Mrs. Erskine would be a brute to refuse you. I will come to call for you at two in the afternoon."

With that, he set her off his knee, stood up purposefully, and clapped his hat on his head. "I had best be off before Mrs. Erskine sets her porters on me and tosses me out into the street."

That night Sarah barely slept. Before it was yet dawn, she had risen from her bed and was contemplating her wardrobe in despair. Going walking with Tom was a far cry from walking out with a butcher. What sort of a dress should she wear for a stroll in the park with a real gentleman? She did not want to make him ashamed of her, or regret being seen with her in public.

She did not admit even to herself that she had other, equally pressing, concerns. Which dress would Tom like best to see her in? What color did he fancy above any other?

Polly, seeing her confusion, kindly came to her rescue. "The green dress with the ribbons," she pronounced almost at once. "It sets off your pretty pale skin, and makes your eyes look even greener. Besides," she added with a giggle, "it is cut so neat that you will not be able to wear a thing underneath it. Poor Mr. Wilde will be driven to distraction thinking about that for the whole walk."

Polly helped her to lace herself tightly into the chosen dress. That done, she paced about the floor unable to concentrate on anything, waiting for two o'clock.

To her relief, Tom presented himself at the coffeehouse at two o'clock on the dot. He offered her his arm and walked her out of the door like any lady into the bright sunshine of a clear afternoon.

"You look as pretty in the afternoon sunshine as you do in the dim light of the gas lamps of an evening," he remarked, as they picked their way over the cobblestones toward the tiny patch of green at the end of the street that called itself a park.

"Is that meant to be a compliment?" She could not help but think that it was a very poor one.

He shrugged. "Not at all. It was simply the truth."

The bright sunshine made her feel more daring than usual. "I would think a man who writes for his living would be able to make a prettier speech to a young woman than that," she teased.

"Do you want pretty speeches? I can make you twenty

such if you please, but I rather thought you would prefer me to pay you the compliment of talking honestly with you."

He was right, of course, though she was more in the mood for compliments this afternoon. "I *do* prefer your honesty."

They walked in silence for some moments until Tom broke it again. "I will not marry you, you know."

His sudden pronouncement took her aback. There was such a thing as too much honesty. "I never expected you would." Expectation was one thing, hopes and dreams and wild fantasies were quite another. She could not deny that in her fantasies, Tom had proposed to her on bended knee, but she knew as well as he did that her dream was unthinkable in reality.

"I cannot afford to set you up as my mistress. Though I can support one household well enough on my income, I cannot support two in any style. You would make a poor showing as my mistress. You'd be better off as a milliner than depending on me for your bread."

She pulled her arm out of his, picking her way through the muddy grass of the park without the support of his arm. Did he think because she was poor that she had no pride? "I am not depending on any man for my bread."

"I have paid Mrs. Erskine for the pleasure of your company for a month, but I really do not know why I am bothering with you."

A cloud covered the sun, making the afternoon suddenly dull and dreary. "Am I that tedious to spend your time with?" Her words were brave, but he had cut her to the quick. "No doubt Mrs. Erskine would give you a part refund if you complained to her of me."

"I cannot afford to keep you to myself indefinitely. I was impetuous enough to pay for the first month, but to pay for a second would be sheer folly. I will have to give you up."

She had never imagined anything different, but still his pronouncement hurt her. "I cannot see what it is to me," she retorted. "I did not ask you to buy my time. Mrs. Erskine will keep me on whether you pay for me or not. There were plenty of single gentlemen in attendance last night who would no doubt have been glad of my company."

A park bench stood at the far end of the tiny park. He took a handkerchief out of his pocket and wiped the seat dry. "That is the problem. There will always be gentlemen glad of your company."

She sniffed dismissively as she spread her skirts and sat down on the bench. "That is hardly a problem for me."

"It is, however, a very large problem for me."

Her tears threatened to choke her voice. "You do not have to make it so."

He tipped her head back to look into her eyes. "If I could prevent it, my dear, I would."

5

Nearly a month of evenings passed. By now Sarah had suffered through twenty-three evenings in a row in which Tom Wilde had teased and tormented her just as much as she had teased and tormented him, if not more so. No longer did he ask her to take him as her lover, and for that she had been grateful. She was not sure that she could live for much longer without giving in to him.

She had started to crave his touch, to live for the moment when she could enter the salon for the evening and he would come forward to take her arm and to claim her as his own.

Twenty-three evenings. It was both too short and too long a time. Too short, for it seemed as if it had been just yesterday when first she met him. Too long, because with every day that passed, one day fewer remained of the time he would spend with her.

Tom tightened his grip on Sarah's arm as he led her to one of the sofas arranged in front of a large curtain. Mrs. Erskine had just announced that the evening's entertainment was to be a play—a new variation on their amusements for the past three weeks and more. He could only hope that it would prove less inflaming to his libido than the usual games.

Sarah still belonged to him for another week, if she didn't kill him first.

He could swear that she had kept him in a state of constant excitement since the day he had first met her, poring over one of Mrs. Erskine's naughty books and stroking her sweet little pussy.

How she'd blushed and stammered when he had caught her out. He'd thought she would be easy game, that she would fall into his hands like a soft, ripe plum ready for the picking.

Hah. He could laugh at his conceit now. There was nothing soft or ripe about Sarah. She was as hard as any common street urchin and twice as remorseless. No woman with an ounce of kindness in her would have kept him on tenterhooks as she had kept him. One moment she was playing the most delightful games with him, undressing for him down to her thin linen shift, allowing him to view her nearly naked body and put his hands under her skirts, sitting on his lap and letting him kiss her on her cheek, her lips, her neck.

The moment he took one step too far, though, she was gone in a flash. Touching her naked breasts was off limits, though she flaunted them in front of him nearly every night by wearing the lowest-cut bodices he could ever wish for. Though she let him stroke her legs whenever he was lucky enough to win a forfeit of her and asked for her stockings as a prize, she would allow him to go no higher than the top of her garters. Just the once, he had reached higher and stroked her pussy. It was dripping wet and more than ready for his touch, but still she had slapped his hand away and pouted for the rest of the evening. And for all that he demanded, even begged, she would not take him to her room and take him as her lover. Her refusals hurt him so much he had finally stopped asking.

He had a week more in her company and then he would have to give her up. Though he made a good living from his scurrilous pamphlets, he was not so wealthy that he could afford to entertain a high-class mistress like Sarah indefinitely. Especially not at the ruinous rates that Mrs. Erskine charged. It was best that he give her up now before he grew addicted to her presence.

His pretty daisy was no longer a poor milliner but an expensive courtesan and out of his reach. He would have to drum that into his head over the next seven days so that it did not hurt so badly to hand her over to someone whose pockets were deeper than his own.

He glared at the gentlemen crowding around them, jostling for a sofa with a good view. Sir Richard Etheridge had made no secret that he was sniffing around Sarah's skirts still. The moment he relinquished her, Sir Richard would come forward and claim her. Sir Richard would claim the right of sitting opposite her in their nightly card games, salivating over each morsel of flesh she laid bare as she stripped down to her shift. He would claim the right to pull her onto his lap and kiss her, to put his fat arms around her waist and nuzzle his grizzled red sideburns into her soft neck.

But, by God, if Sir Richard ever claimed the right to take Sarah upstairs and strip her naked on the bed, there would be trouble. If he ever tried to plaster his gross body on top of hers, to suckle on her white breasts, and to thrust into her pussy with his fat hairy cock, then, by God, he would kill the bastard. If he couldn't fuck Sarah, then no one else would either.

He took possession of a sofa close to the curtain, pulling Sarah down close beside him. The rest of the sofa was quickly taken by a pretty dark-haired girl whom Sarah addressed in a friendly tone as Polly, and her partner, a stiff-necked older gentleman in a morning suit.

The lights were put out and the room became quite dark. He took advantage of the darkness to pull Sarah onto his lap. Judging by the rustling and giggling going on in the gloom behind him, every other gentleman was doing the same.

A light came on from behind the curtain, illuminating the area beyond it. Behind the curtain two shapes appeared with the light behind them, their silhouettes clearly visible as black shadows on the curtains.

At the other end of the sofa Polly, also sitting on her partner's lap by now, clapped her hands together. "A shadow play. Oh, what fun."

The shadows behind the curtain revealed themselves as a man and a woman: the man by the shape of his top hat and walking cane, and the woman by her voluminous skirts. Together they began to strike poses behind the curtain, the gentleman doffing his hat and bowing to the lady, and kissing her hand, and the lady curtsying back in her turn.

Tom yawned and shifted uncomfortably on the sofa. Polly had been a mite too hopeful. So far the shadow play seemed interminably dull to him.

He focused on the woman sitting in his lap. Despite her hard-hearted ways, she was quite delightful. He did not feel the need to put on a show for her or to act as if he were anything other than himself. Early in their acquaintance she had told him quite firmly that she would rather have the truth from him than any foolish lies. He had taken her at her word, and she repaid him in kind. Truth to tell, he had not had such an honest relationship with a woman since his old nurse—who knew all his faults and foibles and every misdeed he had been guilty of as a child—had died.

The shadow couple behind the screen was getting more animated now. The man was kneeling to the woman, his hand on his heart, clearly professing his ardor for her. In short order she was swooning into his arms.

He shook his head at the silliness of it, and surreptitiously adjusted Sarah's skirts so he could put his hand on her stockinged knee. He half expected her to push him away again, but to his good fortune she seemed too enthralled by the silly antics of the shadow people to pay him any mind.

Pushing his luck, he moved his hand a little farther up her leg to caress her thigh. She made no complaint but gave a little shiver and pressed herself more firmly into his lap. Though it was small consolation for the pain he had been in for the past three weeks and more, he hoped she was getting as frustrated as he was. Given that she was inflicting the pain on him, it was only just that she should share in it.

His cock started to rise at the feel of her bottom wriggling against his groin, and he shifted her slightly on his lap so it had room to expand. Before the end of the night his cock would be standing to attention as stiff and as proud as any soldier in the Queen's army. Sarah's teasing ways always had that effect on him.

The actions of the shadow people had changed again. The shadow gentleman, if he was not mistaken, was now engaged in divesting the shadow woman of her clothes, silhouettes of skirts and petticoats appearing behind the screen, only to be tossed to one side. He began to give the shadows on the curtain decidedly more attention. The shadow play was turning out to be more interesting than he had thought.

Garment by garment, the shadow man undressed the shadow woman, to the cheers and shouts of the audience on the sofas, until she was quite naked behind the curtain. The complete outline of her shape was visible, down to the peaking of her nipples at the ends of her pert breasts, and the patch of hair between her legs.

Now she began to take the most suggestive poses, bending over to show off her breasts and rump and opening her legs wide to suggest a sight of what lay between them.

Tom began to stroke Sarah under her skirts, running his hands over her silky smooth stockings. His cock was already getting hard in his trousers. By God, he'd give half of what he owned to have Sarah posing like that for him, to have her naked in front of him displaying her pussy to his sight. No shadow woman could be half as enticing as the hard-hearted woman wriggling on his lap.

Meanwhile, the shadow man was stripping off his own clothes behind the curtain, tossing away his top hat and cane, his jacket, his shirt, his trousers. In a few moments he, too, stood behind the curtain as naked as the day he was born, the silhouette of his erect cock clearly standing up proud and stiff against the light.

Tom could feel Sarah's shock at the sight. She held herself tense in his arms, not moving a muscle, except that a little gasp escaped her.

He hugged her closely to him, his own cock stiffening further under her, until it was nestled firmly between her buttocks. "This shadow play is more entertaining than I first thought," he whispered in her ear.

"It is truly shocking," Sarah mouthed back, but she did not take her eyes from the stage.

He slipped his hand farther up her leg, until he reached the top of her stocking, and then farther again, until his fingers rested against her bare thigh. Her muff was so close he could feel her hairs brush against his fingers, but he did not dare caress her there. Not yet. He did not dare provoke another attack of the pouts.

The two shadows now began to strike poses together. The man took her breasts in his hand, then knelt in front of her and took them into his mouth and began to suckle on them. With his free hand Tom stroked Sarah's own breasts through her bodice, mimicking the suckling on the stage with his fingers, and was rewarded with a shiver of pleasure.

The shadow people held their pose for a few moments and then swapped places, the woman coming to kneel at the man's feet.

Tom gasped as the woman took the man's cock in her mouth and began to suckle on it. He could almost feel the suction of her mouth on his own cock as he watched her. The twin delight of watching the shadow people pleasure each other, and stroking Sarah's naked thighs at the same time, was making him painfully hard.

When they finally moved from their pose, the man's cock had swollen even bigger in size and jutted out from his body like the prow of a ship.

Tom was sure his own cock was at least that big by now. He leaned in close to Sarah's ear. "God, I want you to suck on me like that."

Sarah gave her head a tiny shake. "I am not your whore," she replied in low tones, but her voice was quavering.

Tom smiled quietly to himself and moved his hand a fraction higher on her leg. The shadow play was clearly getting to her as well.

He rubbed his cock between her buttocks, teasing himself with wanting so much more.

The shadow woman was now standing with her legs apart and the man kneeling again at her feet, his head buried in her muff. From the writhing of the woman's shadow and the feminine cries of delight that came from behind the curtain, his tongue was being very well employed there.

Sarah was positively melting in his arms. Tom dared to move his hand higher still, until he was cupping her mound. She tensed up and stopped breathing for a second and he braced himself for a scolding, but it never came. She started to breathe again, a little more heavily than before, and made no protest.

He let his hand lie on her mound, motionless, until she softened in his arms again. Still he did not move, luxuriating in the warmth of her.

Finally the man stood up again and bent the woman over at the waist. He held up one finger, showing it clearly against the curtain, before thrusting it into her cunt and taking it out again. Then two fingers of his were held up before he dipped them in and out of her cunt several times. Finally he held up three fingers against the light and then thrust all of them into her, leaving them there for some seconds before taking them out again.

The shadow woman was wriggling her rump around in delighted fashion and the shadow man's cock was as stiff and as proud as ever.

The shadow man approached her, cock in his hand, and guided it home deep into her cunt. From the shadow on the curtain, Tom could see that he was buried in her up to the hilt. His own cock was aching with desire to do the same. Sarah had kept him so close to the edge for so long that watching them fuck was almost enough to make him come in his pants.

Sarah wriggled against him, rubbing her pussy against his hand and panting quietly. His fingers were dripping with her juices.

At the other end of the sofa, Polly and her partner had given up any pretense of watching the shadow play. Instead, Polly was kneeling between the gentleman's legs and sucking on his cock with noisy vigor.

Sarah glanced at them, spellbound at the sight for a moment, and then looked away again, her face reddening.

"Polly's partner is in luck tonight," he murmured in her ear. If only Sarah would be so accommodating he would be in heaven.

"Don't get your hopes up," she muttered back at him.

It was not only his hopes that were up. His damned cock was about to explode.

Even if he couldn't fuck her and relieve the tension that was building up in him, he could still give her pleasure. He rubbed her pussy a little harder, and was rewarded with an extra wriggle. It was time to try his luck and see if she would welcome a little more.

Her cunt was so slick and wet that his finger slid inside her as easily as winking. Her legs fell open of their own accord to allow him to add a second finger to the first.

She was too far gone in lust to do anything other than welcome him as he fucked her with his fingers, sliding them in and out of her wet cunt, rubbing them over her clit and her pussy, and then thrusting them back inside her.

Polly gave her gentleman one last vigorous suck and his semen spurted into the air, splattering the four of them with tiny droplets.

On the stage in front of them, the shadow man withdrew his cock from the shadow woman's cunt just in time to spurt his cum over her naked ass.

Sarah gave a surprised cry in the back of her throat and he felt the rush of her juices as she orgasmed under his hands.

Tom slowly withdrew his fingers from her cunt, holding her tightly on his lap until her breathing returned to normal. His cock still hurt with wanting to fuck her, or even for the solitary pleasure of stroking himself into oblivion, but he forced his desires to fade to a manageable level. Even more than he wanted release, right now he simply wanted to hold her tightly in his arms and to love her.

For Sarah, the last week passed by at a gallop. At the end of this night, the month was over. Tom's funds had run out and he would no longer be able to claim her exclusive services.

She was a free woman—free to sell her services to the man who tickled her fancy the most, or who tipped her the most generously. If she chose wisely—an older gentleman who wanted the appearance of being a rake more than the reality, for instance—she could earn a few pennies to put aside for a rainy day and still keep herself pure.

She clutched Tom's arm tightly. Why did she care so much about her virginity? She had stripped down to her shift in mixed company, and let Tom touch her everywhere, even there. His touch had given her more pleasure than she had ever known.

In just a few short hours he would be gone from her life. She would never be able to pay him back in kind for the pleasure he had given her.

So why did she feel as though her heart was breaking?

Her thoughts were broken into by the sound of Mrs. Erskine's voice. "Ladies, go hide yourselves."

Sarah picked up her skirts and scampered out of the doorway with a couple of the other girls. Tonight, after Sarah had lost half her clothes to Tom in a few hands of ecarte, Mrs. Erskine had changed the game. This evening they were to play hide-and-seek—with a difference.

Sarah and two of her friends were to hide themselves anywhere they liked on the premises—always excepting the coffeehouse, which was in public view. Once Mrs. Erskine had counted to one hundred, the others were to come and find them. Whenever one of the seekers found one of the hiders, the seeker had to join the hider in her hiding place, until the hiding places were so full that not another body could squeeze in.

Sarah paused at the top of the stairs. "Quick, hide yourself," one of the other girls whispered to her. "They will be coming up any moment now."

Without thinking, Sarah ran to her bedroom, the place she knew best, and shut the door behind her. She considered crawling under the bed, but the floorboards were too cold and uninviting. Besides, she did not want to dirty her white linen shift.

She would not crawl into her bed, either, and hide under her bedclothes—that would be an invitation to the seekers to play all sorts of indecent games with her.

The draperies at the window. They were heavy velvet and came right down to the floor. If she arranged herself artfully she could hide behind them and no one would be able to see her.

Already she could hear the rush of eager feet coming up the stairs. Quick as a flash, she darted behind the curtains, standing right up against the wall and tucking her feet in so that not the barest morsel of slipper peeked out from under the bottom.

Quiet as a mouse she crouched there, hardly daring to breathe. She hardly dared to hope that Tom would find her before anyone else did. And if Tom could not find her, she did not want to be found by anyone else.

The noises in the corridor came closer. Her door opened with a squeak and she held herself as still as could be. In trooped at least three people—she could hear the muted scuffle of two girls in slippers and the heavy thumps of their companion in sturdier walking shoes. A threesome, searching the bedrooms for her.

There was a squeak and a rustle of petticoats as one of the girls sat on the bed. "There's no one here," she said in a voice of mock complaint.

"I am," her male companion said, and the bedsprings squeaked in protest again. "Come and pay me some attention."

"Mmmm, so you are." There was silence for a few minutes, except for some more squeaking, a fair bit of rustling, and more than a little giggling.

Sarah dared to breathe again. The seekers were too occupied with one another to notice her hiding behind the curtain.

The noises went on for so long that she became curious and opened the curtains a tiny fraction so she could peep between them. As she'd guessed, a man and two girls were lying on her bed. The girls were dressed only in their stockings—all their other clothes were discarded at the end of the bed. Their companion was fully dressed still, though in disarray. He had kicked off his shoes and his shirt had come quite untucked from his trousers, which had slipped off his buttocks.

The girls were locked together in an intimate embrace, their arms wrapped around each other and kissing each other with open mouths. He was lying behind one of them, his hands on her naked hips, thrusting in and out of her with all his might.

As Sarah watched, he gave one last thrust and lay still for a few seconds before rolling off the bed and refastening his trousers. "Grab your clothes, ladies," he said to the two girls who showed no signs of stopping. "This isn't going to find us anyone."

"Do you want to find someone else?" The girl's voice sounded definitely pouty. "Aren't we enough for you?"

"Come on. Let's go." The tone of his voice brooked no argument.

Sarah quickly hid her face behind the curtains again as the two girls got off the bed, picked their clothes up off the floor and left.

Her solitude did not last long. As soon as the threesome left, another couple entered.

"This is her room." The voice belonged to Suzanna, a thin-faced French girl with a mean temper and a streak of envy a mile wide.

Sarah stopped breathing again. She dared not hope that the other person in the room was Tom. All the girls knew how much she liked him, and Suzanna would rather sleep on a bed of nails than do a good turn for one of her fellows.

There was a rustle and a clink. "Thank you, my dear."

Sarah gave a start. That was Sir Richard's voice, thick and slightly slurred with drink. Sir Richard must have bribed Suzanna to show him which was her room.

Bother Suzanna and her petty greed. The girl would betray her own mother for half a crown.

She really did not want to be caught behind the curtain with Sir Richard. He would be sure to try to maul and kiss her, and she would have to spend her evening fending off his fat fingers and trying to evade his scratchy red whiskers.

Unfortunately he was not as easily fooled as the threesome. He started to look around for her in earnest, opening her wardrobe, getting down on to his knees and looking under her bed.

"Come on, girl, make yourself useful," he barked at Suzanna, when he did not immediately find anything.

Suzanna's slippered feet scuffled into action. Sarah's heart forgot to beat as Suzanna walked directly over to the drapes and pulled them open. "Here she is." Her eyes glittered with malice.

Sir Richard's piggy eyes gleamed with excitement as he waddled drunkenly over to her. "My dear girl, I am so pleased to be the first one to find you." He shuffled inside the curtain, pressing her close up against the wall with his heavy body. "I have waited for this moment for a long time."

She tried to wriggle away from him, but with his bulk on one side of her and Suzanna on the other, there was nowhere for her to go. She shuffled along the wall away from them, only to find herself at last penned in a corner, like a rat in a trap.

Sir Richard wasted no time in pleasantries. With a gleam of drunken lust in his eyes, he reached up and grabbed at her breasts with his greasy hands. "Very nice," he mumbled, breathing brandy fumes into her face. "Very nice."

She tried to shake him off. "Sir Richard, please. You are drunk."

He gave a snorting laugh and tugged hard on her bodice. "Drunk with love, my dear. I've been watching you for weeks now, wasting yourself on that rascally young Grub Street guttersnipe, stripping in front of him and letting him stare at your breasts and touch and kiss you."

The accusatory tone of his voice and the pressure he was exerting on her bodice started to make Sarah seriously uneasy. "Mr. Wilde paid Mrs. Erskine for my company," she said, tugging her shift away from him. "I could not refuse him."

He snorted again, in disgust this time. "He has no manners and no breeding and I could buy and sell him fifty times over. You are wasting yourself on him, my dear. You deserve a real gentleman to look after you."

All of a sudden her bodice gave way with a loud rip and Sir Richard staggered backward with surprise, a piece of her linen shift dangling from his fist.

Sarah tried to hold the remnants of her bodice together over her naked breasts with both hands. "Sir Richard, that is not the work of a gentleman." Her voice was shaking.

He was advancing toward her, his evil intentions clearly written on his face. "It doesn't matter, my dear," he said, as he deliberately ripped the remnants of her bodice open, letting her breasts spill freely out. "I can buy you twenty more."

His aggression scared her. If he tried to hurt her for real, would anybody hear her if she called for help? Or would they think her cries were all just part of the game? "I don't want twenty more chemises. This is not a game anymore, Sir Richard. I want you to leave my room at once."

His hands were all over her breasts, pinching her skin cruelly with his vicious fingers. "Now then, my dear, don't be so touchy. I just want to play an innocent little game with you. The game that men and women have always played together."

"Please, let me go." She was struggling with all her might, but she could not get free of his hands.

He leaned against her, pressing her body into the wall with his bulk so she could not move, and then reached down to fumble with his trousers. "I'm willing to forgive you for playing around with that Grub Street hack and for not coming to me as pure and innocent as you were a month ago. I lay the blame firmly on his shoulders. He stole you from me, and forced me to bide my time until his money ran out. But you will come to me now and let me taste your sweet naked body."

His cock sprung free from his trousers and nudged up firmly against her mound, making her feel sick to her stomach. His intentions were crystal-clear. He would not be content with mauling her breasts—he was going to rape her.

She gave Suzanna a look of entreaty. "Will you stand by and let him misuse me so?"

Suzanna shrugged carelessly, her face mean and pinched. "You think you're so much better than the rest of us, refusing to spread your legs for the gentlemen. Sir Richard is going to show you that you're no better than the rest of us whores."

Sir Richard was stroking his cock furiously with one hand as he groped under her petticoats with the other. "I'll show you your place, I will," he grunted. "I'll use you as I use my wife, and the slut of a governess she employs, and the housemaids, and every other whoring little bitch who flaunts herself in front of me. I'll fuck every last one of you whenever I please. I'll fuck you all until you scream and beg me to stop, and then I'll fuck you some more."

Suzanna smiled a thin-lipped smile, feeding on Sarah's terror. "And I shall enjoy watching you get your comeuppance as he ruts on you."

"Get down on your knees, girl, and suck my cock."

Sarah whimpered and shook her head. Her only thought was how to escape from this nightmare.

Sir Richard gave her a vicious blow with the back of his hand. "That will teach you to disobey me. On your knees."

Whimpering from shock and from the pain of the blow, Sarah sank to her knees.

Sir Richard poked his cock roughly into her unwilling mouth until she gagged on it.

"Damn you, girl, you're enough to ruin any man's ardor," he grumbled. "Come on, you," he said, gesturing at Suzanna. "Come and show the little whore how it's done properly."

Suzanna dropped willingly to her knees and took his cock deep in her mouth, sucking on it with gusto. "You taste good," she purred when she finally came up for air, throwing a malicious glance at Sarah.

He took his cock out of Suzanna's mouth and thrust it back at Sarah. "Your turn now, girl."

Sarah gagged uncontrollably again as his cock touched her lips and turned her head away. Having his hairy member thrusting down her throat was too disgusting to bear. The risk of another beating was nothing in comparison.

He gave up with a noise of disgust and pulled her to her feet. "Damn you for a sullen whore. I will have to teach you better manners."

"She needs correcting," Suzanna suggested, still kneeling at his feet. "A good whipping would soon sort her out."

He dragged Sarah over to the bed and pushed her down on her back. "I will whip her later." With one hand he held her down while with the other he tore away her petticoats.

She would not let him rape her. She would not. Clawing and biting at him with all her might, she tried to wriggle away from his grasp.

Sir Richard was panting with the effort of holding her. "Come hold the little whore down," he growled at Suzanna.

"Yes, Sir Richard," Suzanna said meekly. She sat at the head of the bed and grabbed Sarah's flailing arms, pinning them to the bed.

Her grip was strong for such a thin, fragile-looking woman. Try as she might, Sarah could not break free.

Sir Richard forced her legs apart with his fat fingers. His thick cock was grasped so tightly in his hand that the purple head bulged threateningly.

Despite her last desperate struggles, she could not get free. Sir Richard would rape her. There would be no escape.

Her stomach heaved and the room began to spin around her. As if from far away, she heard herself scream—an animal scream of pure terror.

6

Tom watched avidly as Sarah scurried out of the room with a couple of the other girls. Damn Mrs. Erskine for choosing this game on the last night he could claim Sarah's company.

There had not even been time to cheat and ask Sarah where she would hide so he could be sure of finding her first—she had been hustled away from his side too quickly for that.

He searched desperately around the room for a friendly face, finally spying Sarah's friend in a corner. He strode over to her. "Polly, where will she hide?"

Polly gave a little smile and shrugged helplessly as her companion glowered in an unfriendly way at Tom. "All our rooms are at the top of the stairs. She will be in one of them, I'm sure—probably in her own."

"How will I know which room is hers?"

"It's blue. Blue curtains and bedcoverings. You can't mistake it."

Tom gave her a nod of thanks and strode over to the door, positioning himself to be one of the first up the stairs.

Mrs. Erskine found him there and drew him aside with a hand on his sleeve just as the call went up to start the hunt.

"What do you want?" he barked at her, itching to be on his way toward his Sarah.

"Come, Mr. Wilde, there is no need to be so hasty," she admonished him. "The night is still young."

"I only have Sarah to myself for one more night," he growled at her. "You're robbing me even of that."

"That is exactly what I wanted to talk to you about," she said. "Come, take a seat."

"Can it not wait?"

"No, I'm afraid not." She seated herself on one of the sofas and waited politely until, with another growl, he sat down next to her.

"You see," she said, with a delicate dab at her nose with a lace-edged handkerchief, "I have another offer for the girl. He wants her from midnight tonight. Which is," she consulted her watch, "approximately twenty minutes from now. Unless," and she gave a gentle cough, "you would be interested in extending your payment for another month. I always like to give the incumbent the right to edge out their competition and extend their terms if they please. It's good for business."

"Another month?" He shook his head. Paying for another month would make a serious inroad into his ready money. He was not so besotted with the wench as to beggar himself on her account. "Out of the question."

Mrs. Erskine gave a gentle sigh. "Then I am afraid I will have to accept the other gentleman's offer." She rose from the sofa and dismissed him with a wave of one heavily be-jeweled hand. "You have fifteen minutes left on the clock. May I suggest you make the most of them?"

Fifteen goddamn minutes. Tom scowled heavily as he raced for the stairs. So much for his plans to spirit Sarah away and keep her to himself for the entire evening. If he didn't find her soon, he would not even have the time to bid her farewell.

Fifteen minutes to find her before she belonged to another man—to Sir Richard Etheridge, he would wager. He could not look on as she was claimed by the disgusting Sir Richard. Bah—he was more like a squat, fat toad than a man.

He took the stairs two at a time, stopping briefly at the top of the stairs to glance around the sitting room.

The sound of giggling came from behind the piano in the far corner.

He strode over and peered behind it.

A number of seminaked bodies were entwined in the small space between the piano and the wall. One of the girls spotted him looking. "Come, you have found us," she cried, holding out her arms to him. "You have to join us."

Sarah was not among them. Ignoring the girl's outstretched arms, he turned away and strode off toward the hall corridor.

One by one he opened the doors to the bedrooms and looked inside. He found a green room, a yellow room, and any number of pink rooms, but no blue room. Most of the rooms were occupied, but he ignored all invitations to join in the games that were going on. His time was running out.

He had just opened the door on yet another orgiastic scene when a terrified scream rang out from the end of the hall corridor.

Sarah's voice—he would know it anywhere.

Taking off at a run, he followed the sound of the screaming, until he burst in on a scene that made him sick to his stomach.

Sarah lay spread-eagled on her bed, screaming wildly. Her arms were pinned down by a monster in petticoats, while Sir Richard, damn every bone in his filthy body, cock in hand, prepared to thrust into her sweet body.

Tom grabbed the first thing that came to hand, an iron candlestick holder from the dressing table, and cracked Sir Richard viciously over the pate.

Sir Richard looked up, astonished, for a moment, then his eyes rolled back in his head and he slumped to the floor. The monster in petticoats took one horrified look at Sir Richard, lying senseless on the floor, and ran for her life.

Sarah was weeping now, curled up on her bed with her face buried in the blankets as if she wanted to hide away from the world.

He took her gently into his arms. "Sarah, my love, don't cry." There was nothing he could do, nothing he could say, that would take away the last few minutes. All he could offer her was his sympathy and his understanding, and the certain knowledge that she was safe in his embrace.

Her weeping eventually subsided into hiccuping sobs. "He hit me. He was going to rape me."

He cradled her in his arms, stroking her hair as if she were a small child. "It's over, sweetheart. He won't hurt you again. I won't let him touch you ever again."

Sir Richard gave a groan and stirred on the floor. Clearly he had not hit the bastard hard enough. It was a shame he ever had to wake up.

She shuddered at the noise. "Take me away from here. Away from him."

He picked her up and carried her down the hallway to a deserted sitting room at the very end where she could recover her composure out of reach of Sir Richard.

Sarah clung to Tom as if he were her lifeline. His warmth and tenderness gave her strength and the feel of his arms around her took away her pain. If only she could hold on to him forever. "Make love to me, Tom."

His mouth fell open and he looked as if she had just hit him over the head with a plank of wood. "What did you say?"

"Make love to me," she repeated, hiding her face in his shirtfront.

"Why? Why now?"

"Sir Richard frightened me." An uncontrollable shudder racked her body as she spoke, but she did not weep. The time for tears was past. "I want to remove all remembrance of his touch from my body. I want to take away those memories of lying helpless under him, and replace them with memories that I can treasure. Please, Tom, make love to me."

"Here?"

"Here, anywhere. What does it matter?" She did not care where—she needed him too badly.

"We cannot stay here. Sir Richard will be furious. He might well be angry enough to have the law on you and have you arrested for assaulting a Member of Parliament."

"But I did nothing to him," she protested, knowing all the while that her innocence would make no difference. The law was not made for poor people. She had dared to reject a wealthy man, a Member of Parliament, and he would have his revenge on her one way or another.

"Sir Richard cannot touch me—he knows he cannot touch me—but you? You are defenseless, a prostitute for all anyone knows, an easy target for his vengeance."

Her heart leaped with fear. The streets would swallow her up after all. "I have nowhere else to go." There was no armor against the resignation of despair that gripped her soul. She'd always known it would come to this in the end.

"Either he will have you arrested or he will try to rape you again. And next time I will not be around to stop him."

He was right—Mrs. Erskine's house was no longer a refuge for her. Sir Richard would kill her. Or he would succeed in raping her next time, and she would kill herself and save him the bother. She shrugged hopelessly. Whichever way she looked at it, the result would be the same in the end.

"Where will you go?"

What did it matter? Her life was over before it had begun. "There is nowhere in this world for a woman like me to go."

Tom looked down at the fragile burden in his arms. His landlady would kick up merry hell if he brought home a strange woman to his lodging house. "You will have to come home with me," he found himself saying. Ah, damn his landlady—he'd never cared much for her anyway.

Sarah acquiesced with a weary shrug. All the fight had gone out of her. She looked like the empty shell of herself, drained of all emotion. "Just for tonight, then," she agreed. "I'll find somewhere else to go in the morning."

No gentleman worth the name would throw a lady out on the streets. Particularly not the lady he was obsessed with, in love with.

Damn it, he might as well admit it—he was in love with her. Head over heels, topsy-turvy in love with Miss Sarah Chesham. Once he had her in his lodgings, in his bed and in his arms, he would not let her go again.

If it meant that she would stay with him and give him the right to protect her from scum like Sir Richard, he would even marry her.

Marriage. He'd not seriously considered it before, but the

more he thought about it, the more it appealed. Sarah would make him a fine wife. Her occupation did not bother him—in fact, he was man enough to admit that it turned him on. He was a grown man and his parents were no longer alive to be shocked by his choice of bride. Nobody else's good opinion mattered to him.

If she stayed at Mrs. Erskine's establishment, she would attract plenty of lovers, men with far more money and status than he could ever hope to aspire to. Any of them would set her up in luxury and she would want for nothing. They might not offer to marry her, but then again, such things had happened before.

If wealthier and more aristocratic men than he was did not blink at marrying a fallen woman, then why should he? Besides, Sarah was no whore, but an abused woman. Only an animal would have no pity on her situation. It was his duty to rescue her from Sir Richard and other men who would take advantage of her.

"Can you walk?" Reluctant though he was to put her down, he could not carry her all the way to his apartments.

She struggled to her feet. "I would crawl on my hands and knees to get out of this house tonight."

They made their way downstairs and out of the front door, unobserved and unmolested.

Arm in arm through the dark streets, they walked to his lodging house. Tom did his best to support Sarah, but she was strong and would not lean on him.

The street was dark, his latchkey was stiff, and his landlady had an ear like a fox. Clad in a voluminous flannel nightgown, a knitted nightcap on her head, and a candle in her hand, she accosted them both on the stairs. "This is a respectable establishment," she hissed at him, looking askance at Sarah's ripped silk shift and low décolletage. "I will thank you to take your fancy piece elsewhere. I want no such she-nanigans in my house."

Tom gave her an icy glare. "I will thank you not to refer to my wife as a fancy piece."

"Your wife?" both women asked at once. Thankfully his landlady's strident squeal utterly overwhelmed Sarah's quiet gasp.

"It is hardly the hour for introductions, but since you insist." He gave Sarah's arm a squeeze to warn her not to contradict him. "May I present my wife, Mrs. Thomas Wilde, until this happy afternoon Miss Sarah Chesham, and daughter of the late, and highly respectable, curate of Wigglesthorpe."

The landlady looked doubtful, but in the face of his insistence, she had no choice but to back down. "Well, if she really is your wife—"

"Which she is," he interjected.

"—then I suppose she is welcome to stay as my guest for tonight." She gave Tom a meaningful look. "We can talk about your rent in the morning." With that, she took her candle and waddled off into her apartments, muttering loudly about Sarah's strange and highly suspicious choice of bridal attire.

As soon as Tom had shut the door into his rooms behind him, Sarah collapsed into a corner of the sofa. The effort of pretending to be strong, of pretending that she was not hurting in every way that she could hurt, was exacting a heavy toll on her. "That was gallant. Unnecessary, but gallant."

He paced around the room, his head averted from her gaze. "Mrs. Fitchett is not known for her kindness to distressed souls. She would have refused you entry if I had made any other excuse for bringing you home with me."

His voice was strangely uncertain. Was he already regretting his offer of a sanctuary for the night? She leaned back and closed her eyes, unwilling to face his rejection just yet. "What will you do tomorrow when she finds out you have told her a lie?"

"There is no need for it to be a lie."

The darkness was a blessing. It matched her mood. "You do not mean that."

"You are wrong. I meant every word of it."

All she wanted was for him to make love to her and remove the taint of Sir Richard from her body. She would not feel clean until every trace, every memory of him was washed away. "Then you are either too foolish or too drunk to know what you have just said." She wanted nothing more from him than his help erasing her memories. She could take nothing more from him.

"I am not drunk, and I make a very good living by my wits, so you should not call me foolish, either."

"It does not matter. You cannot marry me. I would not ask it of you." Her arms ached to hold him. "Come to me, Tom. I will be your mistress for tonight at least, though I cannot be your wife."

"You will marry me."

Her mouth curved in a faintly malicious smile. "Are you that scared of Mrs. Fitchett that you would marry me to escape her wrath?"

"Damn Mrs. Fitchett. I don't care a bean for her."

"Then come kiss me."

"No."

Had Sir Richard's attack on her spoiled even this? She forced her eyes to open, to gaze at his face and read the truth that was in his eyes. "Do you not want me anymore?" His loss of desire was understandable, even excusable. He had seen another man on top of her, preparing to violate her body. The blame for his disgust lay with Sir Richard, not with Tom himself. She would try not to hate Tom for it.

"Of course I want you." He smashed his fist down on the mantelpiece above the fire in frustration. "I've done nothing else but want you from the moment I first met you. I'm just about dead with wanting you."

"Then why won't you kiss me? Why won't you take me to your bed?"

"I am a respectable bewhiskered Victorian gentleman of impeccable morals," he said, his mood changing from frustration to frivolity on the instant. "I will not succumb to your wicked blandishments until you have agreed to marry me."

"You are being ridiculous."

"I don't care."

"You warned me weeks ago that you would never marry me." The memory of their conversation still niggled at her soul. "Why have you suddenly changed your mind?"

"For all the usual reasons."

She raised her eyebrows at him, waiting for an explanation.

"Companionship, a partner to share my life with, children, great sex." He gave a comical leer. "Especially the great sex. I'm particularly looking forward to that part."

Lust was no basis for a marriage. Not the sort of marriage she had dreamed about. "Maybe I won't want to be intimate with you anymore if we get married."

His leer turned into a confident smile. "I have had a month's worth of practice in tempting you to fall into my arms. I am confident I will be able to persuade you into it."

"Maybe I will want to fuck other men," she said, pushing him to see how far he would go with his absurdity. "Consider, I was a coffeehouse girl after all. I may have picked up a taste that you will not be able to satisfy."

His face darkened with distaste. "You enjoyed being beaten and nearly raped by Sir Richard?"

An involuntary shudder wracked her body. "That was not kind of you."

"I apologize." His voice was clipped, but his irritation was directed not at her for baiting him, but at himself for rising to her bait. "It was cruel of me."

She should not allow him to flagellate himself simply for reacting to her provocation. "I accept your apology."

"And my offer of marriage? Do you accept that as well?"

His ability to switch from deadly seriousness to even more deadly foolishness in the space of a heartbeat astonished her. "You will regret it in the morning."

"Never."

She pulled her ripped bodice lower, exposing her naked breasts, tempting him as best she knew how. "Come and kiss me."

Impervious to her nakedness, he stuck his hands in his pockets and did not move away from the fireplace. "No."

Her skirts were easily adjusted to show off her bare calves and thighs. "You will not make love to me until I agree to marry you?" She lifted her skirts higher, almost to the juncture of her thighs. "Are you sure about your decision?"

He gulped at the sight, but turned away resolutely, refusing to be tempted. "I will not."

"Then I suppose I have no choice." She rose from the sofa, clasped the tattered remnants of her clothes around her, and walked with dignity toward the door. "I will not accept charity. If you do not want me as your mistress, I will have to leave."

His solid form blocked the doorway. "You cannot leave."

"You have no right to keep me a prisoner here."

He shot her a reproachful look. "Mrs. Fitchett thinks we

are married. Whatever would she think of me if my new bride deserted me on our wedding night?"

"She would simply realize the truth—that you had the barefaced effrontery to tell her a whopping lie to her face, and the ill manners to introduce her to your whore." The thought of Mrs. Fitchett's horror was almost enough to bring a smile to Sarah's face. "No doubt she would turn you out of doors for it."

"I like my apartments. Mrs. Fitchett doesn't cheat me as much as most landladies would. I do not want to leave."

"Tom, please be serious." The room, which had seemed so comfortable and welcoming before, now felt like a prison whose walls were closing in around her. "This is not a joke to me. This is my life you are playing with."

"I am deadly serious." He ran his hands through his hair. "I like you, Sarah Chesham. I like you more than any other woman I have ever met. I like you enough to want to set up house with you and to spend my life with you."

His plea touched her heart. "I have offered to be your mistress."

"I could not live with the knowledge that you could up and leave me without a thought if you met a wealthier keeper. I want a permanent arrangement, not a temporary one." His hands were on her shoulders and the warmth of his body was a comfort to her. "I want your life entwined with mine, so strongly that our ties to each other cannot be broken. That is why I want to marry you, Sarah. I want to be a part of you as you are a part of me."

Desperately as she wanted to, she knew she ought not accept the gift he was offering her. It was too much for her to accept. "You want a great many things."

"I cannot give you the sort of life you led at Mrs. Erskine's establishment. I cannot give you a wardrobe full of fine silk dresses and a new pair of kid gloves every week."

She shrugged. He did not know her very well if he thought that she hankered after such fripperies.

"I would not blame you if you liked that life too well to want to leave it for me. You are a beautiful woman, Sarah. Such a woman as you will have no shortage of wealthy protectors—wealthier by far than I am. I can offer you so much less."

"I am only a milliner—and a whore. Nothing more. You offer me far more than I can ever deserve."

"And I am a journalist who makes his money by exposing the dirty little secrets of the rich and titled." He shrugged, his body warm against hers. "Marriage to me would not mean an entrée into society. I am tolerated by those on the fringes, and only because they fear the power of my pen. They would not like you any the more for marrying me."

His self-criticism roused her to his defense. "You are more than your profession. They cannot know the real you if they do not love you as well as you deserve."

He gave a self-deprecating smile. "I have a few genuine friends who would welcome you with open arms simply because I chose you. But do not be deceived—they are not society. I doubt your father would have approved of them."

She turned her face to his shoulder. "My father would not have approved of what I have become, either." The thought still pained her, even now.

Taking her face in his hands, he gazed searchingly into her eyes. "All my life, such as it is, I would like to share with you."

Miraculous as it seemed, it appeared he really did want to marry her. She still could hardly believe it, but the truth of it was in his eyes. "You really do want me?"

"You have such strength and resilience that I cannot help but want you."

Her resolve was weakening under his insistence. "Prove it to me. Kiss me and show me just how much you want me."

"Will you promise to marry me in the morning?"

She had no more energy left to fight both him and her own desires. "Yes." The word was barely a whisper in the darkness. Giving in to him felt like she was drowning in Paradise.

His embrace was almost painful in its intensity. "I have had your promise. You will not break your word."

For better or worse she had made her decision and she would stick with it. "I will not break my word."

He had wanted her so badly and for so long that it was sheer torture to have to maintain his self-control. For Sarah's sake, he had to. Keeping a tight rein on his lust, he undressed her slowly, taking as much care of her torn clothes as he would of the finest silk. With his gentleness he would atone for the harm that Sir Richard had inflicted on her. "You are shivering."

"I want you so badly," she confessed to him in a small voice, her arms reaching for him. "I never knew before I met you how much I could want a man."

The knowledge that she needed him as badly as he needed her was a powerful aphrodisiac.

Gently he ran his hands over her naked mound, stroking her pussy as tenderly as he could. "Are you sure you want me to make love to you?" He forced himself to ask the question, though he would die if she refused him now. "Sir Richard did not hurt you too badly?"

She moved her legs wider apart, nudging his hand in between them, encouraging him to explore her body. "He beat me and bruised my wrists, but you saved me before he could hurt me any further. Any hurt he caused me will be gone as soon as you make love to me."

"In that case," he said, picking her up and carrying her into his bedroom, "I had better hurry."

The wax candles beside the bed gave off a muted glow and the eiderdown was soft on his back as he came to lie beside her.

The whiteness of her naked body gleamed in the soft candlelight.

With tender fingers he stroked her breasts, her stomach, her thighs, glorying in the sight of her. Her beauty and her generosity overawed him and made him want to give back to her all that she had given him and more.

This night she would lose her virginity in earnest—not to Sir Richard, but to his own tender loving. He would show her what true lovemaking was all about.

Sarah's fingers were at his shirt buttons. "I want to feel your naked skin against mine," she whispered, as she unbuttoned his shirtfront and slipped his jacket and shirt off his shoulders.

He could not help a smile of satisfaction. He'd waited weeks for her to say those words to him.

Her fingers moved tantalizingly over his torso, touching and caressing him until they stopped at the waistband of his trousers.

If she wanted him to stop now, he would stop, even if it killed him.

"I want to see all of you."

He groaned with relief. She wasn't going to stop him.

With a few deft moves, his trousers and underlinen lay discarded on the floor.

Her eyes grew wide in the candlelight as he approached her. "You are big," she murmured. "Much bigger than . . ." Her voice trailed away into nothingness.

"I will not hurt you."

"I hope not," she said doubtfully, reaching out and stroking him with one fingertip. He arched his back and nearly came in her hand there and then.

"You will soon learn to appreciate my endowments," he murmured, hanging on to his self-control by a thread. Desperate to possess her, he pushed her onto her back and knelt above her, his erect cock nudging between her thighs. "Open your legs for me."

Hesitantly, she did just that, allowing him his first clear sight of her pink cunt lips.

He reached down and touched her there, sliding one finger inside her. Her pussy was hot and warm, and as wet as he could have hoped for. Her hips moved against his hand, urging him on to push deeper into her.

He could not wait any longer to take her. Spreading her legs apart, he nudged the tip of his ravenous cock into her pussy.

Her muscles tensed around him and she gasped, but she did not pull away.

He held himself still, the tip of his cock just inside her, until he felt her relax around him.

"That is n-not so bad," she stuttered.

"Only not bad?" he queried, as he pushed into her a little way farther. "I cannot be doing it right."

Again she tensed up, and again he held still until she melted around him.

"It's better than not bad," she admitted, a little breathlessly. "Indeed, it's r-rather nice."

If it got any nicer than this, he was going to disgrace himself and go off half-cocked. Slowly he withdrew a little way, steeling himself to regain control.

She made a moan of protest and grabbed tightly to his buttocks.

"I'm not going to leave you. Just positioning myself," and he pushed into her more deeply, "for that."

This time she did not tense up against him, but arched into him as he thrust so that he went deeper than he intended until he was buried in her up to the hilt.

Though he was aching to fuck her hard and fast and pound her into oblivion, he held tight to his self-control.

Gently he rocked her back and forth, impaled on his iron-hard cock, wringing every drop of sensation from her. He wanted to show her that there was more to fucking than violence and aggression. He needed to give her pleasure and introduce her to the joy that was to be found in the embrace of her lover.

Droplets of sweat were dripping off his brow when finally she gave a choked cry and he felt her convulse around him. The clenching of her pussy muscles around his cock was too much for his overtaxed restraint. With a cry almost of anguish, he thrust into her hard and fast until the waves of his own pleasure overtook him and he spent his seed inside her until his body was wrung dry.

Exhausted, he collapsed beside her, pulling the bedcovers over them both to protect them from the chill of the night air.

As he drifted off to sleep, he felt Sarah's hand creep into his, and her soft voice in his ear whispered, "Thank you."

Before noon of the following day, Tom stalked in through the open door of Mrs. Erskine's sitting room without waiting to be announced.

Mrs. Erskine was sitting at her desk, scratching away with her pen in a large ledger. She looked up when Tom entered and waved at him to sit down. "Mr. Wilde. What brings you here so early in the day?"

In no mood for pleasantries, he remained on his feet, responding to her greeting with a curt nod. "You will return the money to Sir Richard." His voice was pure steel.

"I will?" she asked, her voice instantly frosty. Her pen lay idle on the blotter, her fingers now steepled in front of her chin. "On whose say-so?"

"On mine."

"Do not be foolish. I gave you a chance to purchase the girl but you refused."

"And I would suggest banning Sir Richard from your coffeehouse in the future."

Mrs. Erskine looked down her nose at him. "Now why would I do that?"

"He attacked one of your girls and very nearly raped her. He would have succeeded if I hadn't arrived just in time to save her."

"Sarah?"

He nodded.

"Ah, I wondered where she had run off to." She gestured to the note on her blotter in front of her. "I was just about to alert the constabulary to the fact she was missing—along with some very expensive clothing she had borrowed from me."

"I took her away with me last night. Thanks to Sir Richard, her expensive clothing is now ruined."

"I will add it to his bill."

"You will allow him to return?"

Her eyes glinted with avarice. "What is it worth to you to have him banned?"

"I will write a short pamphlet that will mention, among other details, how he has been banned from a certain house for ungentlemanly behavior. By the time I have finished with him, his reputation will be in tatters and no respectable person, man or woman, will want to be seen with him." He smiled grimly. Very soon Sir Richard would rue the day he laid hands on Sarah. "For the right incentive, I will make it subtly clear whose house it was, where it can be found, and what services can be obtained there."

She was too canny to smile, but the look of delight that flashed in her eyes betrayed her excitement at the prospect. "The publicity would be worth something," she admitted grudgingly.

"You know perfectly well that it would more than make up for the loss of Sir Richard's contribution. Not to mention, your girls would feel safer if he was banned. It would serve as a warning for other gentlemen not to take what is not freely offered—and paid for."

She gave a decisive nod. "I will inform Sir Richard that his company is no longer agreeable to me. And Sarah? Where is she?"

"My wife," he emphasized, "is in the front parlor drinking a cup of tea."

"Your wife?" The look on her face was of amusement rather than surprise.

"My wife."

"Please bring her in."

Tom hesitated.

"I would like to see with my own eyes that she has suffered no lasting harm from Sir Richard. I am sorry for the girl—I do not countenance such behavior in my house."

Tom felt Sarah's arm tremble in his as he led her through the dark passageway to Mrs. Erskine's sitting room.

Mrs. Erskine regarded her with a mild air. "So, Sarah, you are to be married to this scoundrel?"

"Yes, ma'am."

"You could have done a good deal better for yourself. I was expecting you to snare a handsome young baron at the very least, or an elderly coal merchant with more than enough money to spend on fripperies for a young mistress."

Tom frowned at her.

"But I daresay Mr. Wilde will treat you handsomely enough." She coughed. "As for Sir Richard, he will be dealt with."

"Thank you, ma'am."

"Now that the two of you are to be married," she continued, "I have something I must give you." With one hand she pushed her pince-nez glasses up her nose while with the other she opened one of her desk drawers and rummaged about in it for a minute. "Ah, here it is," she said, bringing out a square of pasteboard and holding it out to Tom.

There was an address written on it in an elegant script—he recognized neither the address nor the handwriting. He turned it over, hoping for a clue to its purpose, but the other side was blank.

"That is my sister's address."

"Your sister?" Sarah ventured, looking over Tom's shoulder at the card.

"She runs an establishment the pair of you might like to explore together," Mrs. Erskine said, a rare smile creeping over her face. "An establishment for the entertainment of adventurous married couples."

Tom shot a sidelong glance at Sarah. Her lips were pursed, but there was a definite gleam of interest in her eye. His cock sprang to attention at the thought that she would adventure there with him. When an opportune moment arrived, he would have to explore that subject a little further.

But not right now. He took Sarah's arm and ushered her to the door. Mrs. Erskine was part of their past, not of their future. "Good-bye."

———

Mrs. Erskine sat waiting as the couple walked out of her office. Had she misread the pair of them? She did not think so, but she *had* been wrong once before. Very, very wrong.

There were sounds of scuffling, and the whisper of a muted giggle reached her from the corridor.

Tom stuck his head back around the door. "We will give your sister your regards," he promised, a merry glint in his eye, and disappeared into the corridor once more.

Mrs. Erskine picked up her pen again, a satisfied smile firmly planted on her face.

She had *not* been wrong. Her sister would be pleased.

LEDA SWANN is the pseudonym for a writing team, the first half of which was born in Tennessee and brought up (mostly) in New Zealand. She has also lived in half a dozen U.S. states, as well as England and Wales. She finally moved back to New Zealand with her life and writing partner. The other half of Leda Swann has also lived most of his life in New Zealand, when he wasn't working or traveling in Asia. These two halves have settled by the beach in a small coastal community in NZ, where they plan to live happily ever after.

Border Lord

Julia Templeton

To my sister Jana,
who shares my love
of romance novels and Scotland.
Love you much!

1

The Priory of Grace, Scottish Borderlands
Present-day

The priory with its amazing Gothic architecture and stained-glass windows caught Terri's eye, and on a whim she stopped.

She needed the time to rest anyway and think about her future . . . now that she knew the truth about her fiancé.

No wonder Elliott had seemed so distant of late. After a restless weekend he had woken at the crack of dawn, saying he needed to get to their London office early.

Certain his worries had to do with the new Egyptian artifact exhibit coming that day, Terri took a shower and arrived to work two hours early to help.

Instead of finding Elliott knee-deep in paperwork, she found him fucking her twenty-year-old assistant, right there on his prized Edwardian desk. The very desk Terri had given him for his fortieth birthday. Stunned, she watched in silent horror as the girl she'd hired some three weeks before reached a staggering climax.

Terri walked out of the museum as fast as her feet would carry her. Feeling as though her heart had been ripped from her chest, she stepped into her Mini Cooper and started driving.

That was two days ago. Now she was in Scotland, confused, angry, and in of all places, an old priory, much like the one in which she had planned to marry Elliott next summer.

There would be no wedding now.

Adjusting the rearview mirror, Terri winced at her reflection. Her red-rimmed eyes were puffy and swollen from crying, and her cheeks deathly pale.

Pulling her blond hair up into a ponytail and adding a spot of blush to her pale cheeks, she joined a tour in progress.

"Please, everyone, no crowding."

Terri glanced at the flushed, middle-aged tour guide, a jovial Scottish woman, who tried with little success to keep the small group in line.

"What's that door there?" an old man with thick glasses asked, pointing toward a solid mahogany door with a heavy board across it.

The tour guide smiled widely. "Ah, good question. That is the door Laird Brochan Douglas broke down to steal away Annabelle MacLellan, Laird MacLellan's only daughter. Legend says that Annabelle's father, knowing Douglas would seek revenge over the murder of his brother, spirited his daughter away from Castle Blackcurn, here to the Priory of Grace. The old laird felt that the only safe haven for his daughter would be here with the nuns."

"Did he succeed?" Terri asked, her interest piqued by the vision of a medieval warrior busting down the chamber door.

"Aye, he did, lass. Though the nuns tried to hide Annabelle's appearance by dressing her in thick habits, her beauty was such that Brochan knew her on sight. It is said he ripped the robes from her body, and left her standing naked in front of the nuns and all his men."

An elderly woman gasped. "What a horrible man!"

The tour guide shrugged. "I'm not so sure he was horrible. He felt he was right doing what he did. After all, MacLellan had killed his brother. And being the great warrior that he was, Brochan sought to hurt Angus MacLellan the best way he could."

"By taking his daughter," Terri finished for her, thinking how she herself would love to get revenge on Elliott.

The tour guide nodded. "Indeed. He knew MacLellan loved his daughter more than life itself. The girl was the laird's one weakness, and so Douglas snatched her from the priory, never to be seen or heard from again."

"Did he kill her?" the old man asked, glancing at the door again.

The tour guide shook her head. "Nay, not that day."

"Why is the door locked then?"

"Because when Laird MacLellan learned of his daughter's fate, he stormed into the priory." The tour guide's voice rose with each second. "So furious was he with the nun who was to protect his daughter, he strangled the poor woman in that very room. From that day forth, strange noises started coming from the room—a terrible moaning, one that sounded much like the murdered nun. Horrified that one of their own might be walking the earth in ghostly form, the sisters closed the door, barred it, and have not entered it since, over seven hundred years ago."

"So no one knows what happened to Laird MacLellan's daughter?" Terri asked, more than a little intrigued by the tale.

"No one knows," the guide said with a shrug. "Some say she was held captive in Brochan's castle, while others say she escaped, back into the arms of her father. To this day her fate remains a mystery."

The tour guide glanced at her watch. "I'm afraid that is all we have time for. We must return to the bus before your driver leaves you all behind. Come, let's hurry."

As the rest of the crowd followed the tour guide, Terri stayed behind, staring at the old, scarred door. How she itched to know what lay beyond. It was a shame the door was closed to visitors, and all because of a ghost.

Terri had always believed in the paranormal after a strange occurrence in the old Virginia farmhouse she had been raised in. At first the hollow footsteps and doors that opened and closed on their own frightened her, but after a while she came to accept the fact that whoever it was would not harm her.

She wondered if the ghost within that chamber would be the same. Just some poor soul who didn't realize she was dead.

Glancing over her shoulder, she looked at the empty hallway behind her. The tour guide's voice faded as a door opened, sunlight filtered in, and long moments later closed.

Silence. Terri chewed her bottom lip. *Do I dare?* Adrenaline rushing through her veins, she took a step toward the door, and paused. Seven hundred years was a long time for a door to be closed. And what if the ghost of the nun was actually in the room when that door opened? Had anyone ever been killed by an apparition?

Stealing a last fleeting look down the long, secluded hallway, Terri lifted the plank and set it aside. Rubbing the soot from her hands onto her jeans, she pressed against the door, and an ominous creak vibrated down the hall.

Just one little peek. That was it, then she would get back on the road and face her future.

Taking a steadying breath, she stepped into the room but could see nothing because of the darkness. Cool air brushed across her skin, making the hair on her arms stand on end. In the corner she could barely make out what appeared to be a cot, and then a chair . . . and something, or rather someone else.

Terri's head hurt like hell.

A horrible pain that throbbed, and sounded like someone pounding. The noise was so loud, she covered her ears with her hands.

"Hurry, or you shall be late," a voice said from the other side of the door.

Terri sat up with a start, looking around the strange room that had a tiny little window, and a huge, thick door. The only furnishings a small cot, a high-backed chair, and a makeshift wood table with a candleholder, where a candle flickered in the waning light.

"Annabelle, wake up."

"Annabelle?" Terri repeated, recalling the name from the tour of the priory. When had that been . . . yesterday?

And was this the chamber she had walked into after the tour? The room at the Priory of Grace in Scotland, where Laird MacLellan killed the nun?

Uneasiness rippled along her spine as she tried to piece together what had happened. Shivering, she ran her hands up her arms and looked down to find she wore a thin chemise, made of rough linen, and nothing else.

She frowned. Where the hell were her clothes?

After a quick search under the cot and about the room, she came up empty-handed. Her jeans, sweater, shoes, socks, and underwear were all missing, and the shapeless black garment flung over the chair must be what little she had in the way of clothing.

Ripping the blanket off the cot, she wrapped it around her and stepped to the window. A secluded courtyard with beautiful roses of varying colors lined a pathway of smooth pebbles. Several ornamental stone benches sat about every twenty feet.

Terri frowned, certain it had looked different during the tour. The courtyard did not have rosebushes, and she could remember little foliage, other than the large tree in the center of the garden, a few benches and chairs.

The knocking at the door persisted. "Annabelle, hurry. Sister Hazel will be furious."

Sister Hazel?

She ran a hand down her face. What the hell had happened to her?

Terri walked to the door, her stomach churning, afraid of what she would find on the other side. "Wake up, Terri. This is just a dream," she said under her breath, and opened the door.

A woman about forty years old, wearing a nun's black habit, stared back at her, a look of exasperation on her face. "You have overslept again. Sister Hazel will be most upset."

"Who are you?"

The woman frowned, her wide brown eyes narrowing. "I am Sister Helena, as well you know, Annabelle. I realize you are not accustomed to our schedule here at the Priory of Grace, but you must conform like everyone else."

"How long have I been here?" Terri asked, glancing down the long hallway where she saw several nuns walking in a small group. They looked at her and all smiled.

Sister Helena rested her hand on Terri's shoulder. "For a

fortnight, my dear, as I am sure you are aware. What is amiss, child? Do you miss your father still?"

Terri's father had been dead for twelve years. "My father?"

Concern marred the nun's brow. "Aye, I know you hate to be parted, but 'tis necessary for now, child. We will keep you safe, Annabelle. We have given your father our word. One day soon you shall return to Castle Blackcurn and to your sire . . . but not until it is safe to do so. When he feels the time is right, he will send for you. Until then, you must abide by the rules of the order. You are a guest, that is true, but you still must work for your care. 'Tis best that way."

Oh, my God! She had stepped into the twilight zone. "Who exactly is my father?"

The nun reached out and touched Terri's forehead with gentle fingers. "You do not feel overly warm." She dropped her hand back to her side and released a heavy sigh. "Laird MacLellan is your father. Certainly you know that."

Terri's stomach tightened with each second that passed. True, she believed in the paranormal, but that didn't mean she believed in time travel. The idea had always held appeal, particularly for someone like herself who loved history, but she also realized that traveling to another place and year was impossible. Wasn't it?

And how could she be this Annabelle MacLellan? She was Terri Campbell from Richmond, Virginia.

"Helena, what year is this?"

The nun straightened her shoulders. "You are to call me Sister Helena, and I fear that given your strange questions, mayhap you should sleep this morning instead of attending mass. I shall tell Sister Hazel you have taken ill."

The nun took Terri by the hand and led her back inside the room, easing her down onto the cot. "Just as we promised your father, I will promise you that we will not let any harm come to you, my dear. We shall protect you as best we can."

Protect her from what?

"What year is it, Sister Helena?"

The nun frowned. " 'Tis the year of our Lord, one thousand two hundred and ninety-four."

"Holy shit!"

The nun put a hand to her chest, her mouth agape. "What say you?"

Terri's heart accelerated as panic took hold. What if she was stuck in this time forever? A life without all the amenities she was used to. Granted, she could never be accused of being high maintenance, but still she loved modern conveniences. Though she had no family left after her father's death, she did have friends who would be worried about her. Then again, many of those friends were Elliott's as well. No doubt the bastard would act the concerned fiancé, while continuing to shag the bimbo. She ran a hand down her face. "This can't be."

"I assure you, it is as I say. Child, what is wrong? You are not acting at all like yourself, even your language is strange."

"I must be dreaming."

"Nay, you are just overwhelmed. Lie down, and I shall call for Sister Hazel." The nun put a gentle hand to Terri's jaw. "Know this, Annabelle, he will do you no harm."

"He?"

"Aye, Brochan Douglas, border lord and chieftain of the infamous Douglas clan. I know you fear for your safety, for he is the devil himself," she said with a shudder. "But we will not let him take you, Annabelle. We will protect you with our lives, I swear it."

The hair on the back of Terri's neck stood on end. She

could not shake the change in the courtyard, or the sudden appearance of the nuns. And they were calling her Annabelle . . . and referred to Brochan Douglas in the present.

If she wasn't dreaming, and this *was* real, then the woman standing before her could very well be the nun who had been killed at the hands of Laird MacLellan over seven hundred years before. The ghostly nun of legend.

The nun who had been in the chamber when she had entered the forbidden room.

A terrifying thought, if ever there was one.

Yes, the nun had been there, standing there, as though waiting for her. And Terri hadn't been afraid, but instead felt as light as a feather before blacking out.

"How did you bring me here?"

The nun looked startled. "I do not know what you mean, my dear. Your father brought you."

"No, I mean from my own time."

Her eyes narrowed. "Your own time?"

"Yes, my own time. In the year two thousand and five I had visited the priory, where this very chamber had been boarded up."

"Child, perhaps some fresh air will do you good."

"I mean it. You were there in the room."

For the first time the nun looked exasperated. "And what did I say to you?"

"You didn't say a word. You just smiled."

Just like she did now, a soothing, comforting smile. Clearly she thought Terri insane.

Realizing she wasn't going to get anywhere with the current line of questioning, Terri asked, "What if Brochan does come?"

Fear flashed in the nun's eyes before she hid it with a smile. "Nay, he will not, lass. No one but your own kin knows of your whereabouts. Your father assured us of such, and he is a man of his word. The Douglas would have no reason to assume you are here."

Though she sounded certain, Terri could still see the wariness in the nun's eyes. She feared Brochan Douglas. His legend had been ominous enough, even with her secure in a different century, but knowing she might face him had her more than a little nervous. The man must be terrifying in the flesh.

"I think I will rest, Sister Helena. Thank you for checking in on me."

The nun's features softened, and she pulled the rough blanket over Terri. "Aye, you are just tired, dear, that is all. Now close your eyes and sleep. I shall return later with a tray. Something soothing for your stomach." With a warm smile, Sister Helena walked out of the room, closing the door behind her.

Terri stared at the door for a long time, her mind racing. For whatever reason she had been thrust back in time, the room she entered was a portal to the past.

No wonder it had been boarded up in her time. Maybe someone else had been sent through time as well?

She ran a trembling hand through her hair. If she was in the portal now, then how in the hell did she get home? She scoured the walls, wondering if there was a hidden opening.

"And how in the hell do I get back home before Brochan Douglas comes?"

2

Brochan Douglas opened the door, his eyes adjusting to the dark room. The inn sat in the shadow of Castle Blackcurn, the keep of Laird Angus MacLellan.

How Brochan hated the man. He would take pleasure in hurting the one thing Angus loved more than life.

His precious little daughter . . . Annabelle.

For two days Brochan had been awaiting word from the castle on the hill. Finally word had come—in the way of a woman, who turned from the window as Brochan shut the door behind him.

About five and twenty in age, the lass was comely, and as she slid the velvet cloak from her body Brochan's cock stirred. Aye, Frederica was indeed beautiful with her long hair and shapely curves. No wonder Angus MacLellan had locked his wife in the solar, while he took this luscious young woman to bed each night.

At the thought of his nemesis, Brochan clenched his fists.

The murderous bastard! He would make Angus MacLellan pay dearly for killing Brochan's brother.

Frederica took a step toward him, smoothing her skirts. Her breasts were not large, but she was slender, and had womanly hips. The green kirtle was made of fine fustian, and complemented her fair skin that turned a flattering pink under his gaze. "Do ye come alone?"

She nodded. "Of course."

"How do I know this is not an ambush?"

"I come alone. I swear it." The woman licked her lips, her gaze moving over Brochan in a familiar fashion. He knew that look. She desired him. In fact, he would have her on her back in a moment's time . . . but first they had business to attend to.

"What news do ye have for me?" he asked, taking a step closer.

"Annabelle has been taken to the priory, a half day's ride from here."

"There are many priories in the Borderlands, lass. Of which do ye speak?"

She folded her trembling hands together. He wondered if fear made her tremble. After all, if Angus knew where she was and with whom, she'd have some explaining to do.

"The Priory of Grace, on the border near Langholm."

"Do ye lie, lass?"

Her gaze slid from his, over his chest and stomach, slowly to the bulge of his sex. He had made sure not to wear his kilt or clan colors in this rival territory, and instead dressed in snug leather braies.

Frederica swallowed hard, her throat convulsing. "Never."

"Is the priory well guarded?"

"Nay, just two of Angus's men. He did not want to garner suspicion."

"Why do ye help me?"

She shrugged, a tiny smile teasing her lips as she once again made eye contact. There was no denying the lust there. "Annabelle is a spoiled little girl, and I am weary of her requests."

"Certainly MacLellan does not favor his daughter over his lover?" Brochan asked, though he already knew the truth. Angus MacLellan spoiled his daughter to the point of obscene. No doubt his lover resented the relationship.

Frederica laughed, flashing white but slightly crooked teeth. "Aye, 'tis one fault I find with Angus. He does not know when to tell his daughter nay. I fear he would go to any lengths to please the brat."

"And ye are jealous that he gives her so much?"

He hit a barb, for Frederica flinched, her smile now forced. "Nay, I am jealous of no one."

"And what of the girl's mother?"

Two bright spots appeared on Frederica's cheeks, and she looked away, toward the closed door. "She lives in the solar."

"Her preference, or her husband's?"

Frederica lifted a brow. "Angus's wife is not well. She has not been well for years."

No doubt because her husband was fucking an attractive young woman half her age. Brochan's gaze slid over her slowly, taking in the emerald earrings sparkling in her earlobes that matched the large stone which lay snug between her breasts. Mayhap a trinket from her lover. She watched him watch her, her nervousness obvious as she shifted from foot to foot.

The pulse in her neck increased as his gaze dropped slowly, inch by inch. The bodice of her gown was tight and low, displaying her small breasts to full advantage. The expensive golden kirtle fit snugly about her hips, emphasizing her woman's mound.

Rumor told that Frederica had been the daughter of a servant in Angus's household. The girl had caught Angus's eye when she was but a child, and became Angus MacLellan's lover when she came of age. He kept her at close quarters, afraid someone else, younger and more robust than the graying laird, would take her as their leman. In truth, Brochan wondered how she had managed to slip away from the castle unnoticed. His men outside would alert him of any activity, he knew that, but it was best to complete their business.

Brochan took the pouch of coins from his pocket and tossed them at her. "For your trouble, my lady." He started for the door.

"You leave so soon?" Her voice, as sweet as honey, hinted at disappointment.

"Do ye wish me to stay?" He did not turn, uncertain if he should stay or go, particularly since his men awaited him downstairs. Then he smiled to himself. He could not resist the chance to humiliate Angus MacLellan further.

"Aye, I would."

He faced her. "Then I shall . . . for a while."

She looked relieved.

He wanted her to make the first move, and he did not have to wait long. Frederica sat down on the bed and lifted her skirts slowly. Fine silk garters encased her long, shapely legs, and she rolled one stocking down, then the other.

Brochan's cock twitched.

She patted the space beside her. "Come, Brochan."

He didn't move an inch, but instead untied his braies, unleashing his rigid shaft.

She stared boldly, shifting on the bed, her excitement obvious.

His fingers wrapped around his erection, and slowly moved up the thick length, then down again.

Her eyes widened as he continued to stroke himself. He sensed her excitement, could smell the musky scent of her sex as she again shifted on the bed, her legs falling apart. She moved her hand from the bed, to her thigh, then through the thick red curls of her woman's mound. Her fingers danced over her clit slowly, then quicker as she found a rhythm she liked. "Come closer, Brochan." Wetting her lips, her mouth opened and she released a groan as she reached climax.

Brochan's cock grew harder with each stroke of his hand. Frederica's fingers glistened with her woman's dew, her scent growing strong as she continued to pleasure herself. Her free hand cupped a breast, her fingers playing at her nipple, teasing it into a hardened peak.

His balls lifted and his hand fell away. He crossed the room, pushed Frederica onto her back and entered her in one fluid motion.

She cried out, biting into his shoulder. Her creamy walls tightened around him with each thrust. His fingers gripped her hair, wrapping it around his fist. She loved his rough play, her fingernails raking the skin of his back, and she groaned loudly, her climax strong, pulsing.

He kept his climax at bay, pulling his cock out, just to where the head lay against her opening. Her hips arched off the bed, and she whimpered. "Please," she moaned, clearly frustrated.

Prolonging her agony, he pulled away each time she arched against him.

"Fuck me, Brochan. Fuck me," she said on a moan, and he entered her, pumping within her in small, fluid strokes. Moments later she screamed, heedless of the thin walls around them. Her channel clamped around him a second time. He thrust three more times, and pulled out, groaning as a steady stream of seed poured onto the linens beneath them.

When his breathing returned to normal, he stood up, wiped his cock with the hem of her skirts, and without a backward glance, turned and walked out the door.

Terri sat on the wooden bench next to Sister Helena, whose high-pitched voice rose into the chapel's high ceiling.

It had been three days since she'd arrived in the year 1294, and still she had trouble wrapping her brain around what was her new life.

This time-travel experience might have been a bit more exciting if she wasn't held captive by a cloister of nuns who thought her one brick shy of a load.

True, the nuns of the Priory of Grace were incredibly kind and understanding, but her every waking moment was spent sewing, writing, reading, or in prayer.

Boredom had become her constant companion.

She had never been any good at being idle, except for weekends when she preferred to stay home and drink a glass of wine while she watched a DVD, rather than socialize with London's elite. Given that she worked twelve-hour days, five days a week, down time always meant a lot to her, and she savored it.

But now she had cabin fever, plain and simple. She learned quickly to make good use of her prayer time, staying in her little room while she searched for a way back to her own time.

She had bruises from where she had ran into the wall, hoping to find a hidden door within the small room.

But there had been no hidden door or window, or latch or trigger, that would take her back to present-day London. She tried not to think of the possibility that she might be stuck here for all eternity.

True, it had sucked being the jilted lover of a man who couldn't keep his dick in his pants. But she could recover from Elliott's betrayal and hopefully fall in love again one day.

Anything was better than her current circumstance.

The nuns abruptly stopped singing, and Terri sat up straight.

A few seconds later, Sister Anna, a usually somber woman, ran into the chapel, her eyes wide in terror. " 'Tis the Douglas! Sisters, you know what to do."

Sister Helena grabbed Terri's hand. "Come, child, we have not a moment to lose."

Terri's heart pounded in her ears as they rushed from the chapel and down the long hallway toward her chamber. Douglas? Did she mean *the* Brochan Douglas?

She recalled the tour guide's ominous words about Brochan Douglas knocking down the door of Annabelle's chamber and ripping the clothes from the girl's body.

That would not happen to her. Not if she had anything to say about it.

Sister Helena pushed Terri into her chamber. "Make not a sound!" she warned, before shutting the door and locking it.

The echo of horses' hooves came closer, then eventually stopped. Men's voices rang out, sending the birds in the courtyard's trees flying.

Holy shit! History was repeating itself, and soon she would find herself face-to-face with the ominous border lord.

Pushing her cot against the door, she started pacing the small room. Terri's stomach clenched as the heavy iron knocker hit the priory's front door. This could be it for her. She could be killed by this border lord if she didn't play things the right way. She chewed her bottom lip, her mind racing. Certainly he wouldn't kill her if she was willing to go with him?

She pressed her back against the wall, sinking down until

she huddled in the corner. Folding her arms around her knees, she waited, her heart pumping madly against her thighs. "This can't be real."

Terri listened intently and could hear voices raised in anger, Sister Helena's rising above the rest. Then a low, deep voice sounded, full of deadly calm. "Sister, ye will open the door or I shall break it in."

A shiver rushed through Terri. Even his voice sounded powerful.

She was so screwed.

"There is no one here," Sister Helena said, her voice losing its shrill quality. "We harbor no girl."

"Ye lie, sister. I have it on good authority that Annabelle is in your care, and I will not leave until I have checked every chamber in this priory."

"Leave here now, Douglas!"

Terri closed her eyes, willing her heart to slow down and her limbs to stop shaking. She had never been so terrified in her life.

"You lift your sword to a woman of God?" Sister Helena asked, her voice cracking. The poor woman.

Terri envisioned Brochan Douglas as a dirty warrior-type with stringy long hair, too-full beard, and yellow rotting teeth.

"Stand away, or ye may be killed!"

Terri jumped when a moment later a loud crash sounded.

"Every chamber is to be searched. Look in every corner, every crevice, until she is found," the male voice ordered.

Terri trembled, waiting as she heard nearby doors open and close.

" 'Tis Sister Ellen's chamber you are upon now," Sister Helena blurted. "I ask you to leave her be. She has not been well."

This was it. Her very life depended on how she handled herself in the next few minutes.

Thank God she was a people person.

"Step aside, sister."

"Nay."

"Step aside, or God's breath, I *will* kill you."

A multitude of gasps followed the threat.

A moment later the door flew open.

Terri held her breath as a large man stepped into the room. Broad-shouldered and narrow-waisted, he wore a black shirt and snug leather braies that covered strong, long legs.

His gaze immediately locked with hers.

Her brow lifted of its own accord. She had seen beautiful men in her life, but none that mirrored this man's stature. At least six foot three, he had dark hair that was plaited in thin braids on either side of his face, the rest hanging in silky waves past his immense shoulders. Forest green, thickly lashed eyes held her pinned to the spot.

She swallowed past the lump in her throat as her gaze shifted to the axe in his hand. "Are you going to kill me, then?"

Surprise flashed across his face before he hid it with a scowl. "Annabelle MacLellan?"

No, I'm Terri Campbell from Virginia, she wanted to say, but knowing it would only piss him off, she instead nodded. "That's what they tell me."

He smiled then, but it wasn't a friendly, welcoming smile, but rather wolfish. A smile that didn't begin to put her at ease. But his lips were nice, full, and he had straight, white teeth. Not at all like the guy she'd envisioned. Not even close.

As he took a step toward her, her heart gave a surprisingly hard jolt.

"Let me guess, you are Brochan Douglas?"

His dark brows furrowed as though she should have known this already. "Aye, I am."

His biceps bulged as he lifted the axe over his shoulder. Every inch of his body looked formed from stone. Hard muscle covered by luscious olive skin.

A man entered the room behind Brochan, a long sword in hand . . . and he looked ready to use it. Dirt covered bits of his face, and his red hair could have used a good brushing. Standing nearly as tall as Brochan, but slighter of build, he smiled on seeing Terri. "Ah, I see ye found the lass." His gaze moved over Terri in a way that made her more than a little uncomfortable.

"Aye," Brochan grunted, coming toward Terri.

She straightened her spine at his approach, noting that he didn't stop until he was just inches away, forcing her to bend her head back to look at him.

"Are you going to kill me?" she asked again, her gaze shifting from his full lips to the dimple in his chin. He had a nice five o'clock shadow. Ironically, she felt the insane urge to run her fingers over that strong jaw, but refrained.

His eyes were really quite astounding, and his lashes so thick and long, they would make more sense on a woman than a man.

"Nay, I am taking ye home."

"To my home?"

The side of his mouth lifted. "Nay, lass. To *my* home, Castle Kildare."

His gaze shifted from hers, down to the habit that covered her from neck to feet. "Where are yer clothes, lass?"

"I don't know."

He cocked his head, green eyes locking with hers once more. "Ye speak strangely."

Her heart fluttered. Damn, the man was sexy. "Do I?"

He nodded. "Aye."

"Brochan, since we have the wench, should we no' leave?" the redhead prompted, looking uneasy as he kept a nun at arm's length.

As though reminded of his purpose, Brochan straightened his shoulders. "Fergus, fetch my cloak for the girl. We dinna want her catching cold now, do we?"

Fergus laughed under his breath. "Nay, we would not."

When Fergus left, Brochan reached out and touched the habit. "My cloak should prove more comfortable than the wool ye wear now." His long fingers brushed against her neck.

Her stomach tightened at the simple touch.

"Take it off."

"Excuse me?"

He lifted a dark brow. "Take it off, or I shall remove it myself." He had the sexiest accent, but even more, the way he looked as he said the words made her nearly scramble to get out of the scratchy, unflattering dress.

Grateful she at least wore a chemise beneath, she pulled the habit up, and over her head, tossing it aside.

His green eyes shifted from hers, to her breasts. The chemise's material was transparent, and she knew he could see her nipples clearly. Though she had always believed men from his time would be too gentlemanly to look at a woman unclothed, he proved her wrong since he made no move to look away or hide his interest.

She crossed her arms over her chest. "You're staring, Douglas."

The side of his mouth lifted the slightest bit. "Aye, lass, I am. And I will do more than look if I so choose."

The look in his eye proved he meant what he said . . . and she might just let him too.

"Do ye know why I am here?" he asked, his voice low and menacing.

She shook her head.

"Your father killed my brother."

She wanted to tell him she knew what it was like to lose someone you loved, but she couldn't. He'd have her locked up and she already had enough problems. "I'm sorry to hear that." He thought her someone else, and she'd best play the part, or she might be dead before she found a way back to the future, a place where men like Brochan Douglas no longer existed.

Back to men like Elliott, who could never be faithful . . . not as long as someone younger and prettier came along.

The thought of her ex brought back bitter memories, and she dropped her gaze to her feet, or rather *their* feet. His large feet were encased in soft leather boots, while hers were bare.

Thankfully, Fergus walked back in. To Terri's surprise, Brochan took the cloak from the man and motioned him away with a wave of his hand.

Fergus frowned, but went back to standing guard at the door.

Brochan placed the cloak around her. She almost sighed as the fur-lined black velvet cloak made contact with her skin. It was a welcome relief from the scratchy habit she'd become accustomed to these past three days. "The hem will drag on the ground," she said, tying it at her neck.

He shocked her by pushing her hands out of the way, and finishing the job himself, tying it tight. " 'Tis brisk outside."

Sister Helena stepped into the chamber, and Fergus grabbed her by the wrist. The ashen-faced nun tried to pull away, to no avail. "Laird Douglas, I pray that you not take Annabelle. She has done you no harm. Do not take your revenge out on an innocent."

Brochan did not break eye contact with Terri. "Her father killed my brother. I *will* take my revenge."

The nun flinched. "In what way?"

Brochan stepped toward the nun, and to the woman's credit, she did not look away. "In whatever way I so choose, sister."

"Laird MacLellan will be angry when he learns the truth of this grievous trespass."

"Think ye I fear the murderous bastard?" His jaw clenched tight, a nervous tic appearing there. "I am counting on his anger," Brochan said, taking Terri by the hand, his large fingers sliding over hers. They were rough hands, callused and as tough as leather. Manly hands. "Tell Laird MacLellan that his daughter is no longer yer concern . . . or *his* concern for that matter. She belongs to me now."

3

Brochan walked past the sobbing nuns, pulling Annabelle with him. Strangely enough, MacLellan's daughter made no fight to stay. Rather, she seemed almost relieved to be leaving the priory, even easing the nuns' concerns by telling them she would be well and write soon.

Quite confident for someone taken hostage by a rival clan.

Little did she know her days were numbered. An eye for an eye, a tooth for a tooth. Nay, Laird MacLellan would never see his precious daughter again.

He had heard the girl had spirit, and would oftentimes do things to irritate her father on purpose, but she seemed to be accepting her fate easily enough.

It unsettled him. Was this a ruse? Did her father wait in ambush? MacLellan had a reputation throughout the borderlands for outwitting his enemy.

His men must be on the lookout for any such event.

Wind rustled the trees, and he welcomed the cool rush of air against his heated skin. He had not expected things to go so well, especially after the nuns had fought so vehemently. Luckily the hostage had been more willing than her protectors.

Helping Annabelle mount the horse, he climbed on behind, settling in for the long ride ahead.

Annabelle immediately leaned back into him, her muscles relaxing, not at all stiff and unmoving.

What madness was this that his captive would act so docile and willing? Even more unsettling than her acceptance of her fate was the blood that rushed to his groin as he inhaled her fresh scent. Like heather.

She glanced back at him, her wide blue eyes showing no fear. Her small nose, with a sprinkling of freckles, tipped up at the end. Full, rose-colored lips looked ripe for kissing.

As though reading his thoughts, her small white teeth bit into her bottom lip as he continued to stare.

Rumored to be just six and ten, she seemed much older, looked older, the slight hint of lines at her eyes speaking of someone a few years out of their youth.

Strange, indeed.

Even at this moment, when most girls her age would not be able to hold his gaze, she stared boldly. She seemed as interested in him as he was in her.

Did this mean she was an imposter? Someone older than the actual Annabelle, who resembled the chieftain's daughter. Someone who accepted her fate?

"You don't mind if I lean against you, do you?"

Aye, would Annabelle ask such a thing from her father's hated enemy?

"Ye sound English, yet different," he said, his voice gruff.

Indeed, her speech was unlike any he'd heard before, yet when he concentrated, he understood the meaning.

"Do I?"

"Aye, ye do, lass."

She tilted her head a little. "Do you not like it?"

"I do not know."

She smiled then, a soft curving of the lips. To his shock, his heart raced like a lad's.

Be wary, Brochan. He could almost hear his brother's voice.

He must be wary of this woman who rested against him, her slender back pressed full against his front, the heat from her body emanating into him, making him sweat. He tried not to think of the body he had seen just a flash of earlier when she'd taken off the horrible habit, but it proved more difficult with each minute.

The chemise had hid nothing from him, and he had seen the full swell of her breasts against the pale material, her nipples pebbling from the cool air.

She had seemed only slightly embarrassed by his stare, but did nothing to hide herself from view, save for crossing her arms over her chest. Her behavior made him wonder if she were chaste. Aye, at least she had made some attempt at modesty.

After all, it was told she had been engaged to a cousin at birth, and upon her next birthday would become his bride.

Mayhap they were already lovers?

The very thought rankled. Brochan had met the girl's cousin in Edinburgh last summer. The young man had been slight of frame, and too caring of his own appearance to be likable, something that disturbed him greatly. A man should not be concerned with such things, to Brochan's mind. Nay, he should take care of his home and his people, for what good were material possessions, other than for flaunting one's wealth?

Vanity was a trait his mother had always frowned upon. Mayhap Annabelle liked her vain betrothed?

Frustrated by such thoughts, he reached for the reins, his arms resting on her thighs.

He did not look at any of his men as he rode past, to the front of the line. They had a long ride ahead of them, which would seem even longer now that Annabelle MacLellan's sweet body rocked against his own.

The last woman he had bedded had been Eva, his lover who lived in the village just beyond Castle Kildare. How different the girl in his arms was from the woman who had warmed his bed for the past few months.

As the minutes ticked away, Annabelle's head fell back on his shoulder, and soon her breathing grew even. Had the wench fallen asleep? Her golden hair tickled his cheek. He brushed it away, his fingers entangling for a moment.

She shifted, and pressed her cheek against his chest.

His cock remained hard for the entire ride, the rocking of the horse not helping in the least. Her soft body molded against his, and his fingers, which held the reins, rested on her thighs, so close to the place where he yearned to bury his cock.

He clenched his teeth, the ache in his cock becoming almost unbearable. How tempted he was to ride toward the trees, to take her against the trunk of one of those mighty oaks. For a moment he imagined her eyes, half closed in passion, her soft sigh as he buried his rod into her heated core.

An image of his brother came to him unexpectedly, taking with it the desire he felt for the woman before him.

At least for the moment. Tristan's death had devastated their clan and family. His brother could make everyone laugh with his quick wit and easy smile. And he could play the pipes like no other.

They rode for hours until they came to a glen, where his men made camp. They would sleep until dawn, and then continue their journey until they reached Castle Kildare.

Certainly the nuns would alert MacLellan to Annabelle's kidnapping. Brochan smiled, imagining the laird's fury upon learning his daughter's fate.

Angus would certainly come with an army.

And Brochan could not wait for that confrontation.

"Annabelle," he whispered, shaking her a little harder than intended.

Her lashes fluttered and blue eyes locked with his. At first she frowned as though trying to place him. Then recognition came slowly, and her lips curved.

His stomach tightened. God's breath, she seemed genuinely happy to see him.

Strange. Unless this was part of her plan. To make him believe she accepted her fate—only to escape once they arrived at his castle.

"I fell asleep," she said, stifling a yawn. "I have to admit, that's the most rest I've had since I arrived in this time."

He frowned, confused. "This time?"

Her smile disappeared. "I meant since I arrived at the priory."

"Ye did not sleep at the priory?"

"The cot was too uncomfortable . . . but you on the other hand, make a most comfortable mattress, Brochan."

Did she jest? Her tone certainly made it sound like she was not at all serious.

He cleared his throat. "I am glad."

Dismounting, he held his arms out to help her down. She placed a hand on either one of his shoulders. Small yet firm arms slipped around his neck, and her body slid against his, every soft curve rubbing against his front. He clenched his teeth, resisting the urge to crush her against him.

"Thank you," she said, her hands moving from his shoulder to his chest.

Jesus! Did the woman have any idea what she was doing to him? He was finding it hard to remember who she was, and why she was here. Her father had killed his brother in cold blood. True, his brother had stolen the man's chattel on a dare, but chattel was not worth his brother's life.

His fingers curled about her wrists and brought her hands down to her sides.

"Come," he said, stepping away from her, toward the camp where his men scurried about. The more distance he could put between himself and the woman, the better off they would both be. By tomorrow night they would be at Castle Kildare and he would keep her locked in the solar, far away from him and his men.

And then MacLellan would come to him.

His men had asked him what he planned to do with Mac-Lellan's daughter, and in truth, he had not known, but he was no murderer.

Nay, mayhap he would bury his seed within her and return her to her father.

His stomach grumbled loudly, reminding him he had not eaten since the day before.

"Are ye hungry?" he asked, and she shook her head.

"No, I am tired though."

He nodded toward the tent that his men had set up. His was closest to the trees. "I shall be there shortly. Fergus will keep watch."

She started toward the tent.

"And Annabelle?"

She turned, her brows furrowed. "Yes?"

"Do not try to escape. I have told my men to kill you if you attempt to leave."

To his shock, she smiled. "I have no intention of leaving you, Brochan."

———

Terri could tell she had shocked him yet again. He had not expected such a willing captive. He didn't know what to make of her—that much was obvious. Even now, confusion etched his handsome face.

Since Annabelle's fate hadn't been common knowledge, perhaps she had a chance at this. If she was kind to Brochan and his men, then it would be harder for him to kill her. Plus, she liked the sexy border lord, and she had an inkling that he might like her a little bit. Even more, she was sure he was the key to returning to her own time. Perhaps history was supposed to be played out before the portal could be opened?

Whatever the case, she wasn't about to leave his side.

She was on her way to his castle, and her fate was now in his hands.

Whatever happened, she would survive this. She had to.

Trying hard not to think about what awaited her, she instead wondered what was taking place in present-day London as she made her way to the tent. Hopefully Elliott was going out of his mind with worry.

The asshole deserved to worry, and more.

To think she'd wasted five long years on the bastard.

When she got back to her own time, she would move her stuff out of his apartment and find a job at another museum. Perhaps she'd find a position in Scotland, and forget that Elliott ever existed.

Fergus stood at the tent, and stepped aside as she approached. The man seemed unsure of her as well, his eyes narrowing as she passed. No doubt they had expected they would have to bring her there kicking and screaming. Furs tossed onto the hard ground would be her bed tonight. Wondering if Brochan would sleep beside her, she lay down, snuggling into the warmth, trying her best to keep focused.

She was in thirteenth-century Scotland, with no idea how to return home. Did she really want to go home, back to an unfaithful boyfriend and credit card debt? There were some good points to living in the past, but wasn't the life expectancy of medieval people something like thirty or forty years?

Suddenly images of her fiancé and her assistant, as she'd last seen them, flashed through her mind. Her fingers dug into her palms. She wondered what old Elliott would think if the tables were turned and he'd seen her and Brochan together.

Elliott and Brochan were complete opposites. Though both of them were tall, and Elliott also had dark hair, that's where the similarities ended. Elliott's hands were as soft as hers, since he wore gloves while handling precious artifacts. Brochan's hands were rough and callused from wielding sword and shield. Elliott's body was athletic, but he could never be called muscular, while Brochan's body rippled with thick muscle and sinew. A true warrior.

The blood in her veins heated as she remembered the feel of his hard body against her back. His chest and abdomen had felt like a solid brick wall. So strong. Honestly, she looked forward to the ride ahead of them, to being cradled against him once more. Now Brochan was a man who made her feel protected. A man who would stop at nothing to keep her from harm.

Warmth filled her stomach, moving down to her groin, her sensitive flesh tingling.

Yes, Brochan was the kind of man that made women think about sex. Even the way he walked was sexy. There was a primal sensuality, an animal magnetism that made her heart rate increase every time she looked at him.

She tried to remind herself that the man had one purpose

where she was concerned. He wanted revenge, and though she felt grateful he hadn't killed her, she had to wonder what would happen to her once they returned to his castle. She was anxious to see the keep.

Castle Kildare. Very ominimous sounding. In all the years she'd been in the U.K., she had never journeyed farther than York.

Little had she known three days ago that she'd be living in medieval Scotland, maybe for the rest of her life.

And Lord knew how long that life might be.

A cold wind rushed through the tent and she shivered, listening as Brochan shouted orders to his men. He had told her not to escape and she had no such inclination. She had no desire to return to the priory and the kindly sisters. No, she would wait this out, be kind, and hope that Brochan wasn't going to kill her anytime soon. Her breath caught in her throat when she heard Fergus just outside her tent. A second later he belched loudly and then broke wind. Maybe men of this time were not so different after all. . . .

Terri smiled to herself. Too bad the tour guide hadn't given more insight into Annabelle's fate.

At least Brochan Douglas wasn't a big, ugly brute of a man.

She closed her eyes and imagined what the Scot looked like without clothing. Ripped, corded muscle, and he definitely had some junk in the front. He would be impressive . . . she knew that. True, men throughout history had done a bit of stuffing when it came to emphasizing certain parts of their anatomy, but if Terri had to hazard a guess, she'd bet that every bit of bulge she'd felt against her back belonged to Brochan Douglas.

Liquid heat flooded her groin and she shifted beneath the furs. She hadn't had sex for three weeks now. Elliott had always come up with one excuse or another. But he had not made excuses the night they had gone out to dinner and drank two bottles of wine. She had made the move on El-liott, straddling him on their couch. After offering a number of excuses, he had given in with a defeated sigh. How could she have been so blind?

She wondered what Brochan would do if she made a move on him?

The flap opened and the man she'd been thinking about appeared. Her heart rate increased, her nipples pebbling be-neath the fabric of her chemise.

She watched him under lowered lids as he kicked off his boots. Warmth spread through her belly. A minute later he lay down beside her, his back to her.

And a wide back it was, broad shoulders narrowing to a defined vee—the thick muscles playing beneath the dark shirt. His long hair curled at the ends and she resisted the urge to touch it, to wrap a lock around her finger and bring it to her nose.

Rugged masculinity, that's what he smelled like. A pleas-ant musky scent that clung to him, surrounded him. She in-haled deeply and smiled to herself, finding it hard to believe she was experiencing an age she had studied, with a man who could only have lived in her imagination.

"Why do ye smile, lass?"

She opened her eyes to find Brochan lying flat on his back, head turned, staring at her. Damn, he was gorgeous. Perfec-tion. Never in all her life had she met anyone like him, and she doubted she ever would again. She squeezed her thighs together, trying to ignore the ache building there.

Of course she couldn't tell him why she'd been smiling, or who she really was, because the last thing she needed was him thinking her insane. No, she needed his complete trust. "I'm just happy to see you."

He went up on his elbow, his eyes narrowing. "Ye are not at all like I thought ye to be."

"Nor are you."

He frowned. "What did ye think I would be like?"

She shrugged. "Mean. Cruel, I suppose."

"Cruel?" He sounded surprised, almost offended.

"Yes," she replied, going up on an elbow. "And what did you think I would be like?"

He watched her for a long time, his gaze searching hers. She had never had someone look at her so intently, and it made her self-conscious. True, she knew she was not ugly, but neither was she a beauty. Rather, she fell into the "cute" category. Her blond hair had always been too wavy, and she detested the freckles sprinkled across the bridge of her nose and cheeks. Honestly, men like Brochan never stopped to look at her twice. Even in school she had attracted the geekier, bookish types, instead of the jocks. So it surprised her to see the interest there.

But maybe Brochan was different from the men of her time?

His eyes shifted to her lips, and her mouth went dry.

Though she was limited sexually, her only partner having been Elliott, she knew the look he gave her now. Desire.

He wanted her and she wanted him. This thirteenth-century border lord. A warrior who lived and died by the sword.

As he continued to stare, moisture pooled between her thighs and her clit became ultrasensitive. What would it feel like to be taken by this man? His rough hands on her, his body moving above hers, and inside her.

As his lips descended on hers, she had a feeling her days of celibacy were about to come to an end.

4

What the hell are ye doing?

Brochan could hear his conscience scream that question, but his body did not seem to care that this woman was his enemy, or that her father had murdered his brother.

Nay, he cared about nothing but the rose-colored lips, and the woman beside him.

From the moment he had looked at her, he had thought of taking her, and take her he would. Over and over again. Get her with child so her father would never forget Tristan's death.

No longer would she be a virgin after this night.

He would see to that.

Her lips touched his, tentatively at first, then aggressively, her tongue sliding along the seam of his lips, prompting him to open. And open he did.

She moaned as her velvety tongue slid into his mouth, past his teeth. She tasted sweet, and as her arms encircled his neck, he pulled her on top of him.

Her curves molded against him, her hips pressing down on his pulsing erection.

He moaned deep in his throat. God's breath, if she kept moving like that he would come before he sank his length into her luscious, lithe body.

His hands moved down her slender back, over her womanly hips, and cupped her high, firm buttocks. She moaned in pleasure, rocking against him, her mound scorching his cock that pulsed with the need to be deep inside her honeyed walls. His fingers dipped into the crevice there, slipping a finger into that heated core.

She moaned again, spreading her thighs, while she pressed hard against his cock.

Sweat beaded on his forehead with the effort it took to hold himself in check. Moisture seeped from the tiny slit of his cockhead.

"You feel so good," she said, and he added another finger into her delicious heat.

She was so tight, so wet.

Her hands moved over his ribs, and then were at the cord of his braies, untying them with nimble fingers. A second later her fingers curled around his shaft. "You're so big."

He flipped her beneath him, pushing his braies down, unable to wait a second longer.

Her beautiful blue eyes were wide, the sides of her mouth lifted in a seductive smile. "I want you inside me."

If this was an act . . . she certainly was convincing.

He slipped his cock inside her molten core and didn't move, savoring the feel of her channel gripping his length.

Her hands moved down his back, cupping his buttocks as she lifted her hips, urging him to move.

He kept the pace slow, in no hurry to end this joining.

Nay, he would savor it, take his time so she would have a difficult time forgetting him.

He wanted this moment branded on her memory.

This enemy of his.

Terri gasped, savoring the feel of Brochan's length stretching her, filling her like she'd never been filled before.

His body was beautiful. Wide chest covered by scars, both short and long. Scars that had faded with time, but marked him as the warrior he was. A powerful, sexy warrior.

He looked at her, his green eyes heavy-lidded, so sensual. Lowering his dark head, he took a nipple into his mouth, his tongue flicking over the peak in slow licks. He suckled hard, his teeth grazing her nipple gently, building a delicious ache that had her fingernails digging into his back.

His hips stopped moving, and she could not keep from lifting her own hips, wanting more of his rock-hard length inside her, but each time she lifted, he pulled away in a cruel game.

She'd never been so aroused in her life.

Two could play at that game.

She reached between their bodies, her fingers finding his sac, finding that sensitive patch she had read about, and stroking it with her thumb.

She smiled when he groaned, a sensual grunt that made her pulse quicken. He thrust deep, followed by long, fluid strokes that had her moving along the ground.

Her head brushed against the side of the tent, and he went up on his knees, pulling her by the hips. His gaze shifted from hers to where their bodies joined.

She looked too, shocked at his size, watching with excitement and exhilaration as he entered her slowly, his rod slick from her dew.

His thumb brushed over her clit, once, twice. She arched

her hips, and he pulled out, just to where the tip of his cock touched her opening.

"Brochan," she said, her fingers curling about his hips, urging him to fill her again.

To her frustration, he didn't budge, but played with her tiny nub, working it. He moved again and she cried out, her body reaching for climax.

Brochan watched Annabelle as she climaxed, her eyes closing, her mouth opening.

He felt the tremors against his cock, her inner muscles gripping him tight, pulsing around him in exquisite harmony. Thrusting deeper, his balls tightened, ready to come.

He pulled out, his seed pulsing onto the hard ground beneath him, falling onto her, trying to control his breathing. Why in the hell had he refrained from coming inside her? Wasn't that the idea behind her abduction?

God's breath, he would have a difficult time sending her back to her father.

Mayhap he would keep her a little while.

Never had he expected to discover in Annabelle MacLellan a vixen who could set his blood on fire. A woman who had obviously made love to a man before, because where else would she have learned to touch him in such ways?

And her body had accepted his eagerly, taking him fully inside her.

Had it been her betrothed who had taken her maidenhead? The vain cousin who had seemed almost too feminine?

Or did she have another lover?

"Why are you frowning?"

Surprised she had been watching him, he looked down, embarrassed to find they were off the furs completely and on the hard ground.

His knees were dirty, as no doubt her bottom would be. He rolled so that his back was against the dirt, and she above him, straddling him.

His cock jerked, already semihard again.

She looked down at him, her lips quirking in a sweet grin that made his insides twist. "Do you have something on your mind, Brochan?"

His gaze shifted from hers, to her breasts, her nipples crinkling beneath his stare. Her fingers encircled his cock, and he jumped, shocked, yet delighted by the bold touch. His hands moved to her slender hips.

Her hand tightened around him in a practiced stroke, up and down in a slow, even rhythm. "You are so deliciously hard again," she said, staring at his cock.

Her folds were swollen, her hair damp from their mingled juices. His fingers slid to her molten core, slipping inside the heat there.

She was drenched, her fingers clasping around him. His thumb brushed over her clit, and she sat up abruptly, his fingers falling away as she positioned herself over his cock.

She took him inside her, sighing when she sat down fast, and then rotated her hips in a slow circle. A smile tugged at her lips as, with hands on his chest, she started to ride him.

Her full breasts bounced with the rhythm, and he reached out and cupped them, a perfect handful, the erect nipples pressing into his palms.

Terri had never been so turned on in her life. Her vagina so slick, stretched more in this position, taking every long inch of him. So stuffed she couldn't possibly take another half an inch.

His thumb brushed over her clit, and he watched her intently. She watched him in turn, and didn't hold back as she reached for release. She climbed higher and closer to peak, riding him harder, faster, her need climbing with every second.

Her insides clamped down hard against him, her muscles pounding, pulling his thick length deep inside.

She cried out, her fingers sinking into the golden skin of his shoulders.

With a low-throated moan, he lifted her, his cream pulsing from his body between them.

Brochan woke to the sound of an owl hooting outside the tent. The owl had been following them from the time they left Castle Kildare. He had made his presence known immediately, and now did again, sitting on a branch outside.

He turned to his side, to find the furs beside him empty.

His stomach dropped to his toes.

Dammit, Annabelle had escaped!

The scent of their lovemaking was still in the air as he pulled on his braies and walked outside.

A fire had been set, and nearby a small number of his men snored. Why had he not posted a guard outside his tent? How humiliating it would be to see his men again, particularly since they had no doubt heard the groans and sighs coming from his tent earlier.

What a fool he had been.

And his men would think no differently.

The girl had fucked him in order to escape. Not because she had desired him, or lusted for him, but because she wanted to flee.

It hadn't been because she desired him as much as he'd wanted her.

Nay, she had known she could use her feminine wiles on him to lower his guard.

And lower it he had.

Cursing under his breath, he was ready to rouse his men when he heard a soft humming coming from nearby.

His heart missed a beat.

Could it be Annabelle?

He walked toward the sound, his heart accelerating the closer he came.

Hope and something resembling relief mingled within him, and as he entered the glade, he saw in the moonlight the silhouette of a woman.

A woman with blond hair and womanly hips.

Annabelle.

She swam the length of the small loch, her voice soft, like the brush of a hand up his thigh.

The excitement he had felt earlier in his tent, when he had taken her beneath him and buried his cock deep inside her heat, came rushing back.

No doubt she had come to wash the scent of their love-making from her luscious body.

He pushed his braies from his hips and stepped into the water.

She turned abruptly. While at first startled, she smiled upon recognizing him.

Like a young lad, his heart skipped a beat.

She stood in the water, her breasts bouncing with the motion, the water lapping at her hips.

Her nipples had tightened into buds, and as she walked toward him, the strip of pale curls glistened from the water.

She jumped into his arms, her legs wrapping about his waist.

"I thought ye left," he said before he could stop himself, voicing his fears aloud.

Smiling, she kissed his jaw. "I have no intention of leaving you, Brochan. I am enjoying myself far too much."

Her words pleased him more than she would ever know. "I am glad to hear that, lass."

He kissed her back, opening to her questing tongue, tasting her, enjoying the feel of her hard nipples pressed against his chest.

He set her back down on her feet and took her by the hand, leading her to the shore. The soft grass on the pond's bank would serve as their blanket. She lay down, pulling him beside her, and he rolled over her, kissing her, tasting her lips, before kissing a trail from her forehead, to her eyelids, to her nose, to her cheeks, and her chin.

He wanted to taste every inch of her.

His lips traveled down her neck, to the swell of her breasts, taking a nipple into his mouth, and sucking gently, using his teeth with care. She arched off the ground, her breaths coming unevenly now, her fingers pulling his hair.

Her thighs fell open, and he moved lower, over her soft belly, his tongue circling her navel, before moving over the wet curls that covered her sex.

He kissed her sensitive inner thigh, before moving to the tiny nub at the top of her sex, tasting her lightly, his tongue flicking over her.

Her thighs opened all the way, her hips arching off the ground. "That feels wonderful," she whispered, her fingers sinking into the skin at his shoulders.

He already had scratches from their earlier lovemaking, and he would have more. Her nails raked him as he licked her slit from one end to the other, coming extremely close to her back passage.

Terri felt like her bones were melting. The man pleasuring her took such exquisite time and care, tasting her and touching her in ways Elliott never had, or ever would.

Brochan's long tongue stroked her folds, taking his time, flicking over her clit again and again, and then sucking hard, but not too hard, and then softer, the tip of his tongue lifting the tiny nub over and over. Her insides tightened, and as her body found release, she pushed at his shoulders, not sure if she wanted more, or couldn't take more. She just felt an intense ache deep inside her core.

The need to be filled.

"Brochan," she said, her voice shallow, almost a plea.

"Yes, Annabelle."

His hard cock rocked against her, impossibly huge, like a stone against her stomach. The head of his rod slid against her opening and she arched her hips, aching for him to take her.

He kissed her, her scent clinging to him. Elliott would never have done such a thing as kiss her after pleasuring her, but with Brochan she felt no shame at tasting herself.

Just arousal.

His long cock slid in and out of her, his rhythm fluid, his strokes strong. Their wet stomachs slapped together, the sound reverberating off the now still water.

His men would think her a slut, but she didn't care. She had never been so attracted to a man in all her life, and if she wanted to make love to Brochan Douglas every day, then by damn she would.

As another climax claimed her, she raked her nails along his back, down over his buttocks, her fingers slipping between his crack.

She sensed his shock, his every muscle tense, but he didn't stop her. But she didn't go further, and instead cupped his tight ass.

And as she fell back to earth, she knew that life with this man was only going to get more interesting.

5

Castle Kildare looked as ominous as its name.

The huge keep made of gray stone rose out of the rugged landscape, ivy clinging to its massive walls. Terri leaned closer to Brochan, seeking his warmth and comfort.

He had gone quiet on her the moment they entered the camp after their tryst at the loch. Brochan's men had watched them, some with knowing smiles on their faces, while others looked a bit angry.

None of them trusted her. Not even Brochan.

Which made her wonder if he regretted making love to her. She hoped that wasn't the case, especially since it had been so wonderful for her. She'd never made love with such intensity before. Secretly a part of her yearned to stay here, with Brochan . . . in this time.

A bell rang, ending the momentary peacefulness of early evening. Shouts sounded from the castle a second before the giant portcullis lifted, and people flooded out, ready to welcome their laird and his men. Medieval men, women, and children, all watching her intently.

Terri swallowed past the lump in her throat as the crowd grew to well over one hundred people. Thankful she had Brochan at her back, she straightened her shoulders.

She had to remember the history here. Remember that she was an enemy to these people. Their laird's brother had been killed by Annabelle's father, and they were out for blood.

And it showed on their faces. She felt safe for now, close to Brochan... but what would happen when he wasn't around to protect her?

"Thanks be to God that you found the wench," an old man said, his gray hair long and straggly, like he hadn't brushed it in weeks. But even with his unkempt appearance, he looked related to Brochan, tall and lean, even for his age. The green eyes the same color and shape.

"Uncle Hamish, I trust ye have kept the castle running smoothly in my absence?" Brochan asked, dismounting. He lifted his arms to help Terri down, and she put her hands on his shoulders.

The blood in her veins warmed as she slid down his body, his long fingers wrapping around her hips, reminding her of their sexual play last night.

They had made love three times in the space of a few hours, and she still burned for him. The sexual attraction to this man was so intense, unlike anything she'd experienced before.

His hands fell away and he stepped back.

"A comely lass, too," Hamish said, his gaze moving over Terri in a way that made her shudder. Catching her reaction, the older man laughed under his breath, while walking around her, checking her out.

Brochan straightened, his eyes narrowing. If Terri wasn't mistaken, Brochan and his uncle were not on good terms.

Hamish lifted a lock of Terri's hair and brought it to his nose. "You smell of heather. Bet you taste as sweet too."

Terri wished she could say the same. The man's breath smelled foul, and a funky body odor lingered in the air.

"Uncle Hamish," Brochan said, his voice deadly calm. "MacLellan's daughter is my prisoner. She is to remain untouched."

His uncle immediately let the curl fall back on Terri's shoulder, his low laugh making her take a step back. The man had "creep" written all over him.

"Forget not who she is, Brochan. Your brother is dead because of her father."

"And well I know it," Brochan said, taking Terri by the hand, his warm fingers wrapping around her wrist. She would rather have had him take her by the hand, but he had appearances to worry about. His clan probably wouldn't take too kindly to hand-holding.

She found strength in that touch, and was grateful when he started walking toward the castle, nodding to the people they passed. Terri didn't look at anyone, but gazed directly ahead, at the drawbridge that had been lowered, and the portcullis overhead that looked like thick, black knives.

The inner bailey was larger than it appeared from the outside, and alive with activity. Many stopped what they were doing to watch them pass. To the right sat a chapel, to the left the great hall, an armory, buttery, and kitchen, and finally the stables. There were two towers, both large and formidable, and she knew even as she followed Brochan into one of them that this would be her prison. Though she told herself she shouldn't be surprised he was throwing her in a cell after making love, it still hurt.

The spiral staircase was steep, and each room they passed she glanced into. There were several good-sized chambers, one extremely masculine. Even the bed was massive, made of dark wood and thick draperies.

She assumed it was Brochan's chamber. Unfortunately they didn't stop at that room, but climbed higher.

They came to the top of the stairs, and he pushed open a door. The small room had one window, but it was narrow . . . so narrow she couldn't escape if she wanted to. Not that she'd ever consider scaling a wall that was four stories high. Then again, she'd never been locked in a solar before. Give her a few days and she might just try it.

"So, what will become of me, Brochan?"

He looked at her, his green eyes distant. Now that he had returned to his clan, she had become the enemy once again. The time they'd had together, just a pleasant memory. "Ye will be locked in."

"What am I to do? Just spend the days looking at the walls?"

He winced. "Ye are a prisoner here, Annabelle. Yer fate has not yet been decided."

In essence she had traded one cell for another. She didn't know which would be better, the priory or Castle Kildare.

"I will see to it that ye are brought embroidery, and other things to keep yer mind occupied."

"I have never embroidered. I wouldn't know how."

His brows furrowed. "All women embroider."

"Well, I don't, so there you have it."

Irritated with him, and disappointed as well, she stepped away, toward the window, closing her eyes as the breeze cooled her flushed skin. She went up on her tiptoes and looked below her.

She could see part of the bailey from her vantage point,

and beyond a large loch, surrounded by purple hills, the heather abundant and fragrant. Any other time she might have enjoyed the view. But the enormity of her predicament hit her like a ton of bricks. What if this really was it for her? What if she couldn't return to her own time and spent the rest of her life here locked away, forgotten?

That could well be her fate. Wasn't that what the tour guide had said? Annabelle had never been seen or heard from again?

What if this was her fate? Dying in a cell, never to be heard from again.

Tears stung her eyes, but she brushed them away. His hand came to rest on her shoulder, and a second later she was pulled up against his length.

She closed her eyes, letting the tears slip down her cheeks and onto her borrowed cloak. His arms encircled her, pulling her close while he kissed the top of her head. "If I could change this, I would, Annabelle. I hope ye know that."

"Why do I have to be locked in the solar? I won't escape."

"You are my prisoner, Annabelle. My people would never stand for ye to walk freely. They do not trust ye. Believe me when I say you are safer here in this room than anyplace else."

"I don't want to be locked up like some animal, Brochan. I can't. I'll go crazy with nothing but these four walls around me."

He turned her in his arms, lifting her chin with gentle fingers, his thumb brushing over her bottom lip. "I will come visit ye every single day."

She knew there was no use arguing. He wasn't about to let her walk free. His clan wouldn't stand for it. He lowered his head and kissed her, without any of the gentleness of the night before.

Rather, there was desperation in that kiss, his hands cupping her face as his tongue stroked hers.

Her stomach tightened as fire rushed through her veins, swooping low to her womanhood. His cock brushed against her, already rock hard, and she thrilled at the knowledge that she excited him in the same way he excited her.

She cupped his sex, her fingers smoothing over the fine material of his braies, molding it against his thick length. He lifted her, walking until her back met the brick wall. Her clit twitched, anticipating that hard cock buried deep inside her heat.

He held her pinned with his weight, while he pushed his braies down, his cock erect, rising against his belly.

He lifted her higher and she sighed when he thrust inside her wet heat. He cupped her ass, his fingers gripping her tight as his strokes increased.

She kissed his jaw, his ear, her tongue stroking the ridge before dipping inside.

His groan filled the room, and she clung to his shoulders as she started the ascent toward climax.

Her entire body trembled as she came, her channel gripping him tight. He nipped at her ear as he held her hips steady, his cock embedded deep inside her.

Nails biting into her tender skin, his strokes increased, harder, faster. Brochan groaned, his head falling back on his shoulders as he thrust and ground into her, not withdrawing this time.

With trembling hands, he set her back on her feet, and she stumbled, her knees weak. "Ye have bewitched me, sweet Annabelle," he whispered, kissing her once more before he pulled his braies up and tied them.

Feeling his absence already, she let her gown fall back into place, glancing at the door to see a guard standing there.

She blushed to the roots of her hair. Had he seen them make love? Chances were good that he had.

"When will you return?" she asked, desperation in her voice. She glanced past his shoulder, to the sparse furnishings in the cell. The bed shoved into the corner, the desk and chair, a large trunk, which hopefully contained a good book or two.

"I will return after dinner."

Was this how she would spend the rest of her life? Waiting for him to come to her? To make love to her? Maybe she should have tried to escape after all?

She should have headed back to the priory to see if she could return to her own time now that Brochan had kidnapped her.

Back to Elliott.

To her horror she tried to conjure up her fiancé's image but failed. All she could think of was the man before her. His green eyes watched her, his jaw clenched tight. Despite their intense attraction the fact remained he didn't trust her . . . or perhaps he didn't trust himself.

She could tell in that look that he didn't want to imprison her any more than she wanted to be locked in this solar.

"I shall see you soon, Annabelle," he said, a soft smile on his face, before he walked out the door, leaving her alone with her thoughts.

Brochan watched his men from his vantage point beside the roaring fire.

The winds had come, and blew with a force that sent embers flying from the giant hearth.

"Even the weather celebrates the capture of MacLellan's daughter," his uncle said, taking a long drink from his leather trencher. Ale fell onto his shirtfront, and he pressed a palm against it. Brochan looked away, disgusted. His uncle had never been known for his manners. His father's younger brother, Hamish had always resented Brochan and even Tristan, his late younger brother. Since Hamish had never married, or had any children, Brochan had hoped his uncle would embrace him as his own child, particularly since Brochan had lost his father early on.

But it would never be. Too much jealousy made it impossible.

"Stories are circulating about you and the girl," Hamish said, a slow smiling spreading across his weathered face. "You've bedded the wench, haven't you?"

Brochan felt a blush rush up his neck. He knew his behavior was uncalled-for. He had not expected to have this attraction toward Annabelle, or for it to be reciprocated. Already he had ravished her a handful of times in one day . . . and still it was not enough. He wondered if he would ever get her out of his blood.

"They are merely stories, uncle."

Hamish snorted. "I do not blame you, nephew. She is a tempting piece, to be sure. I'd not mind giving her a tumble meself."

Brochan cracked his knuckles, right tempted to knock his uncle flat. "The girl will not be touched, uncle." He tried to keep the anger from his voice but failed.

The door opened, and Brochan looked up to find Fergus walking toward him. His friend could always make him smile, and he was in need of a good laugh right now.

"Brochan, the girl is requesting a carafe of wine."

His uncle's laughter burned in his ears. "She is a spitfire, that one. Mayhap Eva can befriend her."

Brochan tried hard to contain his growing temper. Eva, a

seamstress who lived in the village, and who had been Brochan's lover for the past few months since her husband's death, would not take the news that he had found a new lover well.

Though comely, Eva had a temper that had shocked him on occasion. He had visited her hut once a week, and she had satisfied his desires, his physical need, but that was before Annabelle had come into his life. With Annabelle it was more than just sex. They had a connection that went beyond the physical. "Mayhap ye can see that the wine is taken to the guards, uncle," Brochan suggested, tired of his uncle's smug expression.

His uncle came to his feet, and finished off the rest of his ale. "I shall take the wine to the guards then."

Brochan rose, nearly upending his chair in his haste, and put a heavy hand on his uncle's shoulder. "Ye will leave Annabelle be, uncle. Hear me and hear me well. Ye are not to enter the solar or engage in conversation. Speak to the guards only."

The smile left his uncle's face, and his brows furrowed. "Nephew, you mistake my meaning."

"I have said my piece and I will say no more," Brochan added, while watching Hamish walk away.

"You would be wise to send him away, Brochan," Fergus said, brushing a hand through his hair. "He will cause you nothing but grief. In truth, he will probably go to Eva's hut to tell her of Annabelle."

"Eva will not be allowed to get close to Annabelle."

"She will be furious, Brochan. You know that." Fergus rested his elbows on his knees and reached out to the fire. "She is a comely wench, but I would warn you to be careful, Brochan. I say this only because I do not trust Annabelle or her people. 'Tis possible she is pretending, trying to save herself with her feminine wiles. She could be using you."

The accusation felt like a slap to the face, but he knew his friend spoke from the heart. It had always been that way between them. "Aye, I understand yer concerns and I shall be wary."

Fergus nodded. "At one time you said you would as soon kill the girl as give her back to her father. I know you spoke out of anger, because you would never kill an innocent. Tell me, would you still take a ransom for her?"

The idea of parting with Annabelle made him uneasy, which terrified him. What the devil was wrong with him? "I know not what I would do, aside from getting her with child."

Fergus laughed. "Aye, Angus would be mighty furious to know you took his daughter's innocence."

Brochan was not about to tell Fergus that someone else had taken Annabelle's innocence. A fact he'd like to forget himself. And strangely, the thought of Annabelle carrying his babe made him smile.

"Perhaps you will tire of her soon."

"Perhaps," Brochan replied, though he doubted he would ever feel that way. But he would not tell Fergus of his feelings toward the lass. Honestly, he did not understand his emotions where Annabelle was concerned. He just knew he had never been so attracted to a woman in all his days.

"Hamish was overheard by some others saying he would sample Annabelle once everyone fell to sleep. They say he bribed a guard, Brochan. Mayhap you should replace the man with someone more trustworthy?"

Furious, Brochan started for the door. If he had to, he would keep Annabelle in his chamber every minute of the day, locked away, where he could keep an eye on her always.

6

She was completely shit-faced.

Lying on her cot, and staring at the ceiling, Terri had started counting the bricks . . . for the fiftieth time. She always lost count and had to go back to one yet again.

With each sip of wine the gray walls blurred even more.

She had always been a cheap drunk, normally limiting herself to three drinks whenever she went out.

However, tonight she had made an exception to her self-imposed rule. The empty carafe lay on the floor. She had rolled it back and forth, over the uneven wood floor, as she waited for Brochan to come to her.

It had to be close to dawn, and still he had not checked in on her . . . and still she couldn't sleep.

No doubt he could not bring himself to come to her, especially since he had already fucked her once today.

What was the old saying? *Why buy the cow, when you can get the milk for free?* Those words burned in her mind. Would Brochan walk away and forget about her? Let her live out what was left of her life in this stifling solar?

Unfortunately her body still burned for the sexy Scot. Even more so now that she'd drunk the entire bottle of wine. Horny and frustrated, she turned onto her side and started counting the bricks on the far wall.

It was going to be a very long day . . .

Behind her, she heard a door open and close. She glanced over her shoulder, expecting to find someone there. But there was no one.

She frowned. She had clearly heard a door open.

Perhaps it had come from the room beneath her?

A second later she heard a familiar male voice. Brochan, and he spoke to Fergus. She held her breath, wondering if she was just hearing things. "I will see you on the morrow," Brochan said, then closed the door.

Her heart tripped. Could it be Brochan's room beneath her? She remembered passing by the chamber on her way to the solar. Dropping onto the wood floor, she searched the planks. They were large and had no gaps, yet she could hear him moving around beneath her.

Excited, she crawled across the floor, finally finding a place where a sliver of light shone through. She went flat on her belly and looked through the crack, down into the room beneath her. It *was* Brochan's room!

She watched as he undressed.

Her stomach tightened as he slipped out of his tunic and braies, tossing them aside. His cock, now flaccid but still large and thick, sprouted from a nest of dark hair.

Her clit twitched, remembering the feel of that big rod stuffing her. She rubbed her legs together. She wanted him. Desperately. Her body was oversensitive to him. Aching for him. Should she call out to him?

No, that would be too desperate.

A knock sounded at his door, and he seemed irritated as he pulled his braies back on and tied the cord quickly.

He walked across the room, and flung open the door.

A woman stepped in. Dark-haired, wearing a rough-looking gown, she threw her arms around Brochan's neck.

Terri's heart dropped to her toes. Reminded of Elliott's betrayal, she clenched her teeth to keep from yelling some derogatory remark. Could it be that Brochan was married already? She knew nothing about him, and had only assumed he didn't have a wife since they'd had sex.

But since when did marriage stop a man?

"Eva, what are ye doing here?"

The brunette pulled back, her brows furrowed. "I heard that you brought the woman here."

"Aye, Annabelle is here."

"Is she pretty?"

Brochan pulled away, his fingers raking through his long hair, causing the muscles in his bicep to move under his golden skin. "Eva, I am tired and in need of sleep."

"I have come to spend the night with you."

Terri released the breath she'd been holding. She must not be his wife then.

She embraced him again, pressing herself against him.

Terri felt like yelling, *Get off him!,* but she couldn't, and even more, she wouldn't. No, she wanted to see what kind of a man Brochan Douglas was.

Was he like all men, and would he cheat on her with the pretty brunette, who was no doubt his lover?

To Terri's chagrin, he hugged the brunette, kissed her forehead, but then he steered her toward the door. "Not tonight."

The brunette turned and slapped his cheek. "It is because you were with MacLellan's daughter! That whore!"

Terri blanched. Whore? A bold statement from someone who was throwing herself at the man.

"I have no desire to continue this conversation tonight, Eva. I am exhausted."

She planted her hands on her slender hips. "What does she have that I don't?"

Brochan ran his hands down his face, his agitation obvious by his rigid stance. "Eva, ye need to return to the village. I will see to it that a guard walks you back."

She stomped her foot like a child. "Mayhap I shall stay the night in the hall. Perhaps one of your men will be willing to slake my lust, as you are not man enough to."

The words did not have the desired effect. She watched him, waiting for a jealous reprimand, but it never came. Instead, he shrugged. "Do what ye must, Eva. I've made no promise to ye. Ye are free to make love with whomever ye please."

"But I am your lover," she said, her voice shrill and loud. "I want no other man. No one else can fuck me like you, Brochan."

"Lower yer voice," he said, crossing his arms over his chest. "Ye will wake everyone."

"Wake your whore, you mean." She glanced up at the ceiling and Terri held her breath. Thankfully they did not look directly at her. She would be horrified to be discovered eavesdropping. When Brochan lifted his head, she rolled away from the crack, hoping he had not seen her watching.

"It is time ye leave, Eva. I am tired."

Her sobs filled his room, and Terri, too tired and drunk to watch any longer, crawled back to her cot and lay down.

Tonight had been a wake-up call. Though Brochan had turned the woman away now, what about tomorrow or the next night? Maybe all men were alike, and whether she wished to believe it or not, Brochan wanted her for only one thing . . . as a piece of ass. She couldn't fall in love with the man, because she would only be devastated when he replaced her down the road. What she did need to do was find a way out of this solar and back to her own time. Before she lost her mind.

Brochan glanced toward the solar for the tenth time in as many minutes. He had been gone all morning, hunting with Fergus and a handful of his men.

Since his return he had hoped to get a glimpse of blond hair, to see the familiar blue eyes searching for him.

But Annabelle never appeared at the narrow window.

When he had checked on her last night, he had been tempted to enter, to make love to her again, but he didn't. Instead, he replaced the guards at the door with his most trusted men, and returned to his chamber.

Morgar, who had watched her throughout the night, had said she did not make a sound and had requested nothing.

Brochan had sent a tray of food up earlier, knowing she must be hungry.

He would check on her directly, just to make sure she had not taken ill.

Along the castle's battlements his men walked back and forth, awaiting Laird MacLellan's arrival.

Angus would be on his way with a small army directly.

And they would be ready to fight.

Every last one of his men.

To the death if need be.

Will you give her back to her father? Fergus's question still burned in his ears.

Would he give Annabelle back? What if MacLellan agreed

to pay a ransom? Would he be willing to part with her then?

He knew the answer already. Nay.

He thought of Annabelle's pledge to marry her cousin. Would the cousin demand her release as well? Would he come with MacLellan?

The thought of Annabelle spreading her thighs for the man made him curse beneath his breath.

Over his dead body.

He remembered her as she'd been in the moonlight. Rising out of the lake like a pagan witch. Her creamy skin dripping with water. Her pink nipples tightening from the cool water. The strip of hair that covered her succulent treasure, her core so hot and dripping that he had slid right in, stretching her, filling her so completely.

His cock twitched.

He looked toward the solar again.

"Fergus, I shall be back directly."

He didn't wait to see if Fergus had heard him. Last night he had lain awake wondering if Annabelle was all right. After Eva's visit he knew that the wench would not take well to another woman sharing his bed, and perhaps might try to harm Annabelle.

He took the steps two at a time. The guards came to attention, and he nodded at them. "Open the door," he said, and waited, his heart pumping with excitement and something else as the door opened.

He closed it behind him, his gaze immediately going to the cot, where she lay unmoving. Did she still slumber?

The blanket had fallen off, and she lay on her stomach, one leg hitched up, her bottom in the air.

His cock swelled, pressing against his leather braies.

"Annabelle," he said, approaching her.

She turned her head slightly, blinking repeatedly. A moment later her lips curved into a smile and his heart missed a beat.

"Good morning," she said, stretching.

The chemise stretched against her skin, the material hiding nothing from his gaze, only enticing him to look at the dark places in shadow.

The crack of her beautiful ass being one.

Untying the cord of his braies, he stepped out of them and pulled his tunic off. Her eyes widened, but she didn't stop him.

He stood at the foot of the cot, and taking the hem of her chemise, he drew it up and over her bottom.

He groaned as she spread her legs a little, her plump cheeks enticing him. His body covered hers, his cock resting against the cheeks of her firm bottom.

His hands moved beneath her, cupping her breasts, playing with the erect nipples.

She lifted her ass higher in the air.

Adrenaline rushed through his veins like liquid fire. She wanted him to take her.

One hand slipped between her thighs, to find her hot and dripping, so ready.

He entered her, sliding easily inside her wet heat.

She cried out as he moved against her. He was already so excited, he would not be able to hold off for long.

She spread her thighs wider, lifting her hips with each stroke. He slowed his pace, kissing her neck, her spine, enjoying the moan that came from low in her throat.

"You feel so good, Brochan," she said on a moan.

"Do I?" he asked, pleased by her words.

"Mmmm. I could get used to this." Her channel gripped him harder, and the familiar pulsing followed.

He joined her, climaxing, his seed shooting inside her.

With a satisfied groan he fell on top of her, his heart pounding hard against her back.

She turned in his arms, going into his embrace.

"The guards tell me you have not eaten today, Annabelle."

She shrugged. "I'm not hungry."

"Why?"

"I'm bored, I suppose. Nothing sounds good, particularly the greasy venison they brought up earlier."

He brushed back her hair from her face, taking in her flushed cheeks and sleepy eyes. "I know it is not much better than spending your days in this chamber, but how would ye like working in the kitchen?"

Her eyes narrowed as she watched him.

"I thought the news would please you."

"I would like to work in the kitchen. My head just hurts so badly, I can scarcely think. Remind me never to drink wine again."

He laughed, relieved her humor had returned in force. "I will tell Helda to expect you in the kitchen today."

"How about we try it tomorrow instead," she said, rubbing her temples.

"Do you think you are up to it? Helda runs her kitchen with an iron fist."

"I know my way around a kitchen, Brochan. Trust me, we'll get along just fine . . . after I've had about ten hours of sleep. I have never been any good at drinking, and now was not the time to start."

He stood, knowing he should return to his men. Ironically, he had no desire to leave her, wishing instead to scoop her in his arms and take her to his chamber, and make love to her for the rest of the day.

She rolled over, not bothering to cover herself with the

blanket. Oh, but she was beautiful, her curvy hips making him want her again already.

"Brochan?"

He tied his braies and reached for his tunic. "Hmm?"

"Who is Eva to you?"

He had one arm through his tunic, but stopped short, shocked to hear her question. How in the world did she know of Eva? He frowned. "She lives in the village."

She watched him intently, her eyes narrowing a little. "But what is she to you?"

He dropped his gaze to his feet, and realized with a start that she had probably heard the conversation that had taken place last night. The thick boards could only muffle so much sound. Thank God she could not see what was going on. Though he had not had sex with Eva, he still had embraced the woman.

If the tables were turned, and she had been hugging a man in her chamber, he would be furious.

"She was my lover."

She lifted a finely arched brow. "Was?"

He could not help the smile that played at his lips, for there was no mistaking the jealousy in her tone or in her eyes.

"You think it's funny?" she asked, pulling the blanket over her, covering her face. Her anger was confirmed when she rolled to her side, giving him her back.

"Annabelle," he said, walking over to the cot. "Ye are my only lover. Eva was my leman, but she is no longer. I only want ye to share my bed."

She glanced over her shoulder at him, her blue eyes narrowed in suspicion. "Is she beautiful?"

"Not as beautiful as you."

To his shock, he meant it. Though Eva was striking, in a

dark, exotic way, she could not hold a candle to Annabelle's pale beauty and quick wit.

She watched him for a moment, obviously wary, but she smiled, flashing small, white teeth. "Okay, I just wanted to make sure. I don't like sharing you with anyone else. Been there, done that."

Perplexed by her speech, he bent down and kissed her, savoring the moment.

"Oh, and by the way. Thank you for the job in the kitchen. The walls were starting to close in on me already."

He laughed, amazed at her ability to see the best in every situation.

"I shall see ye tonight," he said, heading for the door.

"I'm counting on it," came her reply.

7

The kitchen was hotter than Hades. Between the boiling pots over the hearth and the smell of too many bodies, Terri felt the urge to run and never look back.

Sweating through her thin gown, she tied her hair up in a sloppy bun, and tried to find some relief from the heat. Not easy when it was nearly as hot outside as it was in this furnace.

Discomfort aside, she had to look at the positive. At least she wasn't stuck in the solar counting bricks any longer. Now she had other people to talk to, mainly Helda, the portly cook who had taken a liking to Terri immediately. Thank goodness. The woman had a quick temper and proved it when she hit a page across the knuckles with a wooden spoon.

Pages and servants lined up in the kitchen, taking trenchers and plates of steaming venison and vegetables. Having not eaten a single thing since her drinking binge, Terri couldn't keep her mouth from watering. However, she refrained from picking at the food, certain the cook would kick her out.

"Take a pitcher there, and go fill goblets," cook said, pointing toward the large jug on the scarred wood table.

Knowing she looked frightful, she cringed, glancing down at the dress clinging to her like a second skin. It was made of thin light blue linen, and a sweat ring had formed at her neck and no doubt down her back.

Not sexy at all.

And Brochan would be in the hall, and quite possibly Eva too. This was not how she imagined meeting her nemesis.

Trying not to think of the brunette, Terri did as asked and took the jug, and followed the line of servants out of the kitchen into the bailey.

The cool air felt wonderful against her heated skin and she took a deep breath, walking slowly until she was the very last servant to enter the hall.

Noise hummed in the huge room, people talking among themselves as servants made sure each glass was filled. Terri wondered where Brochan sat. Brushing a curl over her ear, she started pouring.

A man leered at her, his lips quirking. "Aye, lass, yer not so high-and-mighty now, are ye?" His laughter vibrated to the high ceilings.

No doubt they were all enjoying the sight of Angus Mac-Lellan's daughter serving them.

They would have a field day.

And though she was not Annabelle, she still could not help the blush that stained her cheeks red. A group of women sat to her right, laughing. "Well, if it isn't the laird's whore."

Terri's heart missed a beat as she recognized the brunette that had been in Brochan's chamber the night before.

Eva.

To Terri's chagrin, the woman was even prettier up close.

Her dark eyes narrowed. "I would like some ale, servant."

Terri could see jealousy in the other woman's eyes. Though she wanted to pour the entire pitcher over Eva's head, she instead poured ale into the woman's goblet.

"She is not pretty in the least," Eva's friend said, loud enough for Terri to hear her.

Unable to help herself, Terri knocked the goblet over as she went to fill another.

"You idiot!" Eva cried, slapping Terri across the mouth.

Tasting blood, Terri refrained from dropping the jug and hitting her back. Instead, she lifted her chin and met the other woman's gaze.

From the corner of her eye she saw a tall man walking toward them, and knew it was Brochan even before she looked up at him.

Her pulse skittered.

His gaze shifted from hers to the gown, and her nipples pebbled against the rough material, reminding her of yesterday. The way he had taken her from behind, how he had filled her so completely. He had come inside her too, not withdrawing as he had before. No doubt his intention was to get her pregnant so he could return her to Annabelle's father. She'd been on birth control pills for years, but it had been nearly a week now since she'd taken the last one . . . which meant she could very well be pregnant.

Elliott had never wanted kids, and she had never pushed the point, hoping that one day he would change his mind. Thank goodness they didn't have children. It would have made his betrayal even harder.

But now she had Brochan.

His long hair had been pulled back, drawing emphasis to

his finely sculptured features, the sharp cheekbones, strong jaw, and full lips.

Her stomach did a little flip.

Fill and inflame me again, Brochan.

His gaze shifted abruptly to the brunette. "What is amiss?"

Eva stood, putting a hand on Brochan's arm. Her fingers curled around a large bicep. "She spilled the ale intentionally. Look at my skirts."

Sure enough, the ale had left a large, wet spot on the front of Eva's skirt. Terri bit the inside of her cheek to keep from smiling.

"Ye are not to touch this woman again, do ye hear me?" Brochan said to Eva, his eyes as hard as ice.

When she didn't answer immediately he put his hands on his narrow hips.

The woman's cheeks turned red, and Terri was surprised she didn't stomp her foot as she had done the night before in Brochan's chamber.

To Terri's dismay, the entire hall had gone quiet.

She had always disliked being the center of attention, and now she stood in a room full of people who hated her, watching and waiting for Brochan to deliver punishment. He was not in an enviable position, as his people would expect her to be reprimanded.

She was their hated enemy, and though initially she had thought being in this time would be fun, she realized it would never be the thrill she had thought it would be.

Not when everyone here wanted her dead.

Especially the brunette who stood seething, her eyes full of hatred.

"Perhaps I should return to the kitchen," Terri said, dropping her gaze to the floor. No doubt everyone knew she had slept with Brochan.

"Mayhap you are right," Brochan said, pulling away from Eva. "I shall walk you to your quarters."

She walked ahead of him, feeling his gaze on her the entire way. Snickers followed them all the way out the hall, and to her surprise tears burned the backs of her eyes.

What was wrong with her? She had thought this time-travel would be so much fun, but the enormity of possibly never seeing her home again came crashing down on her.

The minute she stepped out into the bailey, she cried.

Brochan's hand encircled her wrist and he pulled her toward him. "Come," he said, walking toward the armory. Inside, armor and swords lined the walls.

Shutting the door behind them, Brochan turned. "Why do ye cry, Annabelle?"

How she yearned to hear him call her by her name, and not Annabelle. "I don't know."

He lifted her chin. "Are ye hurt?" He turned her face to look at her cheek. Gentle fingers probed her tender skin.

"No, it doesn't hurt."

"She will never touch ye again. I swear it."

Brochan's insides twisted as he looked down into Annabelle's upturned face. Her cheek still bore the outline of Eva's fingers where she had slapped her.

In truth, he had not known Annabelle had been in the hall until the sound had alerted him to her presence.

He knew that Annabelle had been roused early to help in the kitchen, but he had not expected her to appear in the hall.

Especially wearing that thin gown, wet with perspiration. Her hair had been pulled up high on the back of her head, the blond tresses hanging about her shoulders, some of the strands wet from sweat.

The kitchens were hot.

Mayhap too hot.

"I don't belong here, Brochan," she said, her voice barely a whisper.

"What do ye mean?"

She looked at him intently. "I don't belong here, plain and simple. No one wants me here. I am your enemy, and what good will come of my being kept prisoner? It won't bring your brother back."

He clenched his jaw. "Nay, nothing will bring my brother back, but at least I will have revenge upon your father."

She lifted a brow. "How will you have revenge? In what way? By getting me pregnant and sending me back in shame?"

His gaze slid to the pulse beating wildly in her neck. He pressed a finger on it, and then ran a trail down to where a nipple thrust against the thin material. He brushed it lightly, and she released an unsteady breath. "You could already be carrying my child. I did not say ye would return to yer village."

"So you will leave me here to work in your kitchen, give birth to your child, and then lock me away at night?"

He wanted her in his bed. To stay with him forever. Mayhap he would even marry her, yet as he stared into her blue eyes, he could not say the words. He had never been good at showing or expressing emotion. "I desire ye, Annabelle. I want ye, and I want ye to carry my babe."

"But only for revenge, Brochan."

At first he had thought of it that way. An excuse to explain why he wanted this woman so badly. But now it had nothing to do with her father, or the death of his brother. It was just about the two of them, and how he felt when he was with her. The need he felt whenever they were together. The intense desire that took hold of him and didn't let go.

He cupped her face in his hands. "I burn for ye, Annabelle. In a way that scares me." His fingers caressed her jaw then fell to her breast, cupping one firm globe.

Her gaze searched his, and the sides of her mouth lifted.

She sat down on the bench, her hands going to the cord of his braies. "I burn for you too, Brochan." Slowly she untied it and wrapped her fingers around his length.

She leaned in and tasted the head of his cock.

His shaft swelled and bucked.

She smiled and took him into her hot mouth, an inch at a time.

Her hot mouth caressed his rod, her tongue stroking the head over and over. She took him deeper into her mouth, and his fingers dug into her shoulders.

Surprisingly she took most of him, her movements slow and steady. Her fingers splayed on his hips, then moved around to cup his buttocks, pulling him even deeper inside her mouth.

His balls lifted.

Her finger brushed against his puckered hole. A place no woman had ever touched.

Yet she did, her slender finger sliding into him.

Unaccustomed to the strange sensation, he pushed her away, his cock sliding from her mouth.

She lifted a brow but said nothing, and leaned forward, taking him into her mouth once again. Her hands returned to his hips and stayed there. She sucked slowly, in no hurry.

He could hear his men outside and knew they risked being caught, but he could not pull away. Not when he was so close to blessed release.

She stroked beneath his balls, her thumb brushing over a sensitive patch, and he was shocked at the climax that rocked his body, his seed shooting into her hot mouth with a force that stunned him.

He groaned as she sucked every bit of his cum from her lips, and tugged his braies back up and tied them.

His legs trembled from his climax. He pulled her up, hugging her to him, his fingers brushing along her spine. How could he return her to her father? This woman whom he could not get out of his blood?

"Brochan, Laird MacLellan and his men were spotted not more than an hour away."

Brochan came awake with a start. At his side, Annabelle stirred.

He had known Angus would come looking for his daughter. He just had not expected it to be so soon.

"I will be there shortly. Rouse the men and have them prepare for battle."

"Right away!" Fergus said, his footsteps receding.

Brochan dressed, and tossed Annabelle's dress at her. "Here, put this on. I want ye to stay here. Do not leave, and do not, under any circumstances, unlock the door until ye hear my voice."

"Brochan."

He turned.

She swallowed hard, and blurted, "Will you give me to him?"

"Ye belong to me, Annabelle. To me and no other."

To his surprise, she smiled. "Brochan, before you go, there is something I must tell you."

His heart missed a beat, terrified of the next words out of her mouth.

"I am not Annabelle MacLellan."

He shook his head, certain he had not heard her right. He remembered how surprised he had been when he entered the priory chamber and saw her standing there, a woman older than six and ten. God's breath, had the nuns at the Priory of Grace duped him into believing one of their own was MacLellan's daughter? "If you are not the real Annabelle, then why is yer father here?"

She came to her feet, wrapping the blanket about her slender body. "This is where it gets difficult." She cleared her throat. "My name is Terri Campbell, and I'm from the twenty-first century."

He watched her for a long moment, shocked she could keep a straight face. His lips quirked. "This is not the time to play games, Annabelle. Yer father is riding here and I am needed downstairs."

"Brochan, I'm Terri Campbell."

"Terri Campbell? An odd name, particularly for a girl."

The smile disappeared from her lips. "Perhaps it is a bit androgynous, but it is my name, and I am from the future, whether you choose to believe me or not."

Misgivings worked its way up his spine. "I do not have time for these games."

She walked toward him and put a hand against his chest. Her expression was earnest, her tone firm. "Brochan, I am who I say I am. One day I left my job, working at a museum in London. Having found my fiancé *sleeping* with another woman, I drove to Scotland. When I came upon the Priory of Grace, I stopped, intrigued by the building."

At the mention of her fiancé he went still, his hands closing into fists at his sides.

"While on a tour of the priory, there was a chamber that had been boarded up. The guide told us the story of Annabelle MacLellan, the young woman who had been brought to the nuns for safekeeping by Angus MacLellan himself. He feared for his daughter's safety after he had killed your brother by mistake."

"He did not kill my brother by mistake. He did it intentionally. Our clans have always been rivals."

"I am just telling you what the tour guide told us. Please hear me out." She dropped her hand back to her side. "I was told that the chamber had not been opened for over seven hundred years, because it was haunted by a nun's spirit, a nun who had been murdered by Annabelle's father. Her spirit haunted the chamber and made the nuns so afraid that they sealed it off, never opening it again."

"And ye opened this chamber?"

She nodded. "I did."

Though the story was entertaining, he grew restless. "And what happened?"

"I woke up in this time."

"In the body of Annabelle MacLellan?"

She shook her head. "No, in my body actually. I wish I could say I was only sixteen years old, but I am actually ten years older than the original Annabelle."

Which made her six and twenty. A prickling began at the back of his neck, growing with each second. From the moment he had met Annabelle, something had seemed wrong. The way she had readily accompanied him, not fighting him, almost being happy to leave the priory and the nuns.

She had not been a virgin either, as the real Annabelle would have been. Nay, this woman knew how to make love to a man. A woman of six and twenty who knew what sexual gratification was.

"Ye believe the chamber is how ye came to be here?"

He could see the relief in her eyes as she nodded. "I thought it was, but trust me, I pushed on every stone in that room. Nothing took me back. When you came, I felt that perhaps you would be the catalyst to help me return to my own time."

"That is why ye came with me, and why ye have—"

"I've always wanted you, Brochan. I still do. That will never change, no matter where I am. If I spend the rest of my life in this time, then that's great . . . as long as you are here to share it with me."

How could it be possible that this woman had traveled through time? A woman unlike any he had known, who spoke so strangely, who knew so much. What if she did not lie, and her story was true? What if he woke up one morning to find her gone? His insides twisted at the very thought. "I do not want ye to leave me, Annabelle."

"Terri," she corrected, and smiled. "You believe me then?"

He sighed. "I don't know. It would explain a lot of things, yet it is still difficult to comprehend."

"Brochan!"

Hearing Fergus's cry, Brochan rushed to the window, Annabelle, or *Terri,* right behind him. A cloud of dust rose on the horizon.

"MacLellan." He turned to Terri and kissed her. "Stay here, and don't open that door. We shall talk about this later. For now ye need to stay safe."

She nodded. "I'll be here when you return."

Angus MacLellan's cheeks were as red as the hair on his head, and he looked furious. "Douglas, you will release my daughter at once!"

Brochan and his men had ridden out to the glen, meeting Angus and his small army before they reached the castle.

He dismounted and walked toward the laird until they stood a handbreadth apart.

"Ye are in no position to demand anything," Brochan said, his fingers curling around the hilt of his sword.

"I did not mean to kill your brother. He came on my lands, and stole my chattel. He was a thief."

Though Brochan knew the man spoke the truth about his brother stealing chattel, albeit on a dare, he believed a human life was far too dear compensation for chattel.

Angus looked past his shoulder, and his lips curved. "Ah, here she is."

Brochan turned, shocked to find Terri sitting before his uncle. Fear slithered down his spine when he saw that Hamish held a knife to her neck.

Angus swore under his breath. "Release her this minute!"

Brochan, knowing his uncle's fury and unstable mind too well, pulled Angus back. "Uncle, what are ye doing?"

Hamish's eyes narrowed as they looked from Brochan to Angus. "Your daughter has been my nephew's whore, a quite willing one at that."

Angus turned to Brochan, his teeth clenched.

"Uncle, release her."

"Nay, I think you no longer can see reason where the chit is concerned. Your lust for her is too great."

"What do you want for her?" Angus asked, ripping his arm from Brochan.

Brochan watched Terri, who stared at him, her chin lifted high. She did not show any fear, but rather sat stiff as an arrow, the blade cutting into the tender skin of her neck.

How he loved this woman.

"I will give you gold coin," Angus said, taking a step toward Hamish and Terri.

"How much?" Hamish asked, greed in his eyes.

"Whatever amount you want." Angus reached into his pocket and pulled out a bag. "Here, this is enough to feed you for a decade."

"She is your daughter, Laird MacLellan. Your *only* daughter. Surely you can afford a bit more than that."

"I will give you lands," Angus blurted out, desperation creeping into his voice. "Whatever you desire."

"How do I know you do not lie?"

"I never lie," Angus said, his voice lethal. "You have my daughter and I will not risk her life for money or lands."

Growing weary of his uncle's game, Brochan stepped toward him. "Hamish, release her now."

Terri had a hard time swallowing with the blade pressed firmly against her throat. Would this be it for her? To die at the hands of a crazy man?

Lord, she hoped not, especially since she believed she had a chance to live the rest of her life with Brochan.

If only she hadn't opened the chamber door. Damn, why had she trusted the madman behind her when he'd said Brochan had been hurt and needed her?

And now she had a blade pressing into her skin. The man behind her was just crazy enough to use it.

Terri had been shocked at the sight of Angus MacLellan, certain he would take one look at her and say she wasn't his daughter. But for some reason, that never happened. Just like at the priory, everyone believed her to be Annabelle. For some reason she had become the woman.

And now the man claiming to be her father watched her with something akin to desperation. He loved his daughter. That much was obvious.

From the moment she had landed in this time, she had known things could end in disaster, one way or the other. And now with the blade slicing into the delicate skin at her throat, she had a feeling she would never again see the man she had fallen in love with. This warrior who made her blood burn and her insides feel like they were melting.

Brochan Douglas, border lord, man, exquisite lover.

She loved him. Not the comfortable love she had felt with Elliott that had grown with time, but the pulse-pounding, "I can't think of anything else" kind of love that comes along only once in a lifetime.

And as easily as he had come into her life, he would disappear.

Like dust in the wind.

Brochan stepped closer, hands out. "Uncle Hamish, let her go. I will give ye whatever ye desire. Castle Kildare and all that goes with it. Just release her. That is all I ask."

The man's grip tightened when Brochan took another step.

"Let her down, Hamish. Let her down now." Brochan stood within five feet of her, reaching up.

The knife bit into her throat at the same time she heard Brochan yell her name, his face a mask of horror.

An excruciating pain made her cry out . . . and then the world went black.

9

Terri woke to a pounding headache, not much different than the hangover headache of a few days before.

She rubbed the sleep from her eyes and looked around the room. She sat up with a start, recognizing her old flat in London. Everything was the same, except that none of Elliott's things were here.

"Brochan," she said, fear and sickness hitting her like a wave. Seeing the flashing light on her answering machine, she hit it.

Elliott's voice filled her bedroom. "Terri, I'm sorry. I didn't mean to hurt you. I hope you know that. I want you back. These past weeks have been hell without you. I can't eat or sleep. I need you back, honey."

Past weeks?

How had she got back to London? Her stomach turned over, and she felt bile rise in her throat. It could not have been a dream! Brochan, the priory, the crazy uncle who had slit her throat.

She reached up and ran a hand over her throat. Racing to the bathroom, she looked in the mirror. A tiny pink scar, no more than three inches long, marred her flesh. Her heart skipped a beat.

It had been real!

The blood rushing through her veins, she raced to her room, pulled a suitcase from the closet and started throwing clothes in it.

After a quick shower, she locked the door to her flat, and jumped in her Mini Cooper and headed to Scotland, and Castle Kildare.

Tears streamed down her face as she relived the moments with Brochan. From the moment he had stepped into the chamber at the priory, to the second she had seen true fear on his face when his uncle slit her throat.

She brushed a finger over the scar.

Her heart raced as hope filled her. There had to be a way back to thirteenth-century Scotland.

Terri watched the sun rise over the heather-strewn hills of Scotland. Castle Kildare was just minutes away, or so said the sign she'd just come upon.

She had no idea what she would find. Perhaps a ruin, and what then?

She crested the hill, and tears choked her throat.

The castle was not a ruin, but looked much as it had that day seven hundred years ago when she'd ridden over that same hill with Brochan.

She remembered his strong chest against her back, and how protected she had felt in his arms.

Please, God, let it be.

The iron gate was thankfully open, and she drove down the gravel drive.

Home.

Putting her car in park, she stepped out, closed the door, and leaned back against it, looking at the castle where she had fallen helplessly in love with Brochan Douglas.

An older gentleman opened the door, and stepped out.

Disappointment nearly choked her. Wearing a kilt, he smiled at her, his dark eyes kind. "Good morning, lass. I fear the castle is not open to visitors this time of year."

He couldn't send her away. She couldn't bear it. "I've come from London."

"So far?"

"Yes, I need to know what happened to Laird Douglas."

He appeared shocked by the request. "The present Laird Douglas is alive and well. He lives here the majority of the year."

"With his family?"

The man shook his head, his eyes twinkling. "Nay, lass. He's never married. A bachelor, he is. We at Castle Kildare hope he will find his soul mate. He says he knows she will appear one day."

Her heart missed a beat.

"Would you like a tour of the grounds, miss?"

What she wanted was to meet Laird Douglas, but she wouldn't push her luck. "Yes, I would."

She walked beside the old man, listening to every word, taking in the castle she loved so much, looking at the solar window, a place she wanted to visit before she left this day. In fact, she wanted to visit every room, every inch of the castle, wanting, no, needing to be here to soothe her aching heart.

So many emotions rushed through her, and she had to keep herself from crying.

"This is where the ancestors are laid to rest." He pointed to the family plot that was surrounded by black wrought-iron fencing. "May I?" she asked, waiting for the man to give her permission.

She stepped past him, to the many graves before her, the hair on her arms standing on end as she walked by each one. The dates went down as she walked, from the most recent, to the previous century. The closer she came to the 1200s, the more scared she became.

Fearful to find the name of her beloved on one of those stone markers.

She came to Tristan, Brochan's brother, then to the graves beside his.

She frowned. Where was Brochan?

Then she caught something else. "This says that Tristan was laird of the Douglas clan. I thought it was Brochan?"

The man's brows drew together. "Nay, lass. You must be confused with the present Laird Douglas."

Her heart nearly pounded out of her chest. "What?"

"Aye, the present laird is Brochan Douglas. You must have him mistaken with James from the thirteenth century. James's middle name was Brochan."

She looked past his shoulder, to the castle.

Could it be?

Was it possible that Brochan had survived, or that he had managed to find his way to her?

"Is Brochan here?"

"I shall see," the man said, wary. "May I tell him who is calling?"

Trembling, she nodded. "Tell him Terri Campbell is here to see him."

Surprise lit his eyes, and his lips curved slightly. "Very well, lass. I shall return in a moment."

Terri watched the man walk to the castle.

She did not want to get her hopes up too high. After all, she would only be setting herself up for a fall.

And a big fall it would be.

Because she wanted this man to be Brochan.

Her Brochan.

Brochan Douglas, the border lord who had come storming into her life, captured her heart, her mind, and her body all at once.

Terri closed her eyes and said a silent prayer.

A minute later the door flew open, and a broad-shouldered man appeared, filling the doorway.

Her keys fell from her hand, to the gravel.

The breath caught in her throat. He was the same, but not the same. Still as tall as she remembered, and as broad shouldered and narrow hipped. No longer did he wear a tunic and braies, but instead a navy cable-knit sweater, and a pair of jeans. He wore no shoes, and his dark hair curled at the collar, not as long as it had been when last they'd seen each other, but still as thick and dark as she recalled. "Terri?"

"Brochan!" Her heart lurched and she ran.

He ran too.

She jumped into his arms and he held her tight. So tight it felt as if he could break her in two, but she didn't care. "I knew ye would come."

His voice slid over her like warm honey. That same intoxicating voice she remembered so well. "I knew it."

He turned in a circle, his laughter loud, like heaven to her ears. "Brochan," she said, hardly believing her eyes. But he was real. Every hard inch of him.

The old man watched them, a wide smile on his face, and as Terri smiled back, he nodded and went back inside, leaving them alone, in the shadow of the castle.

"I knew ye would come," he said again, kissing her.

She kissed him back, desperate to be with him. "Brochan, I can't believe it's you."

He smiled against her lips. "Lord, how I've missed ye."

Brochan could not believe he held Terri in his arms.

His Terri.

It had seemed like an eternity since last he looked into her blue eyes.

An eternity that had been worth the wait.

She stood in his chamber now, watching him as he undressed. Both of them were eager to take up where they had left off.

If possible, she was even more beautiful now than she had been then.

"How is this possible?" she asked, voicing the question he had been wondering about since she'd told him she had traveled through time.

Back in the thirteenth century, when he had seen her on that horse in front of his uncle, he had known a fear unlike any other. She had been so stoic, so brave and courageous, even when his uncle's blade had bit into her skin.

Then she had disappeared into thin air.

He and his men had stared in disbelief, and Angus had yelled his anguish to the heavens. "Where is my daughter? he had roared, looking at Brochan accusingly.

Brochan's heart had slid to his stomach, terrified he would never again see the woman he loved.

In that moment Brochan had known she had not been lying. That she had traveled through time.

He had left Castle Kildare that day and returned to the

priory, to Annabelle's chamber that had been boarded up after Angus had killed the poor nun.

Brochan had ripped the boards from the door and entered the room.

When he awoke, he was in the same chamber, but it was different. He had stepped out into a different world. A strange world that had taken some adjusting to.

He had hoped to find her at Castle Kildare waiting for him, but she hadn't been. Just a staff of kind people who accepted him as their laird, just as Terri had been accepted as Annabelle in the thirteenth century. He did not question the how or why of it. He just hoped and prayed Terri would return to him.

"So how did you find your way back?" she asked, her gaze slipping from his in a way that reminded him of how good they were together.

"The chamber at the priory."

She smiled. "Then you came to the castle?"

"I did, and it was as though I had just been away for a day. My servants knew me as Brochan Douglas. Even friends stopped by, and I didn't know a soul. But I knew, just as sure as ye are standing before me, that I would find ye, or even more, that ye would find me."

And find each other they had.

She undressed, her clothes a pile at her feet.

He pushed his jeans off, and pulled her into his arms, kissing her with all the passion he felt for her.

This woman, his woman, his life.

There was no time for slow pleasure, the need too great. He wanted to fill her body, to experience that wonderful ache that had raced through him from the moment he had first touched her.

She sighed as he entered her, and kissed him. "Brochan, I love you."

He drew back, shocked, yet insanely pleased at the declaration. "I love ye, too."

She searched his gaze, her lips curving. "I don't want to ever lose you again. Not ever."

"Ye have nothing to fear. I will never let ye go. Not ever again."

With that, he showed her how much he loved her.

Julia Templeton read her first romance over twenty years ago . . . and hasn't stopped reading them since. Married to her high-school sweetheart and the mother of two grown children, she resides in beautiful Washington State. Aside from writing spicy historical, time-travel, vampire, and contemporary romance, Julia enjoys collecting research books, traveling, and spending time with friends and family. Please stop by her Web site at www.juliatempleton.com to learn more about Julia and her books or e-mail her at julia@julia templeton.com. She loves hearing from readers!